THE EPHESUS SCROLLS—
THEY WERE A TIME BOMB
THAT COULD MEAN
THE END OF THE CHURCH

For nearly two thousand years, the Ephesus scrolls had lain hidden in a ruined stone hut in the Turkish hinterland. They were written in a language more ancient than Greek or Hebrew. Their author claimed to be the Apostle John.

And the story he told was the secret testament of the Virgin Mary...

The "untold truth" about the man called Jesus...

About the woman called Lael.

A secret that could blow the Church wide open...

And set the world on fire.

Jason Van Cleve knew something had to be done— and done quickly.

"A fascinating concept . . . and a corking good yarn!"

—RAY BRADBURY

"An astounding, off-beat plot—an expert thriller!"

—JEROME WEIDMAN

KEEPERS OF THE SECRET

BARNABY CONRAD and **NICO MASTORAKIS**

A JOVE BOOK

The authors gratefully acknowledge
quotations from the following:
The Gnostic Gospels
by Elaine Pagels, copyright © 1979 by Elaine Pagels,
with permission of the publishers, Random House,
Inc.

KEEPERS OF THE SECRET

A Jove Book/published by arrangement with
the authors

PRINTING HISTORY
Jove edition/March 1983

ISBN: 0-515-05544-1

For Isabel and Kendall

LAEL: Ancient Hebrew meaning "the chosen of God."

—J. V. Robinson, *The Origin and Meaning of Proper Names*

1

To SEE the three men on this sunny Roman morning standing casually by the fountain in the Piazza Novona, one might think they were discussing lofty and esoteric subjects as they contemplated the dancing waters—especially since they were dressed in the robes of office indicating they were cardinal deacons. But one of them, the next-to-youngest of the three, was saying in English:

"I don't say that the old man must be eliminated. Not yet, anyway. Just that we dispatch someone to Izmir immediately to get those photographs from him."

An older cardinal with a gaunt, craggy, and almost handsome face frowned and sighed. "I don't understand. Why, after all these years, do we have to take it upon ourselves to steal this man's property?"

"My dear colleague"—the young man's voice was low and as smooth as margarine—"you know how devastating it would be if the—"

"Yes! Yes, I know! I know about the scrolls! For how many years have we known about those damned scrolls! But why all the excitement about them *now?*"

"Jason Van Cleve," the other man said. "That's why. He's an investigative reporter from America. Skillful man. Likes to expose things. Apparently he exposed one thing too many last year—a labor union involved with the Mafia. Van Cleve's wife was killed, probably as a token of their esteem. He's been reduced to writing travel articles for a while—on a ship in the Mediterranean, at the moment. The old man has been trying to get in touch with him, to tell him the whole story of the scrolls before he dies. Without the photographs, he's just a harmless old man with a ridiculous tale to tell. But with the photos of the scrolls, he's a time bomb."

"Why don't we have them both eliminated?" the third cardinal asked innocently.

The older man said in a shocked voice, "You are joking, Tertius, of course!"

Tertius looked doubtful and shrugged.

The young cardinal spoke up. "We Guardians are prepared for any action. What we must do, we shall do. I'll contact Melnick at once and report back to you. I am sure his reputation—ah, well—you know it. Unsavory, perhaps, but *so* very efficient. Meanwhile, we'd better not be late for the meeting. His Holiness will be there, and you know he misses nothing."

They shook hands solemnly, and, although they were headed for the same destination, they went in three different directions.

The land excursion from the ship was south of Smyrna, or Izmir, as the Turks call it, and the voice over the tour bus's loudspeaker was harsh and crackling:

"Nex' stop he is the house of Virgin Mary!" The guide's Turkish accent made it sound like "Veerchun Mahree."

So now the bus was leaving the ruins of the ancient city of Ephesus, and Jason Van Cleve turned to look again at the majestic columns of what had been the awesome temple of Diana, some two thousand years before.

Jason was lean and good-looking, and the gray coming in at his temples enhanced the dignity of his forty-two years, making his otherwise youthful appearance more interesting. What most women noticed about him was his build, which could easily have been that of a man fifteen years younger. Only the more discerning saw the bitterness lurking behind his eyes. The small scar on his right cheek went back to his college boxing days, but that hurt look in his deepset, hazel eyes was more recent.

The busty, handsome woman next to him said with a sigh as she looked up at the temple, "It's great, I know, but I'm just tired of looking at ruins—plumb ruined out."

About thirty, she was well dressed, laden with gold jewelry, and pretty in a Palm Beach sort of way. Her hair was the color of a saxophone and she laughed easily. As always, she had managed to take the seat next to him. Her name was Vera.

"Now, about Mary's house, I must say I *am* curious about that." She had a heart, as Browning wrote, "too soon made glad," and she had a voice, as his grandfather back in Billings would have said, "that could worm a dog." But Jason barely listened as she rambled on. "Here I am, raised a Catholic, and I never even thought to ask what happened to the Virgin Mary after the Crucifixion!"

Jason wasn't interested in the Virgin Mary's house. He wasn't interested in this shore tour, and not even in this cruise. Friends back in New Haven had persuaded him to take it in the hope that it would help pull him out of his depression after losing his wife. But hell, he hadn't *lost* her, they'd *taken* her, in a phony car accident.

He wasn't interested in Vera, either. He wished he could be. She was nice. He was even getting used to her voice, but he felt nothing for her. She was friendly and he was grateful for it, but that was all.

Mechanically he took out his notebook and began to make notes on Ephesus. It was a magnificent site and it had a colorful and glorious history, but he found it hard to work up enthusiasm for travel writing. Still, it was better than the alternative. He could use a drink about now. His grandfather had always said, "I must have a drink at eleven. 'Tis a duty that must be done./ For if I don't have a drink at eleven, I'll have eleven at one."

"Oh, here we are!" crowed Vera. "I'm getting kind of excited! I guess you can take the girl out of the convent, but never the convent out of the girl."

The bus had pulled up at the foot of a hill and parked alongside three other buses. One of them was still disgorging people, mostly Germans and Japanese, all with long-lensed

3

cameras slung around their necks. There was a straggling parade going up the path and disappearing into the olive grove.

"You go on ahead," said Jason to Vera. "I'll be along in a minute," he assured her as he pretended to have difficulty in worrying his camera case out from under the seat in front of him. He just needed to get away from that voice for a while.

When most of the other passengers had gone on ahead, he opened the leather case, took out the small camera, and went out of the air-conditioned bus into the hot Turkish sun, following the other tourists up the hill.

Along the path were big metal signs, each in a different language, declaring that this had indeed been the final abode of the Virgin Mary, and that a special historical team from the Vatican had verified, in 431 A.D. and again in 1953, that John the Apostle had fled with Mary after the Crucifixion and come here to Ephesus, that John had died and was buried nearby, and that Mary had lived and quite possibly died here in this house at the age of sixty; she was "assumed" into heaven, as the Church taught, since no remains of her body were ever found.

This last resting place of the Virgin Mary was a small house of stone and adobe, incredibly well-preserved for a building dating from biblical times. It must have been restored, Jason thought, or at least partially; it was too perfect. The house looked exactly as the house of the mother of Jesus should look, he thought—as a painter or a moviemaker would conceive of it. Inside, it was lit by candles and was very stark, barren of furnishings, although someone had seen fit to put a rather ugly crucifix in the main room. The floors were of packed earth, and there was little to show the line of demarcation from the exterior soil.

The bedroom was tiny—a mere cell—with an empty niche the only relief from the bare walls. How small she must have been! Jason felt a slight tremor in his body when he stepped into that room, and when he finally left the dwelling, he experienced a definite mystical feeling, almost exaltation, despite his lifelong skepticism toward formal religion.

Jason walked over to the side of a little cliff from which pure water spouted, cupped his hands, and drank some of it.

On their honeymoon, Beth and he had visited Lourdes. Beth had been curious; she wanted to see everything in the world. But here was none of the sickening, gaudy commercialism that Jason had found at Lourdes. There was only one little kiosk with postcards of the house in its lovely setting. He was making a selection to send to Beth's mother in Charlottesville, when a well-dressed man of about forty-five strode up to him.

"Phillips Taylor," he said. His basset-hound eyes flicked from side to side as though to make sure he would not be overheard as he presented his card for an instant and then took it back and pocketed it. "American vice-consul. Talk to you a moment?"

"Sure," Jason replied as the man drew him aside.

Quickly he told Jason about an ancient man who lived in Izmir and who had been on the team that had restored this very house of Mary for the government, around the turn of the century. The old man wanted to talk to Jason.

"What in the world for?" asked Jason.

"You are a writer, aren't you?"

When Jason nodded, Taylor said, "The old boy's got a story he wants to tell. Feels he's dying."

"But . . . why me?" Jason persisted. "There must be other writers around here."

"He doesn't want to work with the local talent. Says he can't trust anyone but 'a writer of the first class.' Well, at least you're traveling first class." He laughed at his own feeble joke. "I got the publicity sheet of the Royal Viking Line from their office in Istanbul."

It was hot in the sun, and the beads of perspiration on Phillips Taylor's forehead seemed static; they did not become rivulets, nor did he attempt to wipe them away.

"This old man," Jason asked, "he's a friend of yours?"

"Friend of a friend, you might say," replied the man. "Met him years ago through a young man who was working with the old boy at the time—an American who needed a passport. I arranged it for him. So the old man figured I could arrange this for him, too."

Jason asked, "Why doesn't he want to work with the 'local talent,' as you put it?"

"Not sure, but I think he's worried about leaks—maybe even problems with the law."

"What is his story?" Jason queried. "Everyone thinks he has a story. I'm really not interested in doing a biography."

"He won't tell me anything, won't tell anyone but 'a writer of the first class,' I told you."

"But the ship leaves tomorrow."

"Not until nine o'clock at night," the man pointed out. "Just see him for half an hour, then maybe he'll stop bugging me."

"I had planned to go to the museum in Izmir tomorrow."

"Just see him for half an hour—fifteen minutes, even— then I'll personally drive you to the museum. I'll bring him down to your ship at nine tomorrow morning."

"Make it eight," Jason said. "Then I can have more time at the museum."

That night on the anchored *Royal Viking Sea,* after high tea, dinner, and a boring Turkish folklore show featuring belly dancers, Jason managed to break away from Vera and get to his cabin before midnight. He tried to read about Ephesus, but he kept thinking about the vice-consul and the old man. He was sure the old fellow wanted his life story written. So many people had come to him over the years and said, "You write the story of my life and we'll split fifty-fifty!" Big, generous gesture! They seemed always to be librarians or accountants. Still, this man was supposed to be very old...

The next morning, Taylor showed up promptly at eight at Jason's stateroom. It was quite a nice room, as he had been given first-class accommodations, courtesy of Royal Viking, in exchange for the publicity they knew his articles would generate.

When Jason's gaze went down to the tiny man next to the American, he thought of Rumpelstiltskin. The old fellow was a troll in a black suit, wearing a black hat with great bushes of white hair coming out at the sides of it. He was clutching a crude portmonnaie made of cowhide, attached to his tiny wrist by a handcuff.

"This is Monsieur Nestor Lascaris," said the vice-consul.

"How do you do?" said Jason.

"I am ninety years old and I am dying . . . that's how I do," he replied in a high voice. He took off his hat and Jason saw a pinched, corrugated face; bright but rheumy eyes gazed out above a hawklike nose and a set, serious mouth.

He sat down in a chair that Jason offered. The vice-consul started to sit, too, but the old man waved him out of the cabin with an impatient gesture.

"I'll wait in the lounge," Taylor said in an injured tone.

When the American had left, the old man took a small key from his pocket and unlocked the handcuff.

"You are a writer of the first class," he said intently in lightly accented English. "I have heard of your books. I have read in *Time* magazine about your brave newspaper articles. You are not afraid of the truth, even if it puts your life in danger."

Even if it killed my wife, Jason thought bitterly.

"You are the man to write this story, the most incredible of stories."

The will and strength of the old man's voice! He did not look like a dying man, nor did he particularly appear to be a crackpot.

"I was born in Ephesus," the man began.

"But you have a Greek name," Jason interjected.

Nestor Lascaris smiled a brown-toothed smile and said, "Just because the cat has kittens in the oven, that does not make them biscuits."

His smile disappeared and he caressed the leather pouch.

"In 1908 I was the youngest on the team of archaeologists assigned to restore the house of the Virgin Mary. Therefore, to me fell the honor of doing all the hard work, the lifting of stones, the digging and hauling away of debris. Thus it was that while shoveling away in the very foundation of the ancient building I came upon this!"

He opened the leather pouch and extracted a large photograph gone yellow with age. It showed an amphora-like jar.

"I saw that there were scrolls in the jar. I quickly threw a sack over it, and the others did not see the jar. That night I came back with a wagon and took it to the humble dwelling of my parents in Izmir. You see, in those days I was young,

7

unprincipled, irreligious, and highly ambitious. I intended to sell my find. I knew I had found a treasure of great price, no matter what was in the scrolls. But then, when I found out what was actually on them!" He whispered fervently, "My God! My God!"

"You translated them when you were that young?"

"No, no! You see, I could not sell them around here. I knew I would have to take them to Istanbul or some big city where I was not known, where I would not be accused of theft. And I could not risk leaving my job, for I needed the money to be able to travel to Istanbul. I kept the scrolls hidden, and it was years later that I found someone to translate them for me. In the meantime I had taken a wife and raised a family. A family man does not run off to Istanbul."

As he spoke, he took two other photos from the leather case; these were obviously of the scrolls themselves, unrolled, with their archaic writing clearly visible, looking not unlike the pictures Jason had seen of the Dead Sea Scrolls, the Qumran discoveries.

"These are two of seventy-six," he said.

"And where are the originals?" asked Jason.

Lascaris blew out a long and terrible sigh.

"My—my daughter—" He looked as though he would not be able to finish the sentence. "My daughter, she is a nun now. She is in convent. She . . . she . . ." He slapped the leather pouch in his anger. "She found my translations! She said they were blasphemy of the most terrible kind. For my protection and that of the scrolls, I do not wish to tell you now where the actual scrolls are, but I have the photographs and I have the translations. I have told no one about them. You wonder why I tell you after all these years? I can no longer keep this to myself! There are those who would kill to suppress this knowledge, but it must be told."

Lascaris bobbed his head up and down as he said, "Only last night I was approached by a . . . how you call it? Gangster? He demanded that I hand over these pictures. I lied, told him that they were burned. I think he does not believe me . . . but he went away."

His rheumy eyes lost their opacity and seemed to darken as

he fixed Jason with a piercing look. He lowered his voice and continued, "This story *must* be told, and I must tell it. I know I am soon to die, and a writer of the first class must tell the world what has been found here. I want no money, if that is what you think. No! I want nothing but that the truth of the Ephesus scrolls be known!"

Then he took out some typewritten pages. As he shuffled them, Jason went to the night table to get the cassette recorder he always took with him in his travels.

"You know who wrote these scrolls?" Lascaris looked around as though searching for eavesdroppers, then whispered, "John!"

"John?" Jason echoed flatly.

"John!" repeated the old man reverently.

"John the Baptist?"

Lascaris rolled his eyes heavenward in impatience at such ignorance.

"John the Apostle! The Apostle John!"

"Oh!" said Jason. This man was crazier than he thought.

"You do not believe me, my friend, I know." Lascaris smiled a little. "I don't blame you. You will doubt more when you hear the story itself. But let us start with facts you cannot doubt. John came to Ephesus after the Crucifixion, afraid, like the other Apostles, for his life. He brought with him Mary. We know John died and is buried here in Ephesus. We are reasonably sure Mary also died here and was shortly afterwards assumed into heaven, as observed in a Church tenet called 'The Feast of the Assumption.' Now, I did not do the actual translation of these scrolls." He looked a little apologetic. "I do not read Aramaic well, so a brilliant American named Paul Krenski made a"—he searched his mind for the words—"free translation in English for me. But the first part, where John speaks to the reader for himself, is exactly as written two thousand years ago." The old man drew from his jacket pocket a pair of steel-rimmed glasses, hooked them over his ears, and read the first of the typewritten pages:

"I, John, bear witness that I was with Jesus in the garden when he went out to suffer. And we were like men amazed or fast asleep, and we fled this way and that. And I saw him suffer,

9

and did not wait by his suffering, but fled to the Mount of Olives and wept. And after he was hung upon the cross, at the sixth hour of the day, there came a darkness over the whole earth. Now that day is long past, but it will live in me each day of my life and I suffer anew, not only for the suffering of Jesus, but for the untruths that abound, for which I myself have been partially responsible.

Now I am close to death and must make haste to bear witness to the truths I know, truths I lived and observed, and truths told to me by Mary herself. She has been my staff, my guiding light, my mother, my friend, my rock through the turbulent days of the trial and crucifixion of her son and through our subsequent perilous journey to Ephesus. It was through her that I learned the truths I now set forth, although I long wondered at the role that Lael had played. Would Lael and Jesus want me to do this act, this setting right of the truth of their lives? Will it not cast a shroud of doubt over the faith of the many who now believe in the ministry of Jesus far and wide, and in increasing numbers?

I have suffered mightily in my doubt whether to reveal or not, but verily I say to you now, Jesus was not the Messiah. Jesus was the son of God, as we all are, but he was not the one chosen by the Father to save all mankind.

Lascaris cleared his throat.

"That is the end of John's introduction. Now this next part of the translations . . . this is where we go into Krenski's free interpretation of the story itself. Believe me, this is the most amazing story never told."

"Well, *tell* me, for God's sake," Jason said.

"For God's sake . . . that is *why* I tell you!"

The old man began to read. For the next few hours, Jason listened, taped, and made notes as the man read in his high, reedy voice the beginning of a most unbelievable saga. Jason was skeptical but intrigued. The story was ridiculous, but he maintained decorum out of respect for the man's age and obvious sincerity.

Shortly before noon the old man stopped. Jason was about to ask him some questions, but Lascaris raised his hand weakly and looked for a moment as if he might faint. Now, indeed, he did look like a dying man. He took a pill from his pocket and put it in his mouth, asking for a glass of water. Then he got up shakily and put on his hat, muttering, in Greek, "Noh-meezoh ohtee eeneh ohra yah toh yehvmah pahmeh . . . lunch, I go home now."

"But I have many questions," Jason protested as he took his Nikon from the night table drawer. "And let me take some pictures of those photographs!"

"After lunch," Nestor Lascaris replied in a drained voice. "I must go home, lie down. I must bite something. My corn flakes . . ."

"What?"

"I must have something to bite . . . to eat . . . my corn flakes." He pronounced it corn "flockies."

Quickly Jason set up the photographs on the bed near the porthole, and began snapping. He took seventeen shots and would have taken more, but by now the man looked so old and sick that Jason helped him handcuff the case to his spindly wrist and called to the lounge to let the waiting vice-consul know that Lascaris was ready to leave. When they went out, Phillips Taylor promised to bring the ancient Greek back at two-thirty.

After they had gone, Jason shook his head and grinned. He'd had a lot of weird stories tried on him in his career, but this one was the winner! Still, he was curious to know exactly what was in those scrolls. He would have the ship's photographer develop his film, then try to find an expert to translate at least some of it when he got to Istanbul.

"It will probably turn out to be the Apostle John's laundry list," he said to himself, and picked up the book on Ephesus.

But then, as he waited for the old man's return, he found himself setting up his typewriter, and then, out of habit, he started transcribing the tape.

First, Lascaris had given a little prefatory lecture of his own, quite proud of his scholarship:

"Since we know from many independent historical sources that King Herod died at the age of seventy, in the year 4 B.C., modern scholars now assign 7 or 6 B.C. as the actual birthdate

11

of the Messiah. But, aside from the writings of His own Apostles, there is no historical record of Jesus Himself—what a pity! We know more about actors and box-fighters than we do about the life of Christ! But the Romans kept good records. We know about Herod . . ." His taped voice sounded gruff and angry as he spat out the name, his hatred spanning the centuries. Then he went on:

"Since the records show that Herod died in 4 B.C., and it was he who ordered the death of the Hebrew children, Jesus had to be alive before then. The mistaken calculations are blamed on the Scythian monk, Dionysius Esigua, who wrote in 533 A.D., centuries later. It is also generally believed that the child was born in September or October, rather than in December, one of the more obvious reasons being that then, as now, the shepherds did not tend their flocks in the fields in the dead of winter; at that time their flocks were in the stables. December twenty-fifth as the date of birth is mentioned in 354 A.D. for the first time. These scrolls, the Ephesus scrolls, confirm both adjustments.

"Modern astronomers further tell us that in 6 B.C., Mars, Jupiter, and Saturn appeared to come together, forming what looked like a single star of dazzling and unique brilliance."

At this point he had jabbed Jason on the chest with a bony finger that felt as sharp as a stiletto.

"Incidentally, astronomers have also determined that the Crucifixion occurred on April seventh, in 30 A.D." Lascaris had chuckled. "I wager you did not know that! That is the only date that would satisfy the biblical statements that Jesus died on a Friday, the day after the Jewish feast of the Passover, celebrated on the first full moon of the spring!"

Jason had interjected, "Then that would have made Him older than most people think."

"Yes," Lascaris said thoughtfully, "somewhat older."

Then the old man had gone directly into the story. It more or less followed the traditional account, but with some interesting deviations.

And when Mary awoke with a cry from the pain of the child in her, Joseph, lying on the straw beside her in the stable, comforted her.

"Is the star still there?" she asked.

And the door of the stable was closed, but even so, through the cracks in it they could see the billiant light.

There came a knock on the door.

"Who is there?" Joseph called out.

And a woman's voice answered, "Becca,"

And it came to pass that the servant girl from the inn aided Mary and Joseph in the birth.

Joseph paced across the straw as Becca helped Mary to bring forth her child. Mary did but once cry out, and her cry sounded almost as though she were in ecstasy instead of pain. One hour later, Becca held up a perfect child.

And then the door was flung open. The wind blew the straw and Joseph trembled, for he knew the proclamation of Herod.

A centurion stood in the opening, saying to his men, "This is the place."

Then Joseph stood between the centurion and Mary and the child. But three soldiers strode in with clanking armor, and one reached for the baby and pulled it from Mary's arms while another held a sword to Joseph's throat.

And they raised the child up to the light of their torches. And the soldier who held Joseph released him and put away his sword.

And the centurion said, "We are wasting time here. This is not the Messiah. This is only a girl."

Jason looked at his watch. Three-thirty, and still the vice-consul and the old man had not come back. He ordered tea and a sandwich and went on with his work.

The language was simple, rudimentary, the Krenski translation free, neither modern nor completely biblical:

After the birth of the child, it came to pass that Joseph and Mary knew doubt and their faith was shaken. For some days they were silent, not daring to look in each other's eyes. Mary feared that Joseph would now leave her, since the prophecy had proved false. She had not borne the Son that was to be the Messiah. Even so, were these not the words of the prophet Isaiah:

"Therefore the Lord Himself shall give you a sign. Behold,

a virgin shall bear a child: and the child's name shall be called Emmanuel." Would this not cause Joseph to doubt her claim that she had known no man?

They looked upon the child with affection, but in their hearts grew deep sorrow. They saw not the truth, for they were simple folk and it brought them much sadness when the prophecy of a divine destiny went unfulfilled.

But the truth shone in the heavens, and three great men from the East, kings, who had followed the star that shone above, were now brought to the stable to honor the child and offer gifts to the Messiah. For had not Isaiah also prophesied: "The multitude of camels shall cover thee, the dromedaries of Midian and Ephah; all they from Sheba shall come: they shall bring gold and incense; and they shall show forth praise to the Lord."

Yet Joseph and Mary watched with heavy hearts, for the coming of the wise men made them feel the pain of deception, but they had not the courage to make known the truth that this child they so revered was but a female.

It would come to pass that in later years Mary would think on those painful moments when her daughter was worshipped as the Messiah and her own tongue was stilled with shame. Had it then been the will of God that the wise men should not know the truth about the child?

Mary and Joseph named the infant after the wise men had gone. Mary had chosen the name Lael, for it meant "the chosen of God." Joseph did agree. "She is the chosen of God, for she could not have a fairer face, but she looks so like you that she should be called Mary." Mary protested that it would be unseemly to name a girl child for its mother. Even so, they settled upon the name, Mary Lael.

As word reached their ears of the deeds of Herod's soldiers, many people saying that both male and female children were slain, Mary and Joseph feared that Lael would not be safe. For did not the wise men find them? Should Herod now hear of this, would he not have the soldiers seek them out again?

Therefore did Joseph take Mary and the infant and flee into Egypt. In Alexandria at that time were many others who had fled—those Jews of the Dispersion—and it was here that Joseph and Mary found friends. Everywhere people spoke of the

14

Messiah, who was said to have been born in Bethlehem and who would some day free Israel from the Roman yoke so that all Jews might return. Egypt too was under Roman rule, but the Jews of Alexandria lived not in the land of their forefathers and cared not whose coffers their taxes swelled.

But here too they could not but fear for the danger that might come to Lael, and thus they moved inland, where Joseph built a modest home for his family.

The child, Lael, grew strong and fair to look upon. Her sweet and happy nature gladdened Mary's heart and her quick mind and curiosity pleased Joseph, and with each day that passed, they set aside the thoughts of the prophecy that their child was to be the Messiah, for she seemed as any other and they could but think of her as their own, not as the child of God. Her beauty filled their hearts with love, and while they had seen that her eyes never blinked and that later, when she walked, she left no footprints in the sand, they did not remark on this.

And it came to pass, when Lael was four years of age, that she was playing with a young goat which had wandered down into a dry river bed, wide and deep. As Mary and Joseph watched, some strangers chanced to come from the other side and did descend also into the river bed. They were not dressed as Egyptians, but in the manner of Mary and Joseph, and they called across to them a greeting in their tongue, and it was returned.

And when all were descended into the depths of the river bed, they heard a roaring sound and they saw a great torrent of muddy water rushing toward them. Then did Mary and Joseph take hold of the child, Lael, and the goat, but they were overtaken by the flood before they could ascend the steep banks. Joseph grasped sedges and, holding Mary with one hand, put his arm around the reeds and supported the goat while Mary did hold up Lael. After the first fury, the torrent subsided and Joseph was able to gain the riverbank.

Lael was the first to sit up. She saw that the goat was alive beside her father. She started to go to the animal when she heard a cry. It was the boy who had been crossing with the others from the far side of the river.

Joseph and Lael walked along the bank and then Lael pointed.

The child was at their feet, but too weak to pull himself ashore. Joseph reached down and lifted the boy from the water. Mary joined them and she did take the child from Joseph's arms.

"I will look for his parents," Joseph said.

Lael watched as her mother swaddled the boy in dry shawls, and she found his face comely and held his cold hands in hers to warm them even as her mother started a fire, for he was chilled and in a swoon.

The boy's eyes were still closed when Joseph came back. Joseph walked to the fire, clasped his hands together, and said, "I went downstream as far as the wide part where the crocodiles gather. It is hopeless if his parents were carried down that far."

Then came Lael's voice as she sat beside the boy, and Mary and Joseph were much puzzled to hear the small child speak these words:

"God is mercy and God is wrath and God is sacrifice, for His name will be glorified not only through life over death, but through death itself."

Then did Joseph and Mary look upon each other with amazement, but in their hearts was rekindled the hope of an old dream.

When the boy awakened, Lael gave him some sips of goat's milk and stroked his forehead with her hand and said, "I will stay with you always."

Mary looked again at Joseph, and he did nod his head, for they both understood that they now had two children to care for.

And Lael asked the boy, "How are you called?"

"I am called Yeshua," he replied. "Jesus."

And thus it was that the lives of Jesus and Lael became intertwined. In the years that followed, the children were as sister and brother, yet was their love even deeper and more constant, and the pleasure they found in each other warmed the hearts of Mary and Joseph.

Fair of face was Jesus, and fairer still was Lael, with her bright hair and comely features. But even as Jesus had a swarthy look, darker by far than Lael, much did they seem to be alike in other ways. They were the same age and their understanding was great, although Lael's understanding was the greater of the two, and often wondrous. Also, they were much alike in disposition, for each possessed a generous and loving nature.

And six years passed, and Joseph and Mary wished to return to their homeland, and they received a sign that it was wise for them to do so when the goat that Lael and Jesus had so loved and cherished died. As Mary and Joseph watched, Lael knelt and looked up to the sky and prayed. And even as she prayed, the animal began to move and opened its eyes and then got to its feet.

It was a sign—indeed, a miracle—and Joseph and Mary could see that Lael did have a great gift. Joseph knew that it was time for them to return to Jerusalem. He knew that she would not be able to exhibit such powers without being regarded as one possessed, but he could foresee that if she were the Messiah, Jesus could be the one through which she might bring salvation to the world. Thus it was that they returned to Galilee and then to Nazareth, and the words of the prophets were fulfilled: "He shall be called a Nazarene."

And it came to pass that the next summer Joseph, while laboring in his workshop, fell to the ground without a sound. Mary ran to him, calling to Lael and Jesus. They went to Joseph and his eyes opened and he smiled and said, "Mary Lael, you are everyone's hope, and you, Jesus, will be one and the same with her." Then he died peacefully. And Mary cried out to Lael, "Save him. Bring him to life again."

But Lael shook her head. And Mary wept and grew angry and said, "You would save your pet goat, but not my husband?"

And Lael said, "This is his time and it is the will of the Father." She too wept for the good man, as did Jesus, and they comforted Mary with embraces and her wrath was lost in her grief.

And then Lael said, "If you bring forth what is within you, what you bring forth will save you. If you do not bring forth what is within you, what you do not bring forth will destroy you."

And Mary did not understand her words. "I do not always know your meaning, but I know you speak as a girl-woman who knows the All."

17

Lael bowed her head and said, "I am you and you are me, and so shall it be all the days of our years. And so shall it be with Jesus. What I am given to know, he too will know, and what I learn, so will he also come to learn."

And she put her arms around Mary and Jesus, and they kissed. And so Lael did not raise up Joseph from the dead, although it was in her ability to do so, for she was almost at the zenith of her powers. She spoke many tongues, though no one knew how she learned them, even did she speak Greek, the tongue of the most learned. And all these things she did teach to Jesus.

The years passed, one upon the other, and in all things the boy Jesus and the girl Lael were as one. All that Lael was granted as the Chosen of God, she shared with her beloved companion, Jesus. Nor was he ungrateful, nor too proud to suffer her teachings, nor did he turn from her to seek others, but basked with pleasure in the greatness of her divine wisdom. As more was revealed to Lael, more then did he learn also, even unto the sacred miracles that he alone would be permitted to perform among the multitudes, for such things did not become a woman and it must not come to pass that she be called a witch, if the word of God was to be made known to all nations.

Thus it was that Jesus could astound the rabbis at the temple with his knowledge and divine reasoning when he was but a boy.

As the followers of Jesus increased in number, so too did the joy in Lael's heart. Always she was at his side, especially when he needed her power, the power that came from the Father, and so it came to pass that many miracles came to be recorded: and thereafter the word spread to the multitudes that, indeed, the Messiah had come.

As Jason listened, he heard the taped voice of Lascaris saying, "Now come many pages we skip by. Nothing very different from the Bible's version of the last months of Jesus, when—"

Then he heard his own voice interrupting. "Sometimes the language doesn't sound very biblical."

"This is not the Bible!" Lascaris's voice said reprimandingly. "This is a free translation by Krenski! Now we go to the end part. Ready?"

"Ready."

And Lascaris began to read again.

And Jesus and Lael met by moonlight in the Garden of Gethsemane, near the oil press at the foot of the Mount of Olives. Only Peter and James and I, John, were witness to the scene.

And Lael, to whom we all referred as "she of Magdala," though we never said this in her presence, just as we never called Jesus "the Nazarene," even though he was known thus far and wide. And again I say, Lael told him that she knew of his conversation with Judas. She agreed that Judas's plan might be a way to save his life, but she told Jesus that if he were to let the world know that he was not the Messiah, all of his teachings would be held in contempt and he would be cast down.

"It is only through their faith in you, as the Messiah, that brotherhood between all men and the resolution of differences in a peaceful manner may come to pass, to keep mankind from destroying itself."

Then Jesus drew himself up and embraced Lael and spoke: "I go to my destiny, not joyfully, but willingly, if it be my Father's will."

You must remember that I, John, did not know at this time the true part that Lael played. I knew only that she was always with Jesus, and so taken were we with the power of his personality that none of us seemed to realize how much he was guided by her, especially in the performing of the miracles. It is true, he raised the dead, he healed the sick, but always was Lael near at hand. There was the time he commanded Lazarus to rise. Lazarus did not rise. He was dead. Then to the scene came Mary Lael, and she stood behind Jesus, and Lazarus arose.

And so it was that Judas directed the soldiers and the Pharisees and the chief priests and the officers of the temple and the elders to the area of Gethsemane where we stood. Judas led the way, for many times he had been to the garden and he knew where to seek us out.

It was near to midnight when they came upon us, bearing torches, and many were the minutes that we stood watching the flames of the torches flickering below as the procession came up the path through the garden. The muttering of voices could be heard, the tramping of feet, and the clanking of the soldiers' armor.

And then we all looked to Jesus, for there was time for us to take flight, but he moved not.

Lael did look to him also, and spoke to him in a low voice, and we heard not what she said. We only heard Jesus reply, "It is but the will of our Father." And so we did take heart, so strong was our faith in Jesus.

Then, as we stood by the fire, waiting, Jesus and Lael on one side, and Peter, James, and I on the other, we could see the faces of the men as they advanced into the firelight. And as I watched, I recognized Judas, and he was talking to the leader of the soldiers, but I could not hear what was said.

Then did Judas step forward, and he did nod to Lael, and then stood for a moment before Jesus. Then did Judas kiss Jesus upon the cheek.

"Dear Judas," Jesus spoke. "I have been waiting for you. Now you see that I tossed the sop of bread to the right person at supper tonight, did I not?"

Then did Judas say to Jesus, "This is not a betrayal, Master. I swear to you! Trust me!"

Jesus turned then to Lael and said, "What must pass will pass."

Then did Jesus step forward into the flickering glare of the soldiers' torches and he spoke, saying, "Who is it you seek here?"

And one of them did reply, "Jesus of Nazareth."

And Jesus said, "I am he."

And then Lael pointed her finger to Jesus and said, "Yes, it is he."

At these words a strange thing occurred: Several of the ranks in the group seemed to stumble backwards, and some fell to the ground. They exclaimed one to another as they picked themselves up and gathered their fallen swords and spears, and as they did, Jesus said,

"Why do you come for me as though I were a thief? Have

I not sat daily with you, teaching in the temple? You could have taken me easily any day there. Why now? Why do you come at this hour of night, with swords and spears? You do not know, but it is all happening so that what was prophesied might come to pass. This is, indeed, your hour, and for now the power of darkness and desolation shall prevail. But I warn you, your hour will be brief."

At this, Malchus, the chief servant of the high priests, having shaken off the spell, drew his sword and, uttering an oath, came forward menacingly.

At the same time, the disciple Peter leapt forward with his sword in hand. He brought the weapon down at Malchus's head. The soldier dodged just in time, and the blade barely sliced through his ear, severing it from the side of his head.

The crowd muttered angrily and moved forward, but Jesus spoke quickly in rebuke:

"Peter, put your sword in its sheath instantly! All those who take to the sword shall perish by the sword! Even now, I could pray to my Father and He would give me more power than twelve legions of angels. But then, how could I do what I was sent to do?"

Lael reached down and picked up Malchus's ear from the ground. She held it a moment in her hand and looked heavenward, then she handed it to Jesus. He took it and then put it to the side of Malchus's head, from whence it had come, and there he held it, taking the man's head in both his hands.

Jesus then did take away both his hands and the ear was in place, and remained there as though no sword had touched it.

A great murmur ran through the crowd, but Peter, James, and I were much used to this, for had we Apostles not witnessed many miracles performed by Jesus, and many far more wondrous than this?

Then did Jesus say to them, "I am the one you want, therefore let the others go."

Yet was there much hesitation. Even so, Sadoc, who had remained in the background, and seeing now the submission Jesus showed, did step forward and shout, "Seize him! Seize them all!"

Peter, James, and I hesitated and looked to Jesus.

"Go," he commanded us.

Then did I withdraw and hide behind a rock. Peter made as if to remain by Jesus' side, but he did say to the fisherman, "You will deny me, Peter, but not yet."

Peter looked to him with anguish, but then he turned and fled. And James did go with him.

Two soldiers followed after them, hampered by their armor. Then Sadoc pointed to the fleeing disciples, saying, "Strike the shepherd and the sheep will be scattered."

Then spoke Lael, "Sadoc, we are glad to see your knowledge, even unto the prophecies of Zachariah."

Closely did he look at her serene face under the hooded white garment that she wore.

"And who are you?

"I am one of God's children," she replied. "Even as you are."

"Are you not called Mary of Magdala, the prostitute?"

And Lael did say to him, "It matters not what I am called. God knows my name."

Then did the soldiers come forth with ropes, but Sadoc shook his head and said, "Not the woman. We have no need of her."

Jesus held his wrists forth to be bound, nor did he resist as they pulled him away down the path, "led like a lamb to slaughter," as Isaiah had foretold so long ago.

Then he looked back to Lael and she called out, "Stop."

And all halted and stood transfixed. And all did watch as she walked down the path toward them. She went to Jesus and put her face near his, and there were tears on her cheeks. But her voice was strong and I could hear her as she spoke unto him, saying, "Now the hour has come. Be strong, my brother, my love, my very life. I am you and you are me forever, from this day forward. Whatever is done to you, so also shall it be done to me." And then did she drop to her knees and kiss his hand.

And Jesus spoke to her, saying, "I shall be strong, do not fear, for it is you who make me strong."

And Jesus was dragged away from Lael, but he looked back to her, and in his eyes were shining tears, yet on his lips was a smile.

• • •

The voice of Lascaris was faltering, and this was when he said he would go home to lunch and would return to finish the story.

But he hadn't returned. And here it was four-thirty. Jason clicked off the recorder and lay down on the bed and thought about the story. Maybe there could be a Sunday feature in it . . . the great biblical hoaxes of history. He could drag in the Turin shroud and other mysteries. But he needed to know more about this. Much more.

And for some reason he felt very disturbed.

2
___

JASON WOKE up in his berth and looked at his watch. It was after six o'clock. He had dozed off.

"They didn't come back," he said aloud.

Why?

Maybe the old man was sicker than Jason had thought. Maybe he'd gone to the hospital . . . or died. What about those remarks Lascaris had made? *There are those who would kill to keep this information secret.*

He sat up and lit a cigarette, then laughed wryly. Kill a crackpot old man over a crackpot hoax? Why would anyone care what that poor, obscure man had to say? If the Messiah was female, the information had been suppressed very effectively for nearly two thousand years, a fine heap of suppression. And a ninety-year-old unknown Greek would be the smallest molecule in a megaton bomb like this one. The Messiah, a woman? A real bomb, all right.

Too bad the whole thing wasn't true; he could use a great story about now. He could see the look on Wild Bill Shiff's face if this story, wired in to the good gray *Times*, came over his desk! It'd be like the old Hollywood movies. "Stop the presses! Scrap that Reagan headline, we're going with 'Jesus Was a Woman!'"

Jason smiled at the vision of Shiff wetting his pants with

excitement, barraging him with dozens of queries, suggesting interviews with the Pope, the translator of the Dead Sea Scrolls, and Billy Graham.

But then Jason's smile faded. Sure, it was a phony, but he smelled a story of some sort here. What if Lascaris and the pimplike vice-consul were crooks in cahoots? What if they had dreamed up this yarn together and shot photos of some kind of scrolls? And the translation that sometimes sounded biblical and sometimes didn't—was that the vice-consul's contribution? That gimmick of the handcuffed briefcase, that was pretty cute. Did they go around from place to place, city to city, bilking people for large amounts of money to "research" the tale? Shake down good Christians to suppress it? Were they well known to the police all over the Mediterranean? Might make a good magazine article if the newspaper didn't want it.

But where was the old man? Where was the shifty-eyed Phillips Taylor?

The Messiah, a woman? Come on! Still, Jason had met a lot of people in his life, and his gut feeling was that Lascaris was genuine. Listening to Lascaris tell his story, it was hard not to believe he had found the scrolls, just as he said. Then the only conclusion would be that the scrolls themselves were a hoax, planted at the site of the archaeological diggings for just such a "find."

But how to pull off a hoax like that, with all the scholars eager to analyze such things? The composing and writing of the script would be no big deal, but where to find the proper time-stained papyrus, the ink with which to perpetrate such a caper? And who would go to such effort? And, more important, why?

Yes, there was a story here.

Quickly Jason put out his cigarette, brushed his hair, straightened his tie, and grabbed his jacket. The ship was not due to depart until nine that night; he had a few hours to try to find the old man.

But where should he start? The consulate? Yes, of course, the consulate. The vice-consul would know how to reach Lascaris.

Jason saw an old taxi waiting at the curb not far from the

gangplank, and he started toward it. Then, suddenly, a newer taxi cut in front of him and the driver reached back and opened the door. The driver of the other cab shrugged and drove off.

"American consulate," he said. "Know where it is?"

The driver growled a reply, tipping his blue cap. He was Turkish, very ugly, with a brown mustache that bristled like copper wires, and obsidian eyes pinched close to his large nose. He looked as though he would kill for a drachma, a congenital assassin. Jason looked around quickly, but now there was no other taxi visible. He stepped in.

It seemed to take forever, through narrow streets and cluttered alleys, to arrive at the consulate.

"When do we get there?" asked Jason at one point, as he nervously checked his watch. It was already seven-thirty.

The man did not answer, but soon pulled up to the curb in front of a small, elegant building with a plaque over the door displaying the seal of the United States.

Jason smiled with relief and asked the driver to wait for him. He received a surly nod in reply.

Jason went to the iron gate in front of the door. There was an electric doorbell button as well as an old-fashioned brass bell with a clapper. Jason rang both. Nothing happened. He rang again. Eventually an old Turk came out wearing what appeared to be a makeshift uniform.

"Yes?" he said in English.

"May I come in? I am an American. I need some information. I'd like to see the vice-consul."

The man shook his head.

"No one here today. Today is holiday."

"But the vice-consul," said Jason. "If he is not here, could you give me his home number? Phillips Taylor?"

Again the man shook his head and said, "No Phillips Taylor here. No vice-consul Phillips Taylor."

"But he *is* the vice-consul," Jason protested. "I met him yesterday."

"Been here for over a year," the man said. "Never heard of a Phillips Taylor."

"But . . . but he brought this old man to the ship. He . . ."

As though relenting, the man said, "Look, you come tomorrow, nine o'clock. Other vice-consul will talk to you, help with your problem. Martin Gray, his name."

Jason nodded. "Tomorrow."

So it all was a big fake, a setup. At least on the part of Phillips Taylor. Never quite bought that one, anyway. Now, what about Lascaris? He turned and went back to the cab.

"Telephone," he said to the driver. "Understand?"

By way of reply, the driver gunned the noisy motor. Again they drove through the interminable streets, taking corners blindly in their labyrinthine progress. When at last they stopped, Jason saw that he had been brought to the post office. He got out and went in. The telephone was on the third floor, and a creaky elevator took him up. On a table of the drab and poorly lit room, he saw some dirty, tattered telephone books. He tried to look up the name Lascaris, but found the Turkic characters unfathomable to him. A ragged urchin of about fourteen was eyeing him.

"You speak English?" Jason asked.

The boy nodded enthusiastically.

Jason handed him the telephone book and, giving him some money, said, "Look up Nestor Lascaris for me."

The boy quickly pocketed the money, took the book, and, frowning in concentration, ran his grimy finger slowly down the page. Finally he handed the book back with a shrug and shook his head.

"There has to be," said Jason, as he looked in the book. "Some other Lascaris, maybe related . . . maybe they could tell me . . ."

He suddenly realized the boy was gone.

No Nestor Lascaris. Strange. But maybe it was not so strange. Not everyone in Turkey would have a telephone, the way Americans did. Also, it was just possible that the boy didn't know how to read. Street children might be able to speak several languages, but not read even one.

The great investigative reporter wasn't doing so hot. *Forget the whole thing,* he thought.

Jason looked at his watch. Eight-fifteen. Time to be heading back to the ship. He walked over to the elevator, pushed the button, and went down to his cab and got in. *Well, it had been an interesting day*, he thought as they headed into the heavy evening traffic. Thank God, he'd soon be back on the ship. They'd be leaving this port in half an hour, and he could relax and forget about old Nestor and his crazy story.

Or maybe he could dress the yarn up to serve as one of those anecdotes the ladies would like: "And now we leave romantic Izmir, ladies and gentlemen, otherwise known as the ancient city of Smyrna. Remember the old song, 'Istanbul Is Constantinople and Constantinople Is Istanbul?' Well, Izmir is Smyrna and Smyrna is Izmir. One of the earliest centers of the Christian faith, Ionian in origin, it also has perhaps the most valid claim to being the birthplace of Homer, and of course the Greeks and the Turks have tossed it back and forth over the centuries during the odd years when the Romans or the Mongols weren't in residence. And I *must* tell you about this little old man with a bizarre tale..."

This damned story was driving him crazy.

As they drove along, Jason tried vainly to find some landmark. He thought he saw the Buyuk Efes Oteli in the distance, but it suddenly disappeared as the driver turned sharply around a corner.

"Where do you think you're going?"

The driver didn't respond.

"Hey!" he shouted. "Do you speak English?"

He thought he heard the Turk say yes, but he was not sure. Then he caught a glimpse of the NATO radar station on a nearby hill, and Jason knew where he was.

"Look, the harbor is down that way. Where the hell are you going?"

The Turk kept looking at him in his little rearview mirror. He smiled and entered the uphill street. Jason was sure he was being taken in the opposite direction from the port. His suspicions were verified by the long shriek of the ship's whistle coming from behind them.

"Stop the cab!" he shouted. "I want to get out!"

He wasn't sure whether the driver was a typical cabbie, circling around to rip him off for extra money, or was intentionally delaying him.

Just then they came to an intersection blocked by a small

crowd of people, shouting and pointing at two cars, which were blocking the street. The driver saw the commotion and slammed on his brakes. Jason saw him start to shift to reverse. Before the gear was locked into place, Jason threw some lira onto the front seat and jumped out.

The driver glanced at the money and hurled a curse after the American. But never mind . . . he could be paid extra when he reported to the foreigner later and collected for the "unavoidable delay." Also, on the next block a little old man was waving for a taxi.

Nestor Lascaris got in the cab and said, "To the harbor."

In five minutes they were there. The great whistle of the *Royal Viking Sea* was sounding as Lascaris dismissed the cab and hurried to the officer who stood at the bottom of the gangplank with a clipboard in the crook of his arm.

"Mr. Jason Van Cleve," he shouted over the roar of the ship's blast. "I have an appointment!"

The officer shook his head. "He isn't going to keep it, sir. He hasn't returned, and the ship's leaving. Right now!"

"But he said—"

"Sorry, sir. Stand back, please. Gangplank's going up."

Lascaris looked up in disbelief at the big ship. Its twin screws were already roiling the black water around its stern into iridescent starbursts.

He walked away from the dock very disquieted and talking aloud to himself—in English, as though Jason were there.

"Why? Why? It is your fault, Nestor . . . stupid old man! You sleep too late. You are too tired . . . too old! Now how will you find Mr. Van Cleve? Why did *he* miss the boat? Must be a good reason. Somebody kidnap him, maybe? Somebody kill him, maybe? Maybe already those accursed scrolls . . ."

He didn't finish, but turned and watched the floating behemoth as it moved away from the dock. The *Royal Viking Sea* had thrummed and vibrated out several yards and was now turning slightly. Lascaris looked around him, expecting to see Van Cleve making a last-minute dash for the boat, but now everyone was walking away from the dock.

Again, Lascaris accused his own stupidity. "I should have had that Phillips Taylor bring me. I do not trust him, but he did get that American writer for me. Now I don't know what to do. Maybe the vice-consul knows where Van Cleve is. I go to the American consulate, maybe they know where he stays if he does not go with the boat."

Nestor Lascaris began to feel sick as he trudged along the dark street, coughing and spitting. He glanced over his shoulder constantly and saw threatening shadows everywhere.

"You are an old fool!" he said to himself. "This is not the cinema, this is life. Who would hurt an old man? Unless . . . unless . . . the scrolls . . ."

He stopped and sagged down on the curb, panting, clutching the briefcase to his bony chest. Then he hauled himself up and continued his journey, praying for a cab to come along. Now he realized that he could not walk all the way to the consulate, so he walked in the direction of his home. As he came around a corner, he heard an ominous rattle. It was the sound of wheels of some sort, chattering over the cobblestones. He flung himself against the side of a house, his briefcase raised as a weapon. The sound increased. Then Lascaris saw him—a legless beggar on a platform on roller-skate wheels. "Go with God," the old man said as he gave the beggar all the change in his pockets.

Staggering with exhaustion, he approached the dark street leading to his house. As he entered the cul-de-sac, the head-lights of a car directly in front of him came on. He threw his arm up against the blinding beams. He could make out the silhouette of a tall, thin man coming toward him. Lascaris tried to run toward the doorway of his home, but the man ran after him and caught him by the belt at the back of his coat. Lascaris whirled, and, with all the strength left in his frail body, he swung the briefcase against the man's head. The man swore and retaliated with a blow with the tire iron he carried. It smashed into the old man's face and he toppled over backwards; his head, slamming against the cobblestones, made a sound like a melon being struck by a mallet.

The assailant bent over Lascaris's body as it lay, small and crumpled, in a fetal position, then struck him in the head once more to make sure the old man was dead. He then took out a large knife, which he snapped open, and tried to cut the handle off the briefcase. The knife went easily through the leather, then struck metal. He went quickly through Lascaris's pockets, but could not find the key to open the handcuffs that bound the briefcase to the old man's hand.

The assassin then pushed back his victim's coat sleeve and slashed at the bony wrist with the knife. Three times he forced the knife against the wrist, to no avail. Then he took the frail arm in both his strong hands, snapping the bones of the forearm, after which he sawed off the bloody hand, and the handcuffed briefcase fell to the ground. The man snatched it up and opened it. By the beams of the headlights he could see the photos and papers in it. His thin lips in his thin face tightened into what was almost a smile. He ran his thin fingers through his red hair.

"Think you just made yourself a bundle," he told himself.

But he would not bother his contact in Rome with the full details of how he got the briefcase. The cardinal was only interested in tangible results, not in methods.

He walked to his car without looking back at Lascaris's body; there was more work to be done. The first thing was to track down the guy who called himself Phillips Taylor. It was not his real name, of course, but Melnick would find him, probably in Istanbul. He had his methods and his contacts—plenty of them.

As he started the car, he chuckled at the thought of that writer guy missing his ship. Better check on him, too.

As the Turk hurled vicious epithets after him, and with the words *"anani sikeyim"* still sounding in his ears, Jason pushed through the crowd and was soon running toward the harbor. He came out on a plaza called Konak Square, and took a street he felt would lead him to the harbor. He was wrong, and after some minutes he realized he was heading the wrong way. He cursed the Turk, Lascaris, and himself under his breath.

"Do you speak English?" Jason asked a man who was sitting outside a doorway in a straw chair.

"Evet," the man replied. Jason kept on running.

The boat's whistle sounded once more in the empty streets, and he had the feeling that it was more distant than before. Suddenly he saw a sign that read ATATURK CADDESI, and he

32

recalled that they had passed that street before; it was the waterfront drive. He sprinted through the strolling crowds along the waterfront, then stopped in his tracks, his arms falling to his sides in resignation.

The *Royal Viking Sea* was a least half a mile from port, heading for Istanbul.

Jason looked around. This area of the city was full of life, people milling in an endless promenade, men grouped together and women grouped together separately.

Although it was nine-thirty, darkness was not yet complete, and the waterfront was bathed in a soft mauve-pink afterglow. Music was coming from horn-shaped loudspeakers—military music, as if the country were preparing for a celebration.

He tried to count the money in his pocket without taking it out, and figured that he had about five notes—almost a hundred lira. He cursed himself for giving the cab driver more than he should have.

He calculated the situation. The boat was heading for Istanbul, which was thirty minutes away by plane and an eternity by bus. He had no plane reservations and not enough money for the fare. The only thing to do was to wait for morning, when the American consulate would be open. With a bit of luck and the vice-consul's help, he'd be able to get the plane for Istanbul and catch up with the boat before it departed for Piraeus.

In theory, it all seemed perfect, especially in the warm summer night, surrounded as he was by interesting sights and sounds and the smell of food. His stomach became particularly interested in the succulent aromas, and began to rumble a reminder that it was long past dinnertime.

As Jason looked around for the source of the mouth-watering aroma, he had the fleeting sensation that someone was looking at him; he felt a pair of eyes nailed to his back. He turned quickly, and caught a glimpse of a man rapidly turning the other way.

You're getting paranoid, he told himself. *That old man's story has sent you around the bend.*

He soon found the stand and saw the sign declaring the prices for sizzling hot bursa kebabi—sliced grilled lamb with tomato sauce and yoghurt, in pita bread. He ordered two kebabi and watched as the man prepared them. His fingernails caught Jason's eyes; they were long, greasy, and filled with dirt. He swallowed hard and looked the other way while he sank his teeth into the juicy meat.

With sixty lira in his pocket and the night falling sticky, humid, and hot over Izmir, Jason realized he'd have to go back to his Boy Scout days in order to survive. But he ruled out sleeping in the streets and decided the next best thing would be a cheap hotel. He was now in a part of the city that seemed dark and hostile. The few loitering figures in the alleys seemed to be brigands out of childhood fairy tales.

He walked briskly toward the brighter lights and kept looking behind him. It could have been his vivid and excited imagination, but he thought someone was following him—that same man?

He passed the train station, turned left, and walked along Anafartalar Caddesi for a block and a half, when he saw a street called 1296 Sokak, and the lights of six hotels in a row. He picked the one with the shortest name, Pension Atlas. As he entered the lobby, the heavy smell of narghiles hit his nostrils. The small room was full of knickknacks, Arabic and Turkish religious plaques, mirrors, tassels, baubles, souvenirs, and even a sign in English, posted right above the tiny desk:

> Whoever you may be,
> Come . . .
> Even though you may be
> An infidel, a pagan, or a
> Fire-worshipper,
> Come.

And, under the copy of this verse from Mevlana, better describing the spirit of the invitation: ROOMS 45 LIRAS.

The sleepy hotel clerk, a one-eyed, unshaven old man, led him to his room. Jason had been informed that prices in rooms with six beds were slightly lower, but he preferred to spend his entire fortune for a single room with a shower; cold, the clerk had said, but if he wished to heat some water, there was a tank where he could build his own fire.

When he was left alone in the miserable room, its decades of human odors mixed with the slightly fresher stench of urine coming strong from the corridor, he looked around to orient himself. The bedding consisted of a sheet safety-pinned to a quilt, very dirty; a bare bulb hung from the ceiling; one dead cockroach lay on the floor; one soiled towel hung from a hook on the wall. He locked his door.

He looked outside the window and instantly pulled back. That same man was standing near a taxi, talking to the driver.

A coincidence? Jason asked himself. He was almost convinced that if he could see in the dark, he'd recognize the driver.

He lay down in his clothes on the hard mattress, kicked the quilt—which fell to the floor, raising a cloud of dust—then, leaving the light on, he shut his eyes and tried to empty his mind. It was difficult to stop the wheels from grinding out visions of all the peculiar things that had happened during the day.

He wondered how long it would be before he was missed on the ship. Vera would miss him. He could see her, a predatory frown on her face, searching the bars, the disco, the lounge for him.

He finally scanned his own mind for the troubled feelings that were beginning to subside as he realized he was not exactly happy; but, yes, he was alive! For the first time in many months, his life had some sort of flavor. Retaining this thought, he fell asleep.

The next morning at nine, Jason was at the consulate, waiting for it to open. Vice-Consul Martin Gray, short, jolly, mustached, sparse hair combed across his pate to hide his baldness—though in fact this had the opposite effect—received Jason cordially in his office.

"Read some of your articles and books!" he said emphatically. "Especially liked the piece on Nicaragua!"

Jason thought he sounded like Teddy Roosevelt; he half expected him to say, "Bully!"

Instead he asked, "What can we do for you?"

Jason told him everything he could, omitting any references to the details of Lascaris's tale.

"Phillips Taylor . . ." Gray said. "I've been here only six months, but that name . . . I have seen correspondence from a vice-consul who was here a while back. I think it was Taylor Phillips, though."

"Maybe that's it!" exclaimed Jason. "Maybe I got the name backwards. Do you have a forwarding address?"

"Check," said Martin Gray as he got up. "I'll check."

He came back from the adjoining room with a slip of paper.

"Taylor Phillips left the service a year ago . . . lives at this address in Istanbul."

"One more favor—I'd better call the ship and let them know I didn't fall overboard."

After half an hour, he had the captain on the phone. Captain Mortensen was a good enough fellow, though acerbic, and he fancied himself a wag, especially in his English, which was serviceable but rudimentary.

"Well, what happened, dear boy? Did Tom T'umb get his t'umb caught in one of those Turkish tarts?"

Jason replied amiably, "Jowett said, 'Never explain, never complain.'"

Then, after telling the captain that he would rejoin the ship later at Istanbul, he added, "Oh, and Captain Mortensen, I'd appreciate something: I wonder if you could see to the security of my stateroom, that my things are . . . intact. I've been worried about . . . well, just about the general security of my things." He added, "I'll explain later."

Jason didn't specify the tape recorder, the camera, or the transcript; he suddenly wasn't trusting anyone, particularly over the phone.

When he arrived on board that evening at six o'clock after the flight to Istanbul and the long taxi ride from the airport to the *Royal Viking Sea*, he was not surprised to see Captain Mortensen waiting for him at the top of the gangplank. A great, bearded, sixty-two-year-old Viking, the husky captain gave a bow and then did a passable impression of Charles Laughton as Captain Bligh.

"Welcome aboard, Mr. Christian. Let's see if your cabin and coconuts lie untroubled."

Jason followed the captain down the corridors to his stateroom.

The captain used his own key to open the door. When they stepped inside the cabin, the captain said, "First, Jason—if I may so call you—you are a fine creative man, and we are proud to have you on our ship. Second, you will probably write about this trip for some magazine, like *Signature* or *Travel and Leisure* or *National Geographic*. We welcome—who doesn't?— good publicity. We do not want you to say that our security was bad. I want you to know that I personally came into your room after our phone call and took inventory. Did you have some two thousand dollars worth of traveler's checks in the bureau drawer?"

Jason nodded.

"They are still there," Captain Mortensen said, jerking open the drawer. "Plus a few hundred dollars in currency from various countries." He pointed to the bureau top.

"Did you also have a typewriter and a camera and a tape recorder?"

Jason was feeling guilty; he'd been too suspicious.

"Yes, and I see they're all here," he admitted.

"Anything else of value, besides clothing?"

Jason shook his head.

"Look, Captain," he started. "I'm sorry to have put you to this trouble, but I was following up the damnedest story . . . if I've offended you . . ."

"We Danes don't offend easily," the captain said. "See you at dinner."

Jason flopped down on the bed. How clean and wonderful a bed it was after the previous night! How beautiful and clear was the air of the room! He was about to doze off, when a strange thought crossed his mind.

He got up and snapped on the tape recorder. The tape was the same, a Maxell 90. He pushed the play button and heard only the faint hiss of blank tape. Hurriedly he pushed the rewind button, and then the play button again. Nothing.

He turned over the cassette and tried that side. Nothing. He stopped to think. Could it be possible that he hadn't pressed the record button while Lascaris was talking? No! But he'd played back that tape while he'd been waiting for Lascaris and the vice-consul to return! He looked at the cassette more carefully. Although it was a Maxell 90, it looked brand-new, and the tape he had used was not; he had been using it the day before he met Lascaris.

He picked up his camera and looked at the exposure counter. The number was correct: seventeen. He wound the film quickly and snapped the back open. The film was the same, Kodak Tri-X. Had they, whoever they were, overlooked the camera? But a closer examination of the cartridge brought a new disappointment. His Tri-X had been a twenty-exposure roll; in the camera now was a thirty-six-exposure roll.

Bingo, he thought. He looked in the drawer for the transcript, knowing it wouldn't be there. It wasn't.

He lay back down on the bed with a groan. Then he said aloud. "That name *was* Phillips Taylor!"

He had his shortcomings, but he'd always been good with names. Names are words, and he'd been preoccupied with words since he'd won his first essay prize back in Billings, Montana, as a sophomore in high school. He had been impressed by the fact that the man's *first* name was Phillips, with an *s*, instead of the usual Phillip.

And another thing: When Phillips Taylor had shown his card as they first met, he had put it back into his own pocket instead of giving it to Jason. Jason remembered thinking that it was probably the last card the man had on him at the time.

The logical way to proceed now was to stay on the ship, go to the Istanbul address given him as the last known address of Taylor Phillips, and check it out in the morning. If that failed, maybe he should forget the whole thing.

But one fact was becoming increasingly clear to him: There was at least one other person besides himself who thought Lascaris's story might be important. Who was it?

3
_____

THE *VAPUR* to Kara-Koy was departing from the bridge and was
almost empty; not many people were using it, as Kara-Koy
was a wealthy area and the rich had their own boats and cars.
And the rich of Istanbul were *very* wealthy.

Jason looked around, but didn't see anything suspicious: an
old woman, holding a cat in her arms—not Turkish, Jason
thought; a few soldiers heading for their homes; three Americans, perhaps on a free day without their wives. The boat was
painted in shades of ochre and green, and smelled of tuna and
sardines. It took fifteen minutes to reach the harbor closest to
Kara-Koy, and as soon as he debarked, Jason looked for a taxi.
He scrutinized the driver of the cab that slid to the curb—
young, smiling, clean-shaven—and, reassured, Jason hopped
in and gave the address in Kara-Koy.

Ten minutes later the cab stopped in front of a small, attractive white house on a hill overlooking the incredible bay
ringed with blue minarets and the ruins of the ancient Greco-
Roman temples that had existed throughout the city's amazing
history.

Jason got out and paid the driver. He walked to the white-
painted iron gate, pushed through, and went up the four black-
and-white marble steps to the door, on which was an untar-
nished brass plaque that read TAYLOR PHILLIPS, and nothing

more. He tugged the chain on the shiny brass bell. He waited. He pulled it again. As he ambled away, wondering what he might do next, a throaty feminine voice said, "Yes?"

A woman stood in the doorway, a beautiful, smallish woman with sun-streaked hair, blue-violet eyes, and tanned skin. She held a book in her hand, her index finger keeping her place. She was wearing white cotton slacks and a white silk shirt; no bra he noted approvingly.

"Yes?" she asked.

"Mrs. Phillips?" Jason asked.

How old was she? Twenty-eight?

She didn't answer.

"Mrs. Phillips?" he asked again.

She nodded slightly.

He noticed that the book she was reading was *Palladio*, by Roop.

"I'd like to speak to your husband."

"So would I," she said. "Any ideas?"

Oh, Lord, thought Jason, *here we go again.*

She saw his distress and said, "I'm sorry. I haven't seen him for two years and he owes me some child support. Who are you?"

"I'm just someone who wants to talk to your husband for about five minutes. You're American?"

She nodded.

"I need to talk to him. I met him as the American vice-consul in Ephesus two days ago, and—"

She laughed—a wonderful, throaty laugh.

"You're kidding! John? A vice-consul? Ephesus? He's a polo-playing, backgammon-playing, woman-playing, stock-market-playing nice guy in Montecito, California, and nothing more. If you want his address, I can give it to you."

Numbly, Jason said, "John?" And found himself repeating it. "John?"

"John Jefferson Phillips the Third," she answered. Then she hesitated before going on, "Look, this is Istanbul, and I don't mean to be rude, but before I give you his address, I'd like to see some identification."

Jason handed her his passport. She scanned it briefly and handed it back.

"I've heard of you," she said as she opened the door wider. "Come on in and I'll give you some coffee and his phone number. He won't accept my calls, but he'd talk to you, I'm sure. While you're at it, tell him he forgot our son's eighth birthday last week." Her face clouded a moment. "Seriously, if you do talk to him, tell him the boy's not been too happy lately. A call from his dad might do wonders."

Jason heard himself saying, "And you? Who exactly are you?"

"Taylor Phillips, ex-vice-consul of the United States, formerly at Barcelona, at Ankara, at Izmir—at your service, sir."

"You?" He stepped through the door. This was Taylor Phillips? But now where was Phillips Taylor?

She showed him into a sunlit living room, octagonal in shape, very white, everything white except for the red tile floor and the terra-cotta niche at the far end, which contained a four-foot-high marble statue of Herakles, minus arms and part of a leg. There was a white *flokati* rug, a white sofa, and above it, dominating the room, a wide-nostriled horse's head of marble, which looked as though it had come from the Parthenon. In the center of the room was a worktable ten feet long, made of a slab of marble from a sarcophagus. On it were piles of drawings and steel engravings of ancient Palladian buildings, as well as manuscripts, books stacked on books, a typewriter, and two projectors—one opaque and one slide.

She gestured toward the terrace, which overlooked a small garden, and he went out and sat down on a chair at a table under a big striped umbrella.

She soon joined him, bringing the coffee she had promised. Sitting across from him, she tipped her head to one side slightly and asked, "So why does a famous writer want to talk to my ex-husband, who never read a book, except maybe *Black Beauty?*"

At one point in his life, a great many people had known Jason's name; now, not so many did. He was inordinately pleased that this beautiful woman was one of the few.

"I don't want to talk to *him,*" he said. God, she was so good-looking! "I thought I needed to talk to you. Now it appears I don't. I'm sorry to have bothered you."

He stood up to go.

"Wait a minute," she said. "You've got me terribly confused. First you want to speak to my husband, then you think you need to talk to me. What on earth is this all about?"

Jason shook his head and said with a wry smile, "I'm afraid I'm just as confused as you are. This whole thing seems so ridiculous to me now."

"What whole thing?" She pushed the coffee cup toward him and said, "Please sit down. You haven't touched your coffee. Why don't you tell me while you drink your coffee? After all, you've interrupted my work, which is fine because I've reached a snag and welcome the interruption. But at least entertain me for a moment by telling me about this. After all, it must be intriguing. The author of *Clay for the Kiln* would not be interested in something dull."

She'd struck a chord. "I didn't think anyone except my mother had ever read that slim little loser," he said.

"It *was* a bit naïve and clumsy here and there. My God, you must have been so young! But overall it was powerful. It knocked me for a loop when I was in college. I also liked your novel, *The Kindness of Strangers,* a lot. So can you tell me a little something of what this is all about?"

Over the dark Turkish brew, thick as delta silt, Jason found himself telling her the whole story, leaving out no details. She listened intently, leaning forward in her chair, her violet eyes wide.

When he'd finished recounting Nestor Lascaris's story of the virgin birth, she breathed, "Jesus." Then, realizing what she had said, she gave an embarrassed laugh.

After a long moment, Jason asked, "Do you believe the story?"

She stood up, arms folded. "Do you really want to know what I think?"

"Of course."

"I think it's an absolutely contemptible premise."

"The old man seems to believe it," Jason said defensively.

"And I used to believe in the tooth fairy."

"But . . . do you think the story *could* be true?"

"I think it's quite possibly the most ridiculous and tacky thing I've ever heard. If I were a better Christian, I suppose I would be offended, even outraged. As it is, I'm just amused. Like a mackerel in the moonlight, it shines and it stinks."

"Not even curious?"

"Not in the slightest. I mean, Mr. Van Cleve—"

"Jason, please."

"Jason. Common sense tells me this cannot be. We do know that Jesus lived—actually lived! Nobody denies that. Sure, the facts are sparse, I'll admit. But he did live around two thousand years ago, and he influenced a great many people, and he was crucified; that we know, if for no other reason than that the Romans left a few records. So who's this girl? Why have we never heard of her before? I'm sorry, this computer rejects the input."

"I don't know."

"You don't know, yet you believe—"

"I didn't say I believe. I just feel something in my gut."

"I've got some Kaopectate," she deadpanned, sitting down.

"Thanks a lot. But someone is going to great lengths to suppress this story. I'll admit it's ridiculous— But why does it mean so much that someone would risk getting caught stealing the tapes and the film? Why was I being followed? Why was old Lascaris afraid? Why didn't he come back? There are just too damned many unanswered questions here for me to write this off. I can't help thinking there is something very important going on here, no matter how ridiculous the story sounds."

She nodded pensively and they sat in silence for a moment, then she said, "I wish I could have seen those photographs you took of the scrolls. There may have been some clues—physical evidence, something to indicate their authenticity." She gestured toward her worktable. "Before I quit the Foreign Service to write what I pray will be the definitive book on Palladian architecture, I was an amateur archaeologist. My marriage was cracking up and I needed something to divert my mind from my problems, so I began to study and do a lot of research in Izmir. I even learned Aramaic. I assume the scrolls are in Aramaic?"

Jason shrugged. "I really don't know. The writing looked like a handful of primitive fishhooks to me."

"If they were in Hebrew or in Greek—if they weren't in Aramaic—then, *ipso facto*, they were phony. And, just incidentally—this will fuel your heretical fires—the ancient Hebrew word for Holy Spirit is *rauch.*"

"And?" he asked, perplexed.

"I shouldn't encourage your preposterous idea—but *rauch* is a noun of the *feminine* gender."

"Well, I don't know about Hebrew, but we can rule out Greek. The old man was Greek, so he would not have needed a translator for that. Wait a minute. I think he said, 'I do not read Aramaic well'!" Jason looked at her, shook his head, and sighed. "You must think me a total fool. But if you'd only been there and heard that old man! It is inconceivable to me that anyone his age, sick and about to die, would try to pull off a hoax."

"Maybe it wasn't his idea to begin with."

"But it was!" cried Jason. "He was the one who found the scrolls in the first place."

"He *says* he found them!" Taylor countered.

"If he says he found them and didn't, we're going back to the hoax theory. And once again I ask why a hoax, at his age? He stated at the beginning that he wanted no money."

Taylor stood up and paced for a moment, frowning.

"Look, Mr. Van Cleve—Jason—this is ridiculous. We're going round and round, and since I didn't see the scrolls or the man, I have nothing to base my arguments on. Except that I too have a gut feeling. And that is that you have somehow been singled out as the patsy in an elaborate and perhaps even dangerous con game. Look—why, if these scrolls are real, why hasn't someone heard of them until now?"

"The Dead Sea Scrolls—which have been authenticated—have been in existence for two thousand years. How come we just heard of them a few years ago? Isn't that the job of you archaeologists, to dig up all this stuff? And another thing. Supposing they are an *ancient* hoax, perpetrated centuries ago. Wouldn't that still give them some value to scholars?"

She stopped pacing.

"All right, touché. I have an idea. I know someone who might be able to convince you a little better than I can."

She went to the telephone and spoke into it in rapid Turkish. Then, to Jason, while she waited for her call to go through, she said, "I'm placing a call to Rome, to an old friend. He helps look after my son, who's staying with my sister in Rome, going to school there. This man's very close to the bigwigs in the Catholic Church. He'll know if anyone does..."

And then the operator came back on the line and Taylor was speaking in Italian, *"Carissimo Padre mio ... qui sua amica Taylor."* Then she went on in English.

After ten minutes she hung up.

"How the hell many languages do you speak?" he asked.

"Eight," she said with a shrug. "But then, so does every headwaiter."

"Eight languages!"

"Don't be impressed. I was an army brat, and my father was transferred to a new country about every other year."

"And what did your Italian friend tell you just now?"

"Actually, he's an American-born Italian." Then she relayed the substance of the conversation: Father Bartolomeo, who had been in and around the Vatican for fifteen years, had never heard of the scrolls. He had heard of other heretical writings over the years, of course. There was little, if nothing, having to do with religion that escaped the Vatican's watchful eye. Something like this would have caused a sensation, even if scoffed at. He said he would investigate further, but...

"And exactly what is his job ... his position in the Church?"

"He's a cardinal deacon."

Jason looked at her questioningly.

"There are three orders of cardinals," she explained, as though to a Sunday-school class. "The most prestigious are the cardinal bishops; they're all members of the Curia and are titular bishops of the six dioceses of Rome. Next in rank are the cardinal priests, you know, like the archbishops of San Francisco or Paris or New York. Then come the cardinal deacons, who—"

"So Father Bartolomeo is pretty far down in the pecking order and may not be privy to something as controversial as this."

"He's a very important person," Taylor said defensively, "and a fine man."

"Is he a scroll expert?"

"He's a very learned man."

"Look, I'm not knocking your friend. I'm just saying that maybe only a very few people know about these damned things and they want to keep it a mighty small fraternity. Maybe even to the extent of bumping off any potential initiates to the club."

"At this point I rather wish I'd never gotten involved with this in any way."

Jason was idly studying a group of photographs on the white baby grand piano. There were pictures of a young boy, of an elderly couple who were probably this woman's parents, of Taylor herself as a young girl on a horse, of Taylor and the young boy on a camel, with the pyramids in the background, of the boy in front of the Parthenon, and others. Suddenly one photo caught his eye. It was a group picture of about a dozen people, in an eight-by-ten standard frame. And one face looked familiar . . . or did it?

"Excuse me," Jason said as he picked up the picture and held it in front of Taylor. "Who's this?"

"Who's who?"

"I think this is my man!" Jason said, pointing to one person in the back row.

"Phillips Taylor," she exclaimed. "I'd forgotten him completely! He was a minor clerk at the consulate in Izmir, fired, I think, for shady dealings in passports and such. This was taken at a little office party for me, just before I left. I remember he and I talked about the similarity of our names but someone later told me that wasn't his real name."

"Lanky, sweaty, with darkish hair and sort of basset-hound eyes?" Jason asked.

"Exactly."

"Do you think he still lives in Izmir?"

"Very unlikely. Since he deals in stolen passports, he's probably right here in Istanbul. Thousands of American passports are lost or stolen in Europe, and most of them find their way to the Persian Divan in the Bey Oglou district, a junction in the railroad of several criminal transportation systems. A man like Phillips Taylor wouldn't get much action in Izmir. He could operate more effectively in Istanbul."

"So, how do I find him?"

"Well, if you could talk to Ali Reza . . . he's the master, they say, of all such dealers. With the bait of some real American dollars—not the ones they print in Tarlabassi—their grapevine can be most effective."

"Fine," Jason said. "I'll go there."

She flashed her charming smile. "You speak Turkish?"

"Fluently. Almost as well as pig latin."

"Then perhaps you'd like me to come with you?"

"Is it safe?" Jason asked, surprised by her suggestion, but aware of the advantage it offered.

"Safer with me than without me," she replied. "I know the crummy area and have a few friends in low places. And I'm afraid that, as a tourist, you may end up having your own passport stolen."

Jason said, "You could have something there, what with all these feelings I've had of being followed. How is it that you know this Mr. Reza, if he's so shady?"

Taylor laughed. "You mean, 'What is a nice girl like you . . .?' Oh, dear. Well, in order to do any excavating, or even trespassing in areas where there are known to be artifacts, one must have permits galore. Once, when I was applying for a permit, there was a terrible ruckus going on down the hall, and I asked what was happening. The young man with whom I had gone through this same red tape before told me that the famous—or infamous—Ali Reza had been brought in and he was highly indignant. I guess I looked a bit stupid, because he said I must surely have heard of Ali Reza, and then he told me about him. Apparently the reason Reza was so upset was that he thought he had the police department in his pocket, but they now had a new captain who hadn't been briefed on the advisability of cooperating with him."

Taylor gave another little laugh and went on, "Then, of all things, as they brought him down the hall and past me, he smiled at me and nodded in a very gentlemanly manner. I said to the clerk, 'He seems quite nice,' and the clerk replied, sarcastically, I suppose, 'Oh, yes, everybody likes Ali Reza!' And would you believe it? Later I was introduced to him at a very respectable cocktail party and he remembered me. He said I had done him a favor, though what it was I don't know."

"And obviously you remembered him," Jason remarked.

"Wait till you see him. He is quite unforgettable, and delightful to talk to, if you like hearing shady dealings made to sound amusing. He told me that 'on the occasion of our initial encounter,' as he put it, he'd been arrested for smuggling three dozen transistor radios and was most fearful of having to wait in jail for perhaps two years before going to court. But he also told me the new captain had a change of heart when he was given six of the radios for his family and friends."

"There seems to be a liberal attitude toward bribery in this part of the world," Jason observed.

"I think being friends with Ali Reza would be far more valuable than being friends with the police captain. In this part of the world, you survive only if you invest in connections." She stood up. "Excuse me while I go freshen up."

Taylor emerged shortly, looking cool, dressed all in white, silky and feminine. And with the addition of a bra, he noticed.

"If you don't mind," Jason said. "I should first explain to the captain that I won't be able to finish the cruise as planned. Would you mind taking me there first?"

Jason suddenly realized what he had done. The words had seemed to come out by themselves, as though he had given no previous thought to them. When had he made that unconscious decision to leave the ship, and why? Sure, Lascaris's tale was a pretty good one, and he'd always loved a good story; no matter how implausible this one might be, it was far more exciting than life aboard a cruise ship. And Taylor was far more alluring than Vera. That, he admitted to himself, was a big part of it. Mrs. Taylor Phillips was a stunning woman as well as an enigmatic and intelligent one. A bit chilly and intellectual and formal on the outside, but on the inside . . . who could tell?

"You're leaving the cruise?"

"Yes."

"For the scrolls and this biblical Wonder Woman?"

"Partly."

"What are you planning—a book called *She, Jesus,* soon to be made into a major motion picture starring Annie Oakley?

"Low blow."

"I semi-apologize."

"I semi-accept."

As they got into her black Citröen, she reached across him to put a scarf into the glove compartment. In the brief instant the compartment was open, he saw a pistol.

She saw him looking at it.

"This is Istanbul," she said matter-of-factly. "I suggest you get one if you're going to be here any length of time."

It was dusk when they reached the ship. Jason went aboard to talk to the captain and remove his baggage. The captain accompanied him to the ramp to wish him well, and gave Jason a bit of a conspiratorial leer when he saw Taylor waiting for him by the car. Jason put his luggage in the trunk, Taylor double-locked it, and they drove away from the dock.

Istanbul was dazzling in the evening light. The sun, setting behind the seven hills on which the city was perched, set the tops of the minarets ablaze. The spectacular Golden Horn bisected by the Bosporus, the squat mosques fraternizing with cathedrals and ruins of temples—all of it was exotically unreal.

"Beautiful, isn't it?" murmured Taylor. "I always think of Kanik's poem:

> *'I listen to Istanbul with my eyes closed*
> *First a light breeze blows*
> *And sets to swaying slowly*
> *Leaves on trees;*
> *From far away comes*

*The ceaseless tinkle of water-sellers' bells;
I listen to Istanbul with my eyes closed.'*

"It's a little tough to hear the tinkling bells over the car horns," Jason said.

"You have to listen with your heart."

"You really like it here, don't you?"

"A very old part of the world, and I find it fascinating."

Jason looked around at the crowded streets, noting the variety of costumes, from western jeans and business suits to flowing robes, interspersed with military uniforms of various countries. "It is that, all right," he agreed. "Also mighty dirty."

"I should have called Ali Reza. There's a cafe up here," said Taylor as she pulled the car to the curb.

The place had no name, but there was a large sign with a rooster painted on it hanging over the two open doors. It was a humble bar and cafe, but decent enough for this part of town.

They went in. "A clean, well-lighted place," Jason commented.

A mustached young man bowed to them from behind the bar. Taylor pointed to the phone, and the man handed it to her.

She spoke briefly in Turkish on the phone, then hung up, looking disappointed. "Not until tomorrow afternoon. I should have called earlier, from home."

"So, let me buy you dinner."

"It *is* about that time, isn't it? I'm so sorry, I should have thought to call before we left. But it probably wouldn't have made any difference." She tipped her head up toward him and smiled. "Yes, you may buy my dinner, on one condition."

"Agreed."

"But you don't know what it is yet!"

"Any condition," he smiled.

"That we do *not* mention those Ephesus you-know-whats—even obliquely."

"Anything else?"

"Hmmm. Yes! That neither of us talks about ex-spouses or ex-spice or the past in general."

"What makes you think I have an ex-spouse?"

"What else is an unattached, attractive man doing on a Mediterranean cruise, except recovering from a divorce?"

"There are such things as widowers."

Her face went serious. "Oh, I *am* sorry! Do you . . . do you want to talk about it?"

He shook his head. "We've agreed not to talk about the past. What the doctor ordered is a night on the town. We can start here and work our way up the social ladder."

"Agreed," she said. "Now, what to drink? Turkish wine is terrible. Their vodka, however, is the best. But I hesitate to tell you the name."

"Why?"

"It'll start you thinking about those damned scrolls again."

"I promise."

"All right, then. Bartender, two Izmiras."

"Izmiras?" Jason echoed.

"Izmiras," she reaffirmed.

They sat at the bar talking, sipping the smooth vodka, and they soon forgot about the "conditions." They talked at length about each other's pasts, and Jason wondered why he'd thought this woman was anything but warm and feminine. She was as lonely as he was, just as desirous of companionship, but wary, like himself.

He found himself opening up to her as he hadn't with anyone for a long time. After he told her about the auto accident in which his wife was killed, he added, "You're probably wondering why I'm chasing after some crazy scrolls instead of the guys who caused the 'accident.' By the time I narrowed the actual perpetrators down to two men in the union, one was in prison and a rival 'family' had taken care of the other. That was lucky, because I think I'd have killed them myself."

"And did you write about what they'd done?"

He shook his head. "No hard evidence against them, the editor said. Take a little trip, he said. Write us some nice, tame travel articles."

"A coverup?"

"No . . . just didn't want to stir up the mud with conjecture."

"What you're on to now is sure going to stir up some mud."

He shrugged. "That's my hobby."

When they finished the drinks, they left the cafe and went

up the crowded, smelly, cobbled street and stopped in front of a garishly painted nightclub. Outside stood a porcine Nubian, preening, naked to the waist and dressed in pantaloons, curved-toe shoes, a scimitar, and an Ali Baba headdress.

"Step right een, gentleman and lady," he chanted. "You jus' een time for beeg belly dancer contest!"

Jason and Taylor looked at each other. "Why not?"

They went into the place, a noisy, dark emporium full of sailors of various languages, uniforms, races, and odors.

They sat at the bar, and Jason ordered more Izmira. On a ramp at the end of the bar, a half-naked belly dancer was bumping and grinding.

When the vodka was placed on the bar in front of them, Taylor said, "Another? I can already feel the other."

"You are a poet," said Jason. "Have always said so. Sure, they're strong . . . but the night is long."

"Gosh, mister, you really are a writer!"

When she smiled, her cheeks got all round and made her eyes almost close. He liked that. He smiled back at her and they clinked their glasses.

"You look like a dog I used to own," he said.

"Thanks," she said, nodding and repeating matter-of-factly, "I look like a dog."

He couldn't help but grin. "Sorry. But he was a beautiful dog. And when he sang—"

"He—he sang?"

"My mother would have these musicales on Sundays—she was a music teacher—and Duggan—that was his name—would smile. Actually smile. And sing along while she played, his eyes closed all the while. You know—*wooooo*."

"Baritone?"

"More of a tenor, I'd say. And he was great, but if any of us laughed, Duggan would stop and glare around the group and walk stiff-legged out of the room, never to sing again that day."

"And"—she peeled the label off the bottle—"I look like Duggan."

"Well," he said lamely, "only that you close your eyes when you smile and—and you are beautiful."

"Like Duggan."

"Like Duggan," he said.

She gave a little laugh and put her hand on his. "You *are* crazy, aren't you?"

He smiled, enjoying the feeling of her hand on his. At that moment another belly dancer came on with a crash of cymbals, trying to outdo her predecessor in the athletic, sensuous movements. The next one, however, was their favorite. She looked like Mickey Rooney and didn't seem to take gyrating her belly in sinuous convulsions very seriously. But the sailors booed her. They liked the following one enormously, a hook-nosed woman whose machine-gun hips worked like an air hammer breaking up an asphalt street.

"Bet I could do that," said Taylor. "Gonna try it when I get home."

She was a little high and very relaxed and happy.

Jason paid the bill and they went out into the street and walked, only a little unsteadily, back to where the car was parked. Jason put his arm around her shoulders and she put her arm around his waist and they laughed. How wonderfully young and happy Jason felt. That such a simple, innocent gesture as having a woman put her arm around his waist could delight his senses seemed nothing less than a miracle to him. How long, how terribly long ago had it been since he'd felt this way?

When they reached the car, Jason turned Taylor slowly toward him. She raised her face for the kiss, first sweet and soft, then hungry and hard. A lurching sailor bumped into them, almost knocking them over.

Silently, Taylor unlocked the car and they got in, and Jason reached over and pulled her to him wordlessly. They kissed and Jason slipped his hand up to her breast. She was wearing a bra, but he could feel her nipple harden as he slipped his hand into it. She put her hand on top of his, not to remove it, but as though to reinforce the gesture. Then she pulled away, suddenly shy, and with a little laugh she murmured mockingly, "'And then he cupped her breast' ... aren't they always cupping someone's breast in those sexy novels you people write?"

Then her voice went serious as she said, "Dear, dear Jason . . . if you only knew how long it's been since I've engaged in such shenanigans!"

Jason straightened up. "We still haven't lined up a hotel for me tonight."

"Home . . . home," Taylor murmured. "I've Jonny's room to offer you. He's in Rome, going to school, staying with my sister." Then she said with a little shrug, "Would you prefer to stay at a hotel? Maybe you'd prefer—"

"You were right the first time," Jason said. "Home."

Once they were back at Taylor's house, she switched on the living room lights and looked around as though momentarily distracted. Then, with the poise and distance he had noted before, she asked, "Want something?"

"You," Jason said. "I want you."

"No more Izmira," she concluded quite definitely, and left the room.

He heard a loud pop, and looked toward the kitchen in time to see her emerge with two glasses and an open bottle of champagne on a tray.

"Taylor," Jason started. "Tell me more about him." He was pointing toward the group photo of the embassy crew.

"Ah-ah!" she chided. "None of that. You promised."

Jason smiled sheepishly and took the proffered glass and sat beside her on the sofa.

"Okay, okay, you win," he said. "Hey, know what—we never did have dinner. And know what else? Who needs it?"

"And this is *good* champagne. French. Left over from my previous husband's splendid—"

"Ah-ah!" Jason cautioned. "We must, by all means, remember the conditions!" He raised his glass. "To the conditions!"

"To the conditions," agreed Taylor. "Certainly we can forget him. I already have."

"Forget? Who . . . whom? Oh, yes, your ex-husband. True. I've already forgotten him too. In fact, I don't believe I ever knew him!"

Taylor laughed and sat down at the far end of the sofa. "Y'know, I'll bet I could do it," she mused.

"Do what?" he asked.

"It," she said.

"It? Almost anyone can. Bees do it . . . up in Boston even . . ."

"Not what I mean!" She bent over with her arms crossed, took the hem of her dress in her hands, and, straightening up, pulled the garment up and over her head, exposing her lovely body in one graceful motion. She picked up two silver ashtrays and, dressed only in her bra and panties, began to gyrate her hips slowly, her eyes downcast sensuously, her lower lip thrust out in the belly dancer's exaggerated pout. She hummed and made little singsong noises that resembled Turkish music. Her hips gyrated faster and faster, and from time to time she banged the ashtrays over her head like small cymbals.

Jason cried out, "Olé! Or whatever one's supposed to say!"

He went over to the piano, and without taking his eyes off her, he expertly picked up her rhythm and played Duke Ellington's "Caravan," the exotic chords jibing perfectly with her movements as her hips snapped first to the right and then to the left, with a bump in between.

"Love that rack-and-pinion steering!" Jason sang.

Then she began to laugh at herself, and finally she staggered to the sofa and tossed away the ashtrays and hugged herself with laughter.

"Not bad for an ex-vice-consul!" she managed to gasp.

Jason was laughing too. Snatching up a vase, he held it up and declared, "La Boobalena . . . ze indisputable winner of ze belly dance!"

He stepped forward to present the brass vase to her, and she flung her arms around his waist and he stumbled backwards and they both tripped and slammed onto the sofa, which then tipped over and catapulted them onto the floor.

They lay sprawled there in the long white hair of the *flokati* rug, arms and legs entwined, bodies shaking with helpless laughter. And then suddenly they weren't laughing so hard, and then they were no longer laughing at all, and Jason was kissing her and she was kissing him back.

"Jason . . ."

"Tay, darling . . ."

"How did this happen? This isn't like me."

He slipped her bra strap off her shoulder. His mouth went

55

to her breast and then his lips moved lower, down to the satiny smoothness of her stomach, and then his fingers were sliding her underpants down over her hips.

And they made love there on the rug—wonderful, gentle, cautious love. Afterwards they lay for a while running their hands over each other's bodies and sharing small kisses, and then Jason lifted her up and carried her to the bedroom and they made love again, but this time less cautiously, less gently, and it had never been so good for either of them.

4

"YOU LOOK so beautiful," he said.

She was wearing a filmy pink dress and her streaked brown hair was pulled back in a chignon that showed off her classic features and tan skin to perfection. Two large, shiny silver clips held her hair in place, and now he stopped with his arm around her and looked into one of the clips, turning her slightly so that he could see what he wanted to see.

"Jason, I'm sure we're being followed."

"You have good instincts," he said. "We've been tailed ever since we left your house."

"Why didn't you tell me?"

"You'd say I was paranoid."

"They say even paranoids have enemies."

He studied the reflection in the hair clip of a burly, bearded man dressed in a long djellabah across the street. He was pretending to be waiting for a bus, but he was the same person who'd been in their vicinity for an hour.

"We'll make a fast exit to the right at the next alley," Jason said in a low voice.

Even though it was a gray afternoon with ominous clouds and heavy with the threat of rain, they'd had a very pleasant day until now—a leisurely morning, slightly hung over and very amorous, and then some brunch with restorative sherry and almost no discussion of the scrolls, as Taylor insisted on showing him the great points of interest in the city.

Her attempts to arouse his interest in the great Hagia Sophia amused him; he hadn't the heart to remind her that he'd been trotting in and out of museums and cathedrals around Europe for the past month. He had preferred walking along the Bosporus hand in hand alone with her until it was time to keep their appointment with Ali Reza. And now this—who was following him now?

They walked rapidly to the mouth of an alley. Once they were around the corner, Jason pushed her ahead and commanded, "Keep going!"

He flattened himself against the wall and didn't have many seconds to wait. The man in the caftan came around the corner at a rapid trot. Jason caught him unawares with both hands at the place in the garment where lapels would have been, had it not been a djellabah.

"Hold it, my friend!"

He held the popeyed, evil-smelling man tightly, lifting him up to his toes. He shook him hard once.

"Now, you bastard, do me the courtesy of telling me why you've been following us for an hour!"

The man answered in a stream of Turkish, the only words of which Jason understood were "Ali Reza."

"Taylor!" Jason called.

She ran back to him and translated.

"He says he is called Mustafa . . . one of Ali Reza's men. Says he was sent by him to see that we would not meet with any unpleasantness and also to make sure that we were not being followed by the junta. I think he's telling the truth."

"Effendi . . . I take you Ali Reza!"

Jason released his grip, and the man sighed and smiled a solid gold smile. Then he looked around and motioned for them to follow him. He set off fast down the alley, then turned down an even narrower path between two old buildings. Jason had to turn sideways to get his broad shoulders through. Then they went down some steep, almost vertical stairs and came out into a grimy courtyard. Under a laundry line, two children were playing a hopping game between chalked squares next to some garbage cans, and a scabrous dog scratched and licked at an open sore. Though the courtyard was open, it looked as though the sun had never filtered down the entire length of the buildings that formed it. It was dark and dank, like the lives of the people who lived there.

Mustafa tousled the curly black hair of the little boy, who paid no attention, and walked on to a door that was unimposing except for a one-inch brass plate where a handle or a keyhole would normally be. From under his garment Mustafa drew what looked like a brass tuning fork, and he made an 'X' on the plate in one quick motion. The door slid to the right and Mustafa motioned them into what appeared to be an elevator. Once they were inside, the outside door glided shut.

A voice in Turkish came over the loudspeaker, and Mustafa answered briefly. The whole side of the cubicle slid back. Bowing deeply, Mustafa ushered them into one of the most beautiful rooms Jason had ever seen. In contrast to the seamy courtyard, this large area was white and light and elegantly decorated in eclectic and contrasting tastes, the whole blending with spectacular success.

They were standing on a museum-quality rug, and over by the piano an antique Isfahan was spread out. A Gobelin tapestry hung from one wall, a painting of a cathedral was on another, and French doors opened onto a small Japanese garden. The elegant effect was marred only by a pyramid of seven television sets in one corner.

"Who said crime doesn't pay?" whispered Taylor.

There came a chuckling voice from behind them. "Not I, my dear. Certainly not I!"

They turned to see coming at them from a side door a great gelatinous shape in a red silk caftan. Ali Reza looked like something out of *The Arabian Nights,* even to the turban and the rings on every pudgy finger. He seemed to undulate toward them in sections, like a quivering and gigantic red aspic, his eyes tiny black buttons in the dough of his face.

His hands were like two abalones, and he enveloped Taylor's small hand in his, then bent and kissed the air five inches over her fingers.

"So good to see you, luv," he said. His English accent was

perfect. "And Mr. Van Cleve," he added.

He gestured to two chairs and seated himself on an outsized ottoman behind a Queen Anne desk.

"I am so sorry, Miss Taylor, not to have been able to see you yesterday. Big troubles!" he sighed. "Never did I have trouble with the police in all the years. Now all this jiggery-pokery. The police—they understand me, and I them. We respect each other's dishonorability, you understand? But this military junta"—he made a retching noise indicating contempt—"one doesn't know where one stands. Simple bribery they have no talent for. Violence is what they know and like best, but violence is what I have always abhorred and avoided. And yet"—he shrugged—"I must mete it out on their terms. It is like a chess game." He gestured toward a silver chess set. "Like a lethal chess game. Last week they took one of my men, one of my important pawns. Last night we had to, er . . . take one of theirs. But they are so many and we are so few. I must be careful. If I have one piece less than my opponent and I exchange pieces, I am certain to be the loser, eh? So I must avoid that, eh, Mr. Van Cleve? When my adversary has sixteen pieces and I have fourteen, I am only one-eighth weaker than he. But when we have exchanged thirteen pieces, he is three times as strong as I. Eh? You see what I mean?"

A costumed servant girl came in bearing a silver tray of baklava pastry and ayran, a buttermilk-like yoghurt drink.

"So now how may I help you, dear, sweet lady?" asked Ali Reza as he stuffed an entire piece of baklava into his mouth. "You once did me a big favor."

Taylor told him quickly about Phillips Taylor.

"And that is all the favor you want from me? To arrange a meeting with this well-known and despicable chameleon?" He was already picking up a gold French-style telephone from its cradle. "I was hoping you wanted a really big favor. My joy is doing favors—big favors—and receiving favors from my friends. But this, this is like . . . how you say? . . . falling off a stick."

"Log," Taylor corrected.

He spoke rapidly in Turkish for a few minutes, his mouth with its fat lips hard, his voice steely, and with no evidence of the charm he had been displaying.

He hung up.

"Done," he said with a grin. "He will be in the Cicek Pasaji district tonight at six-thirty. At a bar called the Golden Sphincter."

"That is some name," Jason commented.

"You will see that it is *some* place," said Ali with a lewd wink.

The Golden Sphincter was a sleazy cafe, located, appropriately enough, in the bowels of the city. When Jason and Taylor stepped off the street into it, they saw that it was patronized at six-thirty on this particular evening by a number of aging homosexuals, several seedy-looking men, and one dwarf. The only touches of class in the odoriferous place were two large, yellowed, and tattered Toulouse-Lautrec posters on one wall, which were nullified by a large reproduction of the Belgian statue of a urinating boy behind the bar, and the fly-embroidered sausages hanging from the ceiling.

Jason didn't like leaving Taylor alone, but he had to go to the bathroom. It was near the bar and was surprisingly large and clean. As he was urinating, a water-closet door opened and a lean Turkish man stepped out. He had a goatee, and from his fly protruded his giant organ, steel blue with its erection. The man smiled. "You like? *C'est beau?*"

"Magnifique," replied Jason as calmly as possible.

Then, for the first time, he noticed a tall, thin man dressed in a business suit and leaning in the corner. Jason couldn't see his face because he was bent over lighting a cigarette, but he had red, spiky hair. Jason went back to Taylor quickly and sat at the table.

Phillips Taylor was only five minutes late, and he looked around cautiously as he came in. He went to Jason's round marble table and slumped into a chair without waiting to be asked.

"Aloha," he said.

"This is Mrs. Phillips," said Jason.

"We've met," she said.

The man looked startled when he recognized her, as though he might bolt. Pearls of sweat were on his forehead.

"Relax," said Jason.

The man recovered his poise and tried to say jauntily, "Ac-

61

tually, I believe I owe Mrs. Phillips a debt. At one point I needed a fancy new name. I heard hers and just turned it around. In fact, I even thought I might call myself E. Phillips Taylor the Third, but maybe that would be *de trop*."

"Maybe," agreed Jason. "We'd like to ask you a few questions."

"And if I don't choose to answer them?"

"We've just come from Ali Reza. Would he be pleased to know that you didn't choose to answer them?"

The man winced a little. "So—what do you want to know?"

"Everything about Nestor Lascaris."

The man hesitated. "Everything?"

"Everything," said Jason emphatically.

The man put on a midwestern accent. "Well, there's folks round here who seem to wish me to be quiet."

"But some who wish you to talk," said Jason. "Quick."

"Well now," the man said slyly, quite expertly slipping into a cockney dialect, "As the vicar's woife said at the choir boys' picnic, oi don't roightly know which way to turn!"

"Ali Reza!" warned Jason sharply.

The man's face went serious. "Ah, yes, Mr. Reza." He sighed, hesitated a moment, and then started to talk.

"Lascaris knew I had acquired a passport for the guy that used to work for him, so he figured that for some dough I could put him in touch with a writer. He wanted only an Englishman or an American. I've got a connection in the travel business. He gave me the Royal Viking list of VIPs, so I got him—you. Okay, so why didn't we come back? Well, that very day the old man joined the turf club, you might say."

"How?"

"Not of old age," he said. "Nor of hemorrhoids."

"How, then?"

The man shrugged and smiled grimly. "Mysteriously."

"How?" Jason persisted.

"I don't know! He said he wanted to take a nap, and that I should come back. He was supposed to have called me. He didn't. Went on his own, apparently. Next thing I knew, they said he was dead. They said he swallowed the key to the handcuffs before he died, but they cut off his hand and took the briefcase."

Taylor sucked in her breath and closed her eyes.

"Who's 'they'?" Jason asked.

"I don't know. I only heard through the grapevine...they don't name names."

Jason blew out a breath and glanced at Taylor.

"That's all you can tell us about him?"

The man shrugged noncommittally. Jason extracted a five-hundred-lira bill from his wallet and put it on the table.

"Come on...anything at all...any little detail."

The man gazed at the ceiling and wrinkled his brow in an exaggerated attempt at recall, while at the same time his fingers deftly removed the bill and slipped it into his trousers.

"Yes...there *was* something. When I was driving him down to the ship to see you, he insisted that we go out of our way to a small photographic shop on the outskirts of Izmir. Stayed there about five, ten minutes. Gotta go!"

"What was the name of the shop?" Taylor asked. "Where was it? And you'd better tell the truth."

"Shit, the address? Who knows? Poseidonos Street, maybe." He took out a pen and started to draw on a paper napkin. "Here's a map showing where it is—more or less. I think it was called Photography Pandora or something like that."

Jason noticed that the tall thin man with red hair whom he'd seen in the bathroom was now at the bar, with his back to them.

Phillips Taylor also saw him.

"Sayonara," he said.

He quickly shoved the napkin toward Jason, got up, and quietly oozed out of the Golden Sphincter. The red-haired man immediately left the bar also, not far behind him.

"Our friend is a jumpy one," said Jason. "And I'm sure with good reason."

"I take it the next stop is Izmir and the camera shop?"

"You can't go! I don't want you to get involved in this."

"But I already am. Terribly." She pressed his hand. "And you get lost in Izmir, remember?"

"No," he said.

"Yes," she said.

• • •

"Phillips Taylor" slunk out of the bar at a normal pace, but once out in the cobbled street he broke into a sprint. He wasn't quite sure who or what he was running from, but he'd spent a lifetime running from something or someone and he knew instinctively when he was marked or being tailed, and for some days now he'd seen that redheaded, thin-faced man in his vicinity too many times.

The street was crowded, but he blended into the crowd, who paid no attention to the fact that he was running while they were walking. This was, after all, Istanbul. After three blocks he stopped and looked back. The man was nowhere to be seen.

"Phillips Taylor," a.k.a. Michael Swenson Redmon, as well as a dozen other aliases, took a deep breath. Then he doubled back on his tracks to an alley he knew. He knew every alley in Istanbul, since he'd been born here, the illegitimate son of a British consul general by a Turkish whore, some forty-five years ago.

The alley was narrow, long, and cool, and it would lead to the street where he lived in a cheap boardinghouse. Whatever money he made, and by whatever means, he did not spend on housing, but rather on clothes, as part of his professional wardrobe for appearances for his varied scams.

As he walked down the alley, trying to avoid letting his new cordovan shoes come into contact with the many piles of animal and humas feces, he thought of Nestor Lascaris and how lucky it was he'd been paid something in advance by the old man before his unexpected demise. What the hell was in those papers, that people would kill for them? Maybe it was some kind of treasure map that showed where to find some buried—

Suddenly a thin, dark shadow appeared out of a doorway in front of him.

"Oh, God!" he gasped involuntarily.

"No," said the man. "It's just me—Melnick."

"What do you want?" he whispered, and he could feel the sweat pouring down his face as he looked into the muzzle of a pistol with a silencer on it. "How'd you get—"

"What'd you tell him?"

"Who, Van Cleve? Nothing. I had nothing to tell him! Except about Lascaris's death."

"I know about that," said Melnick. "All about that. What was all that writing on the napkin?"

"Did you kill Lascaris?"

"What did you write down for Van Cleve?"

"Oh, that . . ." He looked down at the pistol leveled at his stomach. "Christ, you're not going to kill me, are you?"

"'Course I'm not going to kill you," said Melnick. "Not if you tell me what was on the napkin."

"Photography shop . . . P-Pandora," he stuttered. "Pandora Photography . . . or vice versa. Izmir! 'Near the movie house on Poseidonos Street.' Something like that. C-can I go home now?" He pointed down the alley.

"What's in the shop?"

"Pictures of some scrolls or something. Can I go home now?"

"Yes, you can go home now."

The pistol went *spunt-spunt-spunt* . . .

And Phillips Taylor looked down at his stomach in amazement as he convulsed and then sagged slowly to the cobblestones.

The assassin glanced around him, put the pistol inside his jacket, and looked at his watch. He had to get to Izmir before Van Cleve did. He was a helicopter pilot, but it would take too long to rent an aircraft. Luckily he had a very speedy car and was an excellent driver.

He stepped over the body and walked rapidly down the alley.

It was dark on the drive to Izmir, and the otherwise colorful towns of Osmaneli, Bursa, and Susurluk were quiet and pale and mysterious in the moonlight. They bought sandwiches and some rich, thick Turkish coffee at Balikesir, and ate in the car. It was after midnight when they drove into the outskirts of Izmir. Jason had to shake Taylor.

"Time to go to work. You're the navigator on this mission."

She snapped awake almost at once. She knew the complex city well, having once been stationed in Izmir as vice-consul, but it was difficult to make out the hastily drawn map. Nevertheless, they finally found the street and then they saw the photographic store.

"There!"

Incredibly, they saw a fire truck in front of it and another was pulling up, and people were crowding around, many of them in their nightclothes. Smoke was rolling out of the front and billowing up under the yellow Kodak logo, which was larger than the old faded sign: FOTOGRAFIA PANDORA.

"Someone beat us to it!" breathed Jason. "What a funny, funny coincidence."

They parked and got out, and Jason took the napkin the sandwich had come wrapped in and soaked it in the dregs of the coffee. Taking Taylor by the hand, he sprinted for the store. As they came to the entrance, a policeman held out his arms to stop them.

Taylor took out an old calling card that identified her as a vice-consul of the United States, and began to rattle away in Turkish, keeping the policeman distracted as Jason ducked under one of the man's arms and stepped through the open door into the shop.

Taylor's hysterical account of how she thought her father might be in the blazing building enlisted the policeman's sympathy, and her feigned efforts to enter the building herself in search of her father kept him fully occupied.

Smoke was billowing up to the ceiling. Jason tied the wet napkin around his face and bent low as he looked around the room. He could make out enlargements of photos of babies and brides on the walls, and on the counter was a cash register and in the vitrine were rolls of Agfa and Kodak film in their respective blue and yellow boxes. An obviously useless fire extinguisher lay on the floor. Jason pushed open the door to the back room and then dropped to his knees as the smoke poured through the opening. He saw where the actual fire was, for the darkroom and storeroom were flickering with tongues of flame that sprang through the smoke like electric serpents from various places around the room. He could dimly see the firemen attacking the blaze from behind the store, where it had probably originated.

He looked around quickly as he pressed the napkin tight

against his mouth and nose. Above the enlarger and the sinks were shelves, and on them were rows of files in cardboard boxes. They were arranged in alphabetical order, and the flames had already burnt some of the boxes toward the back of the room. The fire had consumed the "H–I" file and was leaping toward the "J–K" box. Jason reached up and pulled down the box that had the letters "L–M" on it.

He started out the back door, but a large flaming beam crashed down from the ceiling, barring the way. He looked over his shoulder toward the front entrance. Now it was a wall of flame. He turned back to the burning beam. Quickly he put down the box and picked up the spent fire extinguisher. Using it like a sledgehammer, he slashed and hacked at the charred beam. On the third blow the wood broke. Jason tossed aside the extinguisher, picked up the box, made a running leap over the flames to the door, and stumbled outside.

Hugging the box to his stomach and trying to conceal it as best he could with his jacket, he ran around the corner until he could see the place where Taylor was still continuing her harangue with the policeman. He whistled once and ran for the car, threw the box in, and got behind the wheel. He started up the Citröen and spun it around in the street as he saw Taylor running to meet him, followed dutifully by the outraged policeman, waving his stick and looking ridiculously like something from a silent movie.

The thin-faced, red-haired arsonist saw neither of them. He had watched Jason go in, but did not know that he had come out the back.

Jason reached across the seat and opened the door, and Taylor jumped in. He jammed his foot down on the accelerator and they roared down the narrow street.

"You okay?" she panted, looking at Jason with concern.

"A little smoky, otherwise okay, thanks."

"You were a fool to do that. I hope it was all worth it. It seemed to me you were in there forever!"

"Thanks for entertaining the Keystone Kop back there. Couldn't have pulled that caper without you."

"Well, don't count on me for any more things like this."

Jason looked up at the rearview mirror. "I think we may

have something else for you to worry about," he said. "What do you make of that car behind us?"

"Could be the police. It has red lights."

"I'm not as afraid of the Turkish police as of . . ."

"As of what?" Taylor looked at him searchingly.

"I really don't know." Jason shook his head. "You think that fire back there was an accident?"

Her face turned serious as she replied, "Yes, it was a bit of a coincidence."

"But how in hell did they know to set that thing just minutes before we got there? The man at the bar? I noticed he left right after Phillips Taylor did."

"He probably offered my reverse namesake another piece of change for the same information he gave us."

"Or saved the money and got it out of him with a gun."

"Maybe Mr. 'Phillips Taylor' is no longer with us. Maybe he too has joined the 'turf club.'"

"I wonder," said Jason grimly, "how much longer *we* are going to be with us, if we keep after the scrolls."

Taylor said, "Well, at least that car that was tailing us is no longer with us. It turned off at the last intersection."

"Good," said Jason. "Back to Istanbul?"

"Back to Istanbul," she said.

"I just had a not-so-good thought," said Jason.

"What?"

"Supposing what's in that box is just something like bills, invoices . . ."

She quickly took the lid off, and in the illumination of a street light they were passing under, she could see the contents.

"Whew!" she said. "We've got good news tonight. They were meticulous—each in its own carefully recorded envelope."

Four-by-five-inch negatives, dozens of them, hundreds of them, perhaps thousands of them, going back decades and decades, depicting the social lives of Izmir citizens whose names began with *L* or *M*. Weddings, births, graduations, funerals, and, occasionally, documents—important documents.

"Now for the bad news," she said. "Ready?"

"Yes?"

"The bad news is that each envelope is not under the name of the client."

"So how are they filed?"

"By number."

"Number?" he repeated.

"In other words, there's a corresponding card file with the name of the people that the photos belong to."

"Which is back in the Pandora," said Jason numbly.

"Burning," added Taylor.

5

"A DISGUSTING idea!" roared Cardinal Michael at the group, spittle spraying from his flaccid lips. There was little reaction from the group of high churchmen.

Cardinal Bartolomeo was bored. He glanced at his Rolex, his only worldly conceit. Meeting or not, he would have to leave for Paris with the Pope in a few minutes.

It would have been a run-of-the-mill conference of businessmen, except for the costumes—black robes, white robes, and red birettas—and the fact that the conclave was taking place in the Vatican's elegant meeting room, oak-paneled and high-ceilinged, amid the paintings and antiquities of centuries. There were some thirty men there, most of them cardinal deacons, but some cardinal priests and abbots were also present. The abbot in charge of finances sat at a long table flanked by two aides with stacks of papers and ledgers before them. The other men sat in the rococo chairs arranged in a semicircle, facing the table. They all had binders and some were taking notes. Most of them had briefcases by their chairs.

"I say it is a disgusting idea!" repeated Cardinal Michael, one of the oldest and most respected members of the See. "What you are suggesting, Monsignori, is that we prostitute the Vatican Radio to the highest bidder. Disgusting, and I say so with considerable heat."

Abbot Elminger sighed and went on with a variation of exactly what he'd been saying all morning.

"Your Eminences, let's get back to the deficit. It is very easy to be noble and above such things, Your Eminence, but still, how is one to run the Church in the style to which the world has become accustomed?"

"I submit, then, that we *change* that style," said Cardinal Michael bitterly.

"Your Eminence would have us go back to the Dark Ages— to all of us living in solitude, as they do at Mount Athos, or becoming wandering ministers with no churches?"

"That is not the worst idea I have heard this morning," said Cardinal Michael. "It was good enough for Our Lord."

"But hardly practical today, Your Eminence."

Another cardinal spoke up: "I, for one, am all for the idea about the radio."

A fat abbot grunted, "And so am I. How else can we afford to help the poor?"

"Quite apart from the poor," said Abbot Elminger, who had briefly been a clerk in a Swiss bank before hearing the call of the Church, and who soon thereafter heard the call of the Vatican, which needed a smart young man in the finance department. "Quite apart from the wonderful work we do, there is the simple problem of maintaining *ourselves*. Take New York, for example. In the vicariate areas of Manhattan, Staten Island, and the Bronx, plus the seven counties to the north, we now have 408 parishes, some 1,005 priests, 393 elementary and high schools with almost 200,000 students, nine hospitals, and seven instutions of higher learning. How are they to be maintained with all the rising costs?"

Cardinal Michael spat out, "Yes, of course we need money. But selling out the Vatican Radio! This powerful, influential voice! Selling it out to political factions, to big business—"

"Your Eminence," said Cardinal Deacon Bartolomeo, "may I remind you, we *are* big business?"

"And so you see," the fat, bespectacled abbot went on, as though no one had said anything about the Vatican Radio. "Or *do* you see? I realize that half of you have not understood a word I've said!" A great sigh. "All right, Your Eminences, let me recapitulate. *Deficit.* Now we all know the word *deficit,* don't we?" He glanced sardonically around the room. "Well, we have a deficit. Now before we truly understand the word deficit, we have to understand another word—*income.* Write that down. I-N-C-O-M-E. A word not to be found in any of our breviaries."

He looked balefully over the group of cardinals. "Income! Now our stocks, as you know or should know, are divided by countries—only ten percent in our beloved Italy, because of tax laws and political unrest, not due to any lack of patriotism. About thirty-five percent, maybe forty, in America. The rest in Europe. Well, there is a bit in Japan. Almost nothing in Latin America and Africa. That is the source, the major source of our income, as you know.

"Secondly, *l'obolo di Pietro*—Peter's pence, as they say— are the offerings of the faithful all over the world. A third source of income is from missions and special collections. Fourth, from rentals and sales of real estate. Fifth, from sales here at the Vatican of coins, stamps, books, et cetera, to tourists. Sixth..."

As he sat with this conclave in the depths of the Vatican, the Brooklyn-born Cardinal Deacon Bartolomeo was bored, and his swinging right leg, crossed over his left, was a sure indication of his growing impatience. Why couldn't these bloody accountants, or rather these esteemed and blessed clergymen, get to the bloody point? He wanted to leave. He *had* to leave in twenty minutes for Paris, but he was obliged to stay so that he'd be able to brief the Pope on what had transpired in this meeting. His Holiness was too smart to attend in person.

Barto, as his few intimates called him, had better things to do than attend this meeting. Church matters, real Church matters—the earthquake in Honduras, the flood in Verona, Cardinal Vincenzo's mother dying of cancer and her last wish to see His Holiness—not the mundane secular business matters of a group of men who, in spite of their titles and fancy clerical robes, were no different than a bunch of Wall Street brokers.

And Taylor Phillips. Just to think of her was a pleasure. What a good friend she had become in the last few years! He had never had a woman friend like her. Before he'd gone into the Church, way back in his Brooklyn days, there had been a woman . . . Angelina Battaglia . . . a lovely young girl whom he had adored. He had wavered between the Church and Angie, but God had made the decision for him, by taking Angie away with leukemia. Since then, he'd never really thought of any woman as more than a parishioner, except the lovely Taylor Phillips, and even she didn't know how often he thought of her, and how tenderly. Now this telephone call from her, asking about some scrolls. How in the world had she become involved with something like that? Of course, her research into architectural relics could have brought her in contact with others interested in antiquities. It had been one of his great satisfactions to encourage her interest in archaeology when her husband left her and her depression was so worrisome to him. And that young son of hers—such a fine boy. Oh, to have a son like that!

He forced himself to look at the speaker and concentrate on his words. But then he found himself looking around and wondering, *What would Jesus have thought if He'd suddenly walked into this room, this marketplace?* Father Bartolomeo chuckled inwardly as the thought piqued his imagination and he visualized the Nazarene walking into this staid and beautifully furnished chamber, dressed in His simple white robe and sandals and addressing the gathering solemnly: "Deficit, brethren? Of course it hath come to pass that ye hath a deficit; yea, verily ye did not buy soybean futures when I advised ye thus!"

Unseemly, unworthy thoughts, Barto, he said to himself. Mother had said early on that his sense of humor would be his ruination. Maybe she was right. Maybe that was why he was only a cardinal deacon instead of an archbishop or even a Pope.

He glanced at his watch. He'd give it a few more minutes. He brushed his fingers through his leonine mane of gray hair. Except for his thick lips, he was a good-looking man of sixty-four. With the unlined face and athletic body of a man twenty years younger, he walked with a limp that was not the result of age but rather of a piece of metal that was still embedded in his knee, a souvenir of the Second World War, when he had been a chaplain on an aircraft carrier. He'd received the Purple Heart and other medals for that episode, when, his leg spouting blood and his uniform afire, he had dragged an unconscious man from the cockpit of a flaming Helldiver. He wished he had taken the surgeon's advice and had the second operation to remove the chip that had been missed in the initial emergency surgery, but he'd been young then, and the leg hadn't even slowed up his tennis game. Funny how these things caught up with you when you grew older.

Time to go. Father Bartolomeo stood up for a moment, letting the circulation in his bad leg improve before attempting to walk.

"Yes, Cardinal Bartolomeo?" the abbot's abrupt voice was directed at him. "What do you think, Your Eminence?"

"I think," said Father Bartolomeo, making an elaborate gesture of looking at his watch, "that if I don't leave this august body of savants right this moment, His Holiness will bust me back to altar boy."

Under the ripple of laughter, he took his briefcase and limped out of the conference room. As he stepped out into the hall, he saw two cardinals huddled in conversation. There was something about both of them he'd never liked—something almost sinister, especially about Cardinal Tobin. He was an unattractive man. Very small and trim, he came from Ireland, but was as dark as any South American Indian. His black hair was combed down over his forehead and his manner was brusque, dictatorial, detached, and authoritative.

The other was Tertius, a brown-haired, cadaverous fifty-year-old Neopolitan. He was considered an intellectual, possibly because he spoke five languages and wore glasses with lenses as thick as the ends of cola bottles. It was rumored that he was a pederast, and Bartolomeo always felt a little discomfited in Tertius's presence. The two greeted Bartolomeo with pasted-on smiles and he nodded back.

As he hurried down the hall, he saw a familiar form at the end, by a drinking fountain whose water gushed forth from the mouth of a leaping porpoise. As he neared, the man looked up.

"Barto!" he called out with obvious pleasure.

In the See, there were more than a hundred cardinals, but only this one called him by his nickname. They had known each other since St. Catherine's, back in Brooklyn, where they once had served together as altar boys. They didn't see each other often these days, and Bartolomeo regretted it.

"Georgie!" countered Cardinal Bartolomeo. "Just the man I need to talk to. Walk along with me!"

He had called Patrick Furst "Georgie" when, as a youngster, Patrick had admired the movie actor George Raft, and, indeed, he had resembled the star in his sleek, dark good looks.

"So, Barto," Patrick said with an easy smile, "how goes it? Pretty grim back there with J. P. Morgan and Sons, eh?"

In the Vatican, Patrick Furst was called Cardinal Patricio. His mother was Irish-American and his father a Jew, Polish-born, who had come to America prior to the First World War. His father had been employed by a large corporation and sent with his family to Germany because of his ability to speak German. When the Nazis came into power, he was "relocated." Patrick managed to get his mother and himself back to the States, where they later learned that his father had been "relocated" to Auschwitz. His mother was convinced that her husband's fate had been God's way of punishing her for having left the Church, since her husband had not even become a naturalized United States citizen and had no intention of abandoning his faith when they married. She atoned for this lapse by persuading their only child, Patrick, to become a priest. He became, and remained, fanatically religious, growing more zealous as he got older.

Father Patricio was a handsome man of sixty-three, his once patent-leather hair was only slightly gray, and his deepset eyes were those of a melancholy dreamer and ascetic.

"Boring, deadly boring," agreed Bartolomeo. "Maybe it's age. I used to find everything about the Church, even the seamy financial workings, interesting. But now all I think about are my bum leg and my liver. I don't even play tennis anymore. I tell you, Georgie, old age is no place for sissies. After fifty it's just patch, patch, patch!"

"But you, Barto," Father Patrick said. "You look a lot better than most of us. We're all marching down the road, though." He slipped his arm through the other's as they walked. "Let's just think of our age as life's test score—the closer we get to a hundred, the closer we get to perfect."

"I'm glad to have this chance to talk to you, Patrick. You know all about the history of the Church. I had a phone call from Istanbul, from Mrs. Taylor Phillips."

"Ah, a lady friend, Your Eminence?" Patrick chided. "Seems to me you've mentioned her before."

"I may have. I am very fond of her...lovely person...sometimes this damned uniform..." He indicated his Cardinal's robes. "But anyway, we are good friends and I keep an eye on her boy, Jonny, who's been staying here in Rome with Taylor's sister, Jean Hudson."

He then told Patrick about Jason, Lascaris, and the story of the scrolls.

Father Patricio was suddenly a little pale and shook his head vehemently. "Wish I could help you, Barto, but it sounds to me like just another hoax. I know of no such scrolls. Sorry."

"Thanks, Georgie. I'm sure you'd know, if anyone would. I'll give her a call and tell her our resident expert says it's baloney. Well, I've got to run. Can't keep His Holiness waiting."

"Have a good trip, Barto."

Patrick waited until Bartolomeo went around the corner, then walked back quickly to find Tobin and Tertius. They were no longer in the hall, so he went to Tobin's office and knocked on the door. He could hear a rustling of papers.

"Who is it?" asked Tobin.

"Patricio."

"One moment."

The door opened and Patrick walked into the small office. Tobin quickly closed the door and locked it. There was a glint of triumph in the little man's eyes, and Cardinal Tertius had a pleased smirk on his face.

"Look, my friend, and tell me whether or not the Guardians still know how to get things done!" Tobin said as he went to the desk.

"It just arrived," added Tertius. "By, one might say, special courier."

Tobin took out the briefcase with the locked handcuff still dangling from it. "A little present from Izmir!" he said as he brandished it. "And wait till you see its contents!"

"Why the handcuff?" Patrick frowned. "I trust there was no violence connected with the assignment."

Tobin assumed a hurt look. "My dear Patricio, it is a violent world outside our Vatican. Besides, we Guardians never inquire about details. The overall image of Christ is all we care about." He opened the case, saying, "And what were you and our beloved *confrere,* Bartolomeo, talking about? Something interesting?"

Patricio hesitated, then said, "Something very interesting indeed. We did not get that briefcase in time. Lascaris got to Van Cleve. Photographs were made. Bartolomeo's friend was involved, the one whose child he looks out for here in Rome."

Tobin cut him off. "Van Cleve is alive?" His little black eyes went squinty. "I had reason to believe he died in a fire in Izmir."

Patricio looked hard at Tobin, then said, "I wouldn't count on it."

"What else did your friend Bartolomeo tell you?" asked Tertius.

Father Patricio said, "He only wanted to know if I had ever heard of the Ephesus scrolls."

"And what did you tell him?" Tobin demanded.

"That I had never heard of them, of course."

"Who is this child you mentioned?" Tobin asked. "Who is this friend of Bartolomeo's? What have they to do with this?"

"The woman is a Mrs. Phillips, and it is her son that is here in Rome, living with his aunt while going to school here . . . Jean Hudson. Bartolomeo has mentioned before that he looks in on them. Apparently he's known Mrs. Phillips for some time. She was once vice-consul of the United States in Izmir."

"I repeat, what does she have to do with this?" demanded Tobin.

"It seems she has taken up with this Van Cleve," said Father Patricio.

Tobin nodded to Tertius. "That must be the woman we were told about." Turning back to Patrick, he asked, "Does Mrs. Phillips agree with Mr. Van Cleve's crusade to find the scrolls?"

"I think not. She is a good Catholic."

"As we all are!" said Tertius. "Perhaps she might be very helpful to us, should Van Cleve's American zeal and investigative powers lead him to the original scrolls. Perhaps we should urge her to cooperate with him."

"And then what do we do with the scrolls?" asked Patrick. "Destroy them, I trust?"

"Ah," said Tobin. "We will decide that detail once we get our hands on them. Our Lord will help us decide what to do with them." Cardinal Tobin then took a small black book from his desk drawer, saying, "If you'll excuse me, gentlemen, I have some phone calls to make."

Patrick said, "I must go anyway," and left the room.

Tertius had not intended to leave, but Tobin waited with feigned patience until Father Tertius realized he was no longer welcome and left.

When both men had gone, Tobin picked up the phone and made two calls: one to San Francisco, to a clergyman, and the other to a professional criminal, a specialist in kidnapping who lived on the outskirts of Rome.

The one to the clergyman was delivered in a cheery, offhand way.

"Bless you, Edward. How goes the battle? You are well? Thank God for His blessings! I am well also, thanks be to Him. Ah, traveling, are you? Spread that special gift of yours to communicate the Word as far as possible."

"Now"—Cardinal Tobin's voice went down an octave as he became serious—"I trust this line is, well, inviolable, as we say? You're sure? Truly private? Good! Problems? Yes, you can imagine. Now, with reference to our previous conversation, we've found a good man for the assignment. His name is McCue. We'll have him contact you soon. He must be engaged, but misled. Tell him Melnick recommended him. So if he is apprehended or gets in trouble with the authorities, it is Melnick who is to blame, understand? I thought you would. You received the photos? Good. Give McCue the money and brief him. You'll have all the data by tomorrow. What? Don't worry about any previous orders from Cardinal Furst; he's as soft as eiderdown. The New Guardians are about to take over, believe me, and will run things in the traditional way, the way they used to be run in the old days. Be prepared.

"Now remember, emphasize to McCue that he should not simply go there and perform what we might call an ordinary task. No, it is far more complicated, and in fact, depending upon the circumstances, it may not be necessary for him to do *it* at all. He must be made to understand that. We must try to be civilized. We will let Van Cleve find the scrolls if he has the know-how and the desire. But don't tell McCue how much the scrolls mean to us—that they represent power and that we can use them as a fulcrum to form the New Guardians, which will continue the heritage of our forebears. Under no circumstances must they be returned to Cardinal Furst—or, God forbid, to the Vatican directly. I must go."

He started to hang up. "What? Oh, you mean if Van Cleve does indeed find the scrolls? Well, then, tell McCue to . . . you are sure that this line is secure? Well, then, Edward—*Eduardo, mi amico*—for Jason Van Cleve, it seems to come down to . . . *requiescat in pace*, eh? *Buona sera*, my friend, and may the spirit of Jesus fill your heart."

6

"I DON'T know," Taylor said, pacing up and down in her living room. "I really don't know!"

They had spent the whole day in the house, taking turns making coffee and running the negatives through the projector, looking at every slide in the "L" section, beginning with the year 1914.

Weddings, funerals, anniversaries, baptisms, baby pictures, honorary testimonial dinners, mayoral elections, war heroes, championship soccer teams, closeups of soccer stars, even some mild porn.

Jason tried to make light of it. "Here's a cute little naked baby, probably dead of old age by now—and here, looky here now . . ."

At one point Taylor exploded, "Did any of these pictures ever mean a goddamn thing to anybody?"

Jason patted her hand. "Calm, calm . . . such language!" he said. "Didn't the nuns teach you better?"

"The Catholic faith is something I espoused when I married, along with the man. Fortunately, it was more faithful than he was, so I didn't give it up when he departed."

"Look we're both tired, but let's try a bit longer, okay?"

But while several more amusing old photographs emerged, they found nothing that could have any bearing on history or antiquity. And still, the quantity of negatives remaining to be viewed was numbing to contemplate.

"Hey!" Jason suddenly said. "Look at this tombstone!"

But that was all it was—a tombstone.

Then Jason said wearily, "I'm getting punchy. I give up. We're just grasping at straws anyway."

Taylor sighed in agreement. "You look beat. Why don't you go get some sleep?"

"Join me?"

"Later."

He kissed her and shuffled off to the bedroom. He was exhausted and his intelligence told him that this long shot was not coming in for him.

He eased his body gratefully down onto the bed.

There came a light tap on the door and Taylor asked in a low voice, "Jason, are you asleep?"

He sat up. "No, not yet."

Her face was slightly flushed with excitement. "I'm sorry to bother you, but I think we've been going at this ass-backwards!"

Jason gave her a puzzled look.

"Look, sure the negatives are old, made years ago . . . way back when. But why did the old man stop at the shop just before he met you at the boat? Because he had ordered some new prints made from the old negatives, correct?"

Jason nodded.

"Then it was a *new* order! We started at the wrong end!"

Jason leaped up and pulled on his slacks, and together they went back into the living room and started viewing negatives from the other end of the box.

In ten minutes Jason exclaimed, "There it is!"

Part of an ancient scroll flashed on the screen, then another and another.

"I'm not crazy! That's it!"

"Aramaic!" Taylor exclaimed. She examined it for a moment, and translated the first few words: "'And it came to pass that Jesus was led . . .'" Her voice trailed off to a trembling whisper. After a moment she flashed another image on the screen, this one of a page of a writing in English.

After studying it for a few seconds, Jason said, "That's it! That's exactly as he read it to me—word for word! This must be the translation someone named Krenski made for the old man years ago."

More English translations appeared, apparently picking up the narrative where Lascaris had left off.

"This is probably the part he was going to tell me if he'd been able to return that afternoon. Poor old Lascaris."

Taylor's deep violet eyes were wide, and she said softly, in a voice filled with wonder, "God, now I'm beginning to understand why people would kill to suppress these things."

They continued to project the slides and watch the story unfold...

And so it came to pass that Lael watched Jesus as he was led across the brook of Cedron and through the streets of Jerusalem, and through the Gate of Sheep near unto the temple, where the sacrificial animals were passed. First to Annas, father of the wife of Caiaphas, the high priest and presiding officer of the Sanhedrin, was Jesus taken...

Annas then did order Jesus to be taken to the palace of Caiaphas, he who had instructed the Jews that it would be good that one man should die for the people. In the palace and bound like Jesus was the murderer Barabbas, also on trial.

Then were brought forth witnesses, an old man among them, and thus was he questioned:

"Say you not that you had palsy all your life and that now you do not? Who then did heal you of this affliction?"

And with his staff did the old man point. "He who stands before you."

"And how is he called?"

"Jesus of Nazareth."

Then spoke Caiaphas: "And did this man say unto you that he was the son of God?"

"He said only that he did God's work. And behold, my hands no longer shake."

Then did the hearers say much among themselves in low voices, and they did look to the old man with wonder. And then did Caiaphas make haste to call forth other witnesses.

And many were those who bore witness to the acts of Jesus, and after each did Caiaphas turn to Jesus and say, "How say you?" And ever did Jesus stand silent and say naught.

Then did Caiaphas, the high priest, grow wrathful, and he did say unto Jesus, "Swearest thou that thou art the son of God?"

And Jesus did say unto him, "This only I say unto thee: Henceforth thou shalt see the Son of Man seated at the right hand of God."

Then was Jesus beaten, and then was he dragged before the Procurator, Pontius Pilate, there to be sentenced.

But Pilate did only speak thus to Caiaphas and say, "Do with him what you want, for he is your prisoner."

And Caiaphas beseeched Pilate and spoke thusly: "For us it is unlawful to put a man to death."

And Pilate answered, "Thus it is left to us to do your bidding."

And Jesus stood before Pontius Pilate, and the soldiers did make mockery of him and dress him in purple robes and call him King of the Jews in jest, but Jesus did stand silent, with head bowed and sorely marked by blows.

I, John, was among the throng who sat by Lael, and we were in the front row before Pilate, and I could study his countenance, and it was that of a man much hated, for he was the sixth Procurator of Judea since the conquest, and had been so for ten years, and each year was he more hated and despised by us. Many were the things he had caused to be done as the representative of the Emperor Tiberius, whose statues were brought by night and set up in our temples. Confiscated were our treasury funds and murdered were many of our people, for reasons never explained. I did search his face for some sign that would give me hope; none did I see. Yet did it give me hope that the hearing was not within the house of the governor, for then we would not have entered, as we would not defile ourselves by entering the house of a Gentile before Passover. Also did the multitude who had gathered give me hope, for they were mostly Jews.

Then did Pontius Pilate speak to the multitude in mockery, saying, "You may have your king." And he looked down upon us.

And as he did look from one to another of us who were near to him, he looked also at Lael. And his gaze did stay upon her, for she was beautiful to behold.

And Lael raised her hand in blessing as he gazed upon her face and he spoke to his soldiers, saying, "Why does this woman of Judah bless me when all others curse?"

And none among them could answer.

Then did Pontius Pilate speak to the multitude, saying, "I find no case against this man. No more did Herod, for he sent him back to us. This man has done nothing to deserve death."

Then did my heart become joyful, for our prayers were to be answered, and so great was my relief that I did not hear the unrest of the multitude behind us. And yet did my heart wonder at such charity, for Herod Antipas was the son of Herod the Great, who had caused the slaughter of the infants, and wise was I to wonder, for Herod Antipas had his own reasons to keep Jesus alive, as he wanted some miracles performed. Thus was he little better than his father and his uncle, Herod Agrippa, who later had my friend James, also an Apostle, put to death. This Herod Antipas was known to be worldly and sensual, and had left his wife and lived with his brother's wife. For this, John the Baptist had condemned him, and thus Herod Antipas had John put to death.

And as I sat thus with my head bowed in prayer of thanksgiving, I heard a voice cry out, "Crucify him!"

And yet did I go on with my prayers of thanksgiving, for well I knew that most of the multitude behind me were also Jews, and none but a Roman would cry out thus.

Then did I lift my eyes to Lael and there saw her anguish, for many were the voices that were crying out, "Crucify him!"

In haste I looked up to Pilate as he sat watching over the crowd and listening to their cries.

And then Pilate spoke, saying, "It is the custom to be generous during your time of Passover. One prisoner may be spared. I leave it to you to choose. Which of these men would you crucify?" And he did point to the murderer Barabbas, and then to Jesus, and it was when he pointed to Jesus that my heart turned to stone, for the multitude called out as one, "Kill him!"

Then did Pilate look to Lael, and seeing the bowed head of flaming hair, he again spoke to the multitude, saying, "Flogging would befit this man more, for he has done no wrong."

But the people only cried louder, "Crucify him!"

Then did Pilate speak to his men, saying, "Take him away."

Again I turned to look at Lael, but her face was in her hands and she wept, much as any other woman.

After the trial, we disciples were sore afraid and most of us did hide. But Lael was ever steadfast, and she feared not for herself, but only for Jesus. And Mary, too, did counsel her to leave Jerusalem, for the mood of the people she understood not, and she was fearful that harm might come to Lael. But Lael stood by Jesus and would not leave.

And it came to pass that during the terrible ordeal, Mary and Lael and I followed as Jesus bore his cross and trod the long way to the hill of Golgotha, and sick I was to see his face as the blood did come from the thorns of the rude crown that had been placed on his head in mockery. And my heart was heavy laden to see him hanging there on the cross, and I was numb with sorrow.

Long we knelt watching while Jesus suffered, and then those who had followed Jesus to see him crucified did go their ways, and so we were but few left on Golgotha.

Then did Lael go forth, and the centurion let her pass, and she came near to Jesus and then his voice cried out, "Lael, Lael, lama sabachthani!"

A priest, standing not far from Mary, was heard to say, "Hear, he says, 'Eli, Eli, lamma sabachthani!'" And so it has been repeated over and over again through the years: "Eli, Eli, why hast thou forsaken me?"

But only Mary and I did know that he spoke to Lael.

And then Jesus looked upon Mary and spoke to her, saying, "Woman, behold thy daughter," Yet that has come to be repeated as, "Woman, behold thy son." Even so, I, John, know that I heard what I heard.

And then the skies grew dark and the rain came down upon us, and out of the body of Jesus drained all life.

Then came Joseph of Arimathea, for he had permission to place the body of Jesus in the tomb of his family. And we did place the body of Jesus upon a roll of linen that was rich with *the odor of spices, and we did roll the linen about his sorely wounded body, and we did lay him down according to custom, with his face toward Jerusalem.*

Then did I find Lael upon her knees, praying, and . . .

It was at this point that the scrolls and their translation came to an abrupt end, and Jason said, "I guess that's it. Wish we could have known how it ended."

"But you do. You've heard it many times, even if you don't attend church," Taylor said.

"Not this version."

"Parthenogenesis," Taylor mused as she sat, still staring at the now blank screen.

"What?" Jason watched as she got up and went to the bookcase.

"Parthenogenesis," repeated Taylor. "Means 'virgin birth' . . . from Greek *parthenos*, meaning virgin, and *genesis*, as in the Bible, meaning 'beginning.' I've just read an article on it. I still have it around here somewhere. I think this *Scientific American* . . . yes, here it is. You might want to read this while I get us some food. You must be starving."

"Sounds good," Jason said as he took the magazine from her.

"And here's a book too, on some other newly discovered scrolls," she said as she handed him *The Gnostic Chronicles*. "Let me add that I don't find it very believable."

Jason started to read, but glanced up from time to time to watch Taylor as she prepared the food, finding it amusing to watch her head bobbing from side to side to the tune she was humming as she put the oranges in the squeezer. She was quite a woman, and he wondered what could have happened to her marriage. His own marriage had been very comfortable—perhaps not sensational, by some standards, but good and easy. They'd had a few fights, but divorce? As his grandfather had said about his own happy marriage, "Murder, yes—divorce, never!"

He was really tired now, and the excitement of finding the negatives of the scrolls had taken its toll of his energy. It was difficult for him to concentrate on the dry parthenogenesis literature, but he kept trying. He read that numerous plants reproduce themselves by parthenogenesis, and that some insects—greenflies, wasps, and honeybees—give birth asexually. He read of the famous hen turkeys of the U.S. Department of Agriculture Research Center at Beltsville, Maryland, that reproduced without male participation. Then there were the Belgian hares that reproduced "if they could barely smell the male, even if his cage was no nearer than twenty feet away."

The article went on to say that parthenogenesis in humans had been reported in many cases since the Virgin Mary, and had been reliably documented by a team of scientists who found that a shock to the body was sufficient to make a woman's cells divide, multiply until nine months latter, a baby—a duplicate of the mother—was born.

Jason read on. He couldn't believe the number of case histories reported in which women swore they had not had intercourse to give birth, their stories supported by extensive medical and lie-detector tests.

"Learn anything?" asked Taylor as she set the table.

Jason looked up. "Always the same," he said thoughtfully. "It's always the same."

"What do you mean, always the same?"

"They always had offspring of the same sex—female."

"Really?" She frowned. Then she put down the utensils. "Wait a minute. There was something about..." Taylor went to her bedroom and Jason could hear her saying, "This book...it's about something else entirely...where is it? Here..." Her voice trailed off as she riffled through the pages while walking slowly back into the living room.

She sat down beside Jason and continued to search for the information.

"It's only a few sentences. I can't seem to find it now, but I do remember that it said *every* fetus starts out as a *female!* Then it requires the stimulation of the male sex hormones to begin the changeover at about the fifth week of pregnancy. That would mean, wouldn't it, that in the case of parthenogenesis, the offspring could *only* be female!"

"So," Jason said, "without the introduction of the male sex

hormones, the offspring will always be an exact duplicate of the mother!"

"And in the translations, it said that Lael looked exactly like Mary had looked as a child! Then Lael . . . ?"

"Right!"

"There's only one trouble with all this." She frowned.

"Yes?"

"We're trying to come up with all these rational explanations for the story."

"So?"

"We're forgetting that religion is not rational. There's something called *faith,* you know."

Jason thought for a moment.

"Tay . . ."

"Yes?"

"Supposing it is true. Would it be the end of the world? Does it matter, really, who thought out and taught the great concepts of the Christian religion? Supposing we found out definitely, for example, that Bacon wrote Shakespeare's plays—or that Mrs. Bacon wrote them, for that matter—what difference would it make? The plays are still there, not a word could be changed or have another connotation. The plays would not be one whit diminished."

"Ah, but this is so different, Jason!" Taylor said. "There the works stand alone, apart from the author, about whom we know virtually nothing. But with the Messiah, the words He left us with cannot be taken separately—they cannot be divorced from the man, from His life, from His miracles, from His sacrifices, from His Crucifixion and Resurrection. Yes, it would matter."

"We don't know the whole story yet—the new version."

"Are you going to try to tell me this Lael ends up on the cross too? How very strange that no one has ever seen a painting or statue of a crucified woman."

"I'm not trying to tell you anything, because I don't know any more than you do. But I'm sure as hell curious, and what I want to do now is get to an expert and have this checked for authenticity, or at least antiquity."

"But I wonder if your curiosity may not end up simply jeopardizing the faith of many, many people. I think *I* could accept it, if it were the truth. In fact, I'm sure I could. But obviously some people out there don't think the rest of the Christian world would."

"You mean the global repercussions, the domino principle, the lowering of the power of the Vatican, the social and political implications?"

"True or not, it could cause chaos—a moral A-bomb," Taylor said.

"Somebody out there certainly seems to agree with you, and will go to any lengths to suppress the story. That's just what is keeping me hooked on this thing. Who are they? Don't you understand, Taylor? I really don't care all that much about these scrolls, true or not. What I care about is the real story, the story about the people who don't want this to come out, and are apparently willing to resort to murder to see that it doesn't."

"In other words, the case of Mr. Nestor Lascaris."

"Exactly. But it's not quite as simple as that. The fact that the man was murdered shortly after talking to me means that they may now believe I know more than I do."

The phone rang. Taylor picked it up and spoke first in Turkish, then in Italian and English.

When she hung up she said flatly, "There goes your story. My friend at the Vatican says that Cardinal Patricio, who knows more about Church history than anyone, says he's never even heard of the scrolls."

"But—but you just saw them! Did you tell him that?"

"He said that was like the man who claimed he rode around the world on a bicycle and kept pointing to a bike saying, 'If you don't believe me, there's the bicycle.'"

"In other words, there are the scrolls, but that doesn't make the story true. All right, I'll buy that. But the scrolls still exist, and some people will kill for them!"

Captain Elev of the Istanbul homicide department had been helpful enough, once ten thousand lira were slipped into his sweaty palm by Jason. The dossier was opened and Captain Elev, tugging at his Fu Manchu moustache, provided superfluous information, accompanied by an array of sickening details.

It appeared that one Nestor Lascaris, aged over ninety, had been attacked by thugs on a side street of Izmir, near the home of his relatives. The thugs had smashed the victim's skull with a blunt instrument, possibly a tire iron, and his right hand had been severed with a surgically sharp knife.

The Turkish police, Captain Elev went on loftily, had repeatedly advised the citizens of Izmir and Istanbul to avoid walking in the streets while conspicuously carrying cases and purses that might provoke thugs. The captain also said it was doubtful they would find further evidence that might link anyone to the crime. He regretted the incident, offered his condolences, gave them the address of the nephew who had claimed the body for burial, and then dismissed them curtly.

"Shows the quirks of their mentality," said Jason as they walked out of the station. "One would think it would have been easier to cut off the handle of the briefcase."

Taylor gave a low moan of revulsion.

"Lascaris told me he had a daughter—a nun," said Jason. "I think we ought to talk to her, but he didn't tell me where she is."

"Why don't you just forget the whole thing, Jason? I think you're asking for trouble. Big trouble!"

"I told you, running away won't help. And the nephew lives here in Istanbul. He might know which convent she's in."

"I could drive you there," she offered finally.

The house was in a narrow alley in the heart of the city— an odoriferous, short street that stank of rotten melons and a thousand human urinations and dog excrement. After parking, they went to the door, which had a tile with the number twelve sunk into it, and they knocked with the heavy lion's-head knocker.

A young boy shyly opened the door.

Inside they could see that the house was surprisingly well furnished, though dark. A bald man with a paunch, wearing an undershirt, came up behind the boy, frowning suspiciously. He had a newspaper in one hand, a cigar in the other. He didn't invite them in or even greet them.

"Sir, do you speak English?" Jason asked.

The man nodded and growled, "What you want?"

"Nestor Lascaris..." Jason began.

"My uncle dead."

"Yes, I know and I am sorry. I met him the very day he died."

"Ah," the man said enigmatically. "That what you say."

"We had some unfinished business. He was anxious for me to collaborate with him on a book."

"Now my uncle dead. Crazy bullshit scrolls. Trouble for my uncle, trouble for me, my family... you keep on, trouble for you!" He started to close the door.

"He mentioned a daughter," Jason persisted.

"My aunt," the man said.

"Is she here? Could I see her?"

"Eugenia not see you even if she here. But she not here. Not live here. Not live in Turkey." He pronounced it *toor-kee*.

"Mr. Lascaris told me his daughter lived in a convent, on an island, Mykonos."

"You crazy. Eugenia live on Tinos."

"Of course... I meant Tinos."

"She not see you... she not crazy."

"What can *you* tell me about the scrolls?" Jason asked.

"I already tell you all I know—trouble! That all I know. You see Eugenia, and I no think so, you tell her about Uncle Nestor. Tell her he had good funeral."

"She—she hasn't been told?"

"We no want her to see how he die. We tell her later he die of old age."

He slammed the door.

They walked down toward the car.

"Clearly, a graduate of the Idi Amin school of charm," Taylor said.

"At least I now know where to find Eugenia."

A dying newspaper caught Jason's eye as it lay in the gutter, fluttering its wings. Something about a photograph on one page looked familiar, and he reached down and picked it up. "That's Phillips Taylor!" he said as he held it up for Taylor to read. "What does it say?"

"Oh, Lord," Taylor said as she scanned the Turkish letters. "It says he was shot and killed in the streets!"

"When?"

"The night we met with him at the Golden Sphincter."

"Oh, great," Jason muttered.

They walked in silence back to the car.

"Where is Tinos?" asked Jason.

"Near Athens."

"How near?"

"Well, it's an island, like Mykonos. I'm not sure how far."

"Mind driving me to the airport?" he asked.

"Yes, I would. I'd mind a whole lot," she said angrily. Then she looked over at him for an instant and said, "I wish—I really wish you wouldn't. I'm afraid for you."

"And *I'm* afraid for *you*. I've told you what happened to my wife. I'd better get away from you before they associate you with me. At least that way I can be pretty sure I'm the only one they'll follow. And whoever they are, I might be able to bargain with them if I can get them out in the open. Those photographs of the scrolls should give me some leverage."

Taylor drove on in silence, and just a bit too fast.

"You should be reasonably safe in your house, but it might be a good idea to ask your friend Ali Reza for another favor . . . like a security guard," Jason suggested.

"I don't think that will be necessary," she snapped. "I've been taking care of myself very adequately for years."

"Anyway, if I have to go to Athens to get to Tinos, I'll be able to stop by to see Yanni Elias. Ever heard of him? An ecclesiastical and political reporter for a big Athens newspaper. Used to be a stringer for the *Times*. He did some research for me by mail years ago, and then he looked me up when he came to the States. Quite a guy. Maybe he can shed some light—"

"Maybe he can make you *see* the light," Taylor said. "Make you cease and desist all this cloak-and-dagger stuff. Make you accept the Christian religion as it's been for two thousand years. I feel like that comic strip where Lucy says she'd have made a good evangelist because she'd convinced the kid who sits behind her that her religion was better than his, and when Charlie Brown asks how she did that, she says, 'I hit him with my lunch box.'"

She shot an angry look toward Jason and said, "I wish I had a very large lunch box now."

"Madame," he replied, "I have a very hard head. Anyway, all I'm going to do is go see a harmless old nun and then have a drink with an old newspaper reporter. Nothing very dangerous about that. And you may be right. Yanni may tell me I'm just wasting my time."

The pickup truck had circled the house twice—a small, well-kept white house with a red-tiled roof, on the outskirts of Rome. Two American boys, Jonny Phillips and his cousin, Rob Hudson, were playing soccer in the big front yard. Four Fanta cans marked the goal areas. Jonny, a good-looking eight year old with an explosion of blond hair, was two goals up on his older cousin.

For the first time in their intensely rival lives, Jonny was beating his cousin.

"Hey, spastic!" laughed Jonny. "Use your damn foot!"

"You better not let my mother hear you talk like that!" Rob warned with a scowl. He took his soccer and his tennis and his swimming very seriously; he took everything very seriously except his studies, at which Jonny excelled.

The truck stopped and one of the two men in it stepped out. With a big smile, he walked over to Rob, and said a few words.

"Hey, Jonny, he wants to talk to you!" Rob called out.

The boy amused himself by bouncing the soccer ball on his head while Jonny came over.

"Hi, Jonny . . . how goes it?"

He was a big, ruddy man with graying hair, and his English was perfect—a bit *too* perfect. He said "Jawnie" instead of "Jonny."

"Fine, sir," said the boy, his brow wrinkled questioningly. What was this about?

"Want to talk to you," said the man with his toothy smile.

"Something wrong? Mom?"

"No, nothing too serious. Just that your friend, Father Bartolomeo—well, he fell and broke his hip."

"Gee, that's too bad!"

"Oh, he's doing fine, but he'd like a visit from you. He's at a hospital near here. Won't take long."

Jonny hesitated. "Well, sure, but let me ask my aunt."

"Well, there's a problem—he's about to go into surgery. You'll be back in twenty minutes."

Jonny looked back at the house, then turned to his cousin and said, "Got to see a friend, Rob. Be right back. Practice up while I'm gone—you need it!"

He waved cheerily as they drove off, and Rob thumbed his nose at his cousin in return.

7

JASON HAD only been gone an hour when the telephone rang, and Taylor answered it. Long distance from Rome. What would her sister be calling about at this hour? But perhaps Father Bartolomeo had learned something more about the scrolls.

"Mrs. Phillips?"

The man sounded businesslike and strange.

"Yes?"

"Mrs. Phillips, are you alone?"

"Not exactly. Why? Who is this?"

"Mrs. Phillips, who is there with you?"

"My cleaning woman, though I can't see what business it is of—"

"Mrs. Phillips, put down the phone and go to another phone where she can't hear your conversation."

"What *is* this?"

"Another room, Mrs. Phillips," the voice commanded harshly. "And quick. It's about your son."

She put the phone down fast and picked up the extension in the bedroom.

"I'm alone."

"Mrs. Phillips, I'll be brief. We have your son."

"You have my—" she echoed.

"We are decent people, Mrs. Phillips, and we will not harm

him. We just want to be assured that you will work with us. It won't be long—only for the duration of Mr. Van Cleve's stay in Istanbul."

"But he's gone. He left today!"

"Where did he go, Mrs. Phillips?"

"Who *are* you? Why do—"

"Remember, we have your son."

"Athens," Taylor answered, then asked, "Please, please . . . may I speak to my son?"

"Yes, of course, Mrs. Phillips," said the voice smoothly, "One moment . . . here he is."

"Mom?"

"Oh, Jonny! Is it true? Are you all right?"

The eight-year-old voice sounded strong and confident. "Sure, Mom, I'm okay. I'm in a nice place . . . don't know where . . . but the people are okay to me and nobody's hurt me or anything. Just do whatever you have to do . . ."

The other voice came back on the phone.

"Very good, Mrs. Phillips. Now about Van Cleve—we're not asking you to do anything difficult or illegal. We just want you to keep an eye on him and tell us about his movements. I'm sure you will want to cooperate because you love your son and want to see him again." The voice sounded calm and reasonable as it asked, "And now, do you know where Mr. Van Cleve might be going in Athens?"

"Well, actually . . ." She hesitated.

"Yes, Mrs. Phillips, go on."

"Actually, he was going to Tinos, and I really don't know where—"

"That's very good, Mrs. Phillips. Now there are a few things I must caution you about. First, you will not call the police or your sister, or let anyone else know about our conversation. I know you can understand that police intervention would only endanger your child's life. Second—and this is very important—do not answer your phone. When we wish to contact you, we'll call, let it ring once, and hang up. We will then call back. Let it ring twice and then pick it up on the third ring. You will not speak until we have spoken first. Third, Mrs. Phillips, we would like you to go to Athens. Have you any idea where Mr. Van Cleve will be staying?"

"I don't know. He didn't say."

"Well, probably the Hilton. In any case, we'd like you to check in at the Hilton, locate Van Cleve, and stay close to him, you understand?"

"Yes," Taylor said in a voice near to breaking. "May I please speak to Jonny again?"

"Why, of course, Mrs. Phillips. Jonny?"

"Mom?"

She stifled a sob. "Jonny . . . oh, darling! We'll be together soon . . ."

Her son's voice was quavering. "Don't worry, Mom. I've got to say goodbye now, Mom."

The line went dead.

Taylor sat holding the instrument and looking at it, still in shock.

The old cleaning woman peered in at her and asked in Turkish, "Something wrong, madam?

"My son," said Taylor, trying to pull herself together. "He's not well."

"Oh, I am sorry. I'll make you some coffee."

"Thank you," said Taylor, then went into the bathroom to cry.

In San Francisco, California, it was eleven-thirty in the morning. The man looked nervously out at the lobby of the Hyatt Regency Hotel, where a twenty-year-old bovine girl was crossing the huge, plant-festooned room. She had an aloof, puckered mouth and the largest breasts he'd ever seen in his life. She was very aware of them, and it looked as though she were leaning backwards, either to keep her balance or to make sure that no one in the world would ever miss her only distinguishing feature. She sauntered over to the elevators—glass cages that slid up and down on the outside of the walls like yo-yos. She disappeared momentarily, then reappeared inside one of the rocketlike capsules. The man's mouth opened slightly as he adjusted his weight on the chair to accommodate the tumescence the girl's appearance had caused, then the elevator stopped and she disappeared forever from his life.

McCue sighed. He would like to have known her, to have touched those incredible breasts, however briefly. Maybe even to have kissed the nipples. He would think about her, about her pouty mouth and enormous breasts; he would think many times about that woman who hadn't even known he had observed her. When he was beaten next in the Athens brothel, it would be her in his fantasy, but without a blouse.

He glanced at his watch; it wasn't good to be late with these types, nor early either. He finished his drink and took the elevator up through the cascading greenery to the seventeenth floor. He was a short man, slightly effeminate-looking, an insurance man neatly dressed in cheaply fashionable clothes, with eyes that seemed overly moist. His nose ran continuously and he dabbed at it regularly with a folded white handkerchief. He could have been a bookie, a car salesman, or a disposer of cemetery plots.

He stepped out of the elevator with a polite "excuse me" to the other passengers, and went down the hall to room 1710. He only had to knock once before the door was opened. A robust man in his late fifties, bald on top with a halo of white hair, and a kindly round face, greeted him.

"McCue!" he exclaimed.

"Yes, sir," said the smaller man with a hint of an Irish brogue. "I'm McCue," he admitted, almost apologetically.

"Liz," said the big man to a bespectacled secretary sitting on the sofa with a pile of papers on her lap. "Same time tomorrow, eh? Want some M&Ms before you go?"

"Bad boy, sir," she said as she gathered up her things. "You know too much sugar's bad for you."

"But there are so few things left that are good for me," he laughed as he watched her go.

He took from his trousers pocket a brown and yellow paper bag of candy and offered it to McCue. "Some M&Ms?"

He was stalling for time while the secretary made her exit, and when McCue shook his head, the large man poured some of the polychrome candy pellets into his own hand and popped them into his mouth.

Then he arranged his pear-shaped bulk in his chair and said, "So you're McCue, eh?" Then, pointing to another chair, he said, "Sit down, sit down! So you're McCue?"

The little man sat down. Who was this fat old fart? He'd try a joke. "Well, if not, I'm sure having a ball with his wife."

There was a silence.

"I was given to understand that you were not married," the older man said, suddenly unjovial.

"That was just a little joke, sir."

"But you *are* McCue?"

"Oh, yes, that I am," McCue replied. Shit, the man was a mummy.

"And *do* you have a wife?"

"No, sir. Really. That was just part of my joke, sir."

"No relatives, children, people close to you?"

"No, sir."

"No girl, no woman you live with or take out? No one you confide in?"

McCue put his folded handkerchief to his forehead after he wiped his nose. "No, sir."

"Who knows you are here, right now, this moment?"

"No one in the world. Except a connection in Rome—"

"Yes, of course. A connection immediately forgotten, right?"

"Yes, sir, that's right." He'd play it any way the old boy wanted. "Forgotten already."

With a benign, grandfatherly smile he said, "You come highly recommended."

The younger man looked more uncomfortable. He was not used to compliments. Do the job, get paid, get lost. No compliments necessary.

"So what am I supposed to do? I mean . . . who?"

The big man, who was dressed in a white silk shirt, black trousers, and shiny black shoes, got up and paced as he talked.

"McCue, my friend, my new friend, you realize of course that your position is precarious from this moment on. One word to anyone about this meeting, this conversation, this assignment—one word, just one word—and you will be . . ." He gestured at the window and smiled genially. "You will be defenestrated."

"Don't understand," said McCue.

"You will be thrown out the window," said the big man

with a chuckle. "Oh, not literally, perhaps. But it behooves you not ever to divulge what we are going to talk about in the next few minutes. Furthermore, it will be denied and disproved that you and I ever met, much less conversed. And as for Monsignor X, who put us together, I'm sure you realize there is no such person. Understand?"

"Got it," said McCue.

The fat man beamed and held out some candy. "I am delighted that you have 'got it.'"

McCue took a candy and nodded. "I don't talk."

"So I've been told, my son. Most commendable. That's one of the reasons you have been chosen to handle this job. And you are reliable too, I'm told, very good at your calling. Like the proverbial Mountie, you always get your man."

The little man nodded as he took out his handkerchief and touched his nose gently.

"Now you want to know your assignment, of course. I think you will take to it willingly, more so than most of your jobs. You are, I presume, a good Catholic?"

"Don't know how good, sir, but—"

"But still a Catholic, yes? Any Catholic is a good Catholic to me! All right, there is a conspiracy afoot—a conspiracy designed to destroy the Catholic Church! I'll wager that your mother is a very fervent member of the Church, right? Right?"

"What's that got to do with it?" The man seemed confused. "She died about—"

"Sed en altre mane," said the older man charmingly, not listening to McCue. "'But on the other hand,' as they say in Latin. Catholics are always apologizing, have you noticed? They're always saying, 'Well, I went at Easter and I went at Christmas.' Well, if this maniac is allowed to go on, there just might be no Easter or Christmas as we've known them. You yourself may not be the best churchgoer, but people like your mother will have their worlds devastated by this maniac!"

"What maniac, sir?"

The large man popped some candy into his mouth.

"His name is Jason Van Cleve," he said.

Placing his hands on the arms of the chair he dropped into moments before, he heaved his bulk up, went to the desk and picked up a folder from which he extracted a sheet of paper and a photograph.

"This is he, and here is where he is at this moment, and here is his dossier."

McCue took the paper and the photo and said skeptically, "How could one man destroy the Catholic Church, sir?"

"Possible," said the big man solemnly. "Not only the Catholic Church but every branch of the Christian religion. Two thousand years, down the drain."

"Wow...heavy."

"And time is of the essence. But understand this—do not, uh, get him immediately."

McCue shook his head. "I'm supposed to get him but not get him?"

"You are supposed to *find* him and stay with him! And then be ready to...to do the job at any moment!"

McCue seemed genuinely upset. "I don't...well, how do I know when and what?"

"Your instructions are in this envelope with half of your fee. I understand it is usual to give a retainer, and then when the— Let me put it this way. A long time ago my mother had a cherished parrot, and one day I stopped by, looked at the empty cage, and said, 'Mums, where's Caruso?' And she, gentle lady who could never face the truth about anything, said, 'Oh, dear, I came down yesterday and it was, well, dear Eddie, it was sort of a leggies-up situation."

McCue nodded. "So this is—"

"Leggies up."

"May I ask...I mean, am I allowed to know just who's giving me all this bread? The Church? The Vatican? The Pope?"

The big man looked a little hurt. "Friend McCue, you must be crazy. The Church would never condone an action like this. The Church is above this sort of thing. No! It is an agency...an agency that protects the Vatican's interests. It's a committee of anonymous devoted Catholics, laymen who have quietly realized what harm this maniac could do to our religion."

McCue shrugged. "Guess I better get going."

"One more thing," the older man said as he went again to the desk and brought back another photograph. "Take a good look at this. This woman is a new friend of our target, Jason Van Cleve. Now get this straight—under no circumstances is this woman to be harmed. Understand?"

McCue took the photo and studied it. "Why not?"

"She is working for us."

"Oh." McCue nodded, showing no emotion. "Okay."

"Good luck, and God be with you."

Half an hour later, a large man in a cardinal's robes emerged from the lobby of the Hyatt Regency. A long green limousine was waiting, and the chauffeur jumped out of the front seat and held open the door for him.

"Thank you, Fred," said the man pleasantly. "Off to the cathedral!"

As he got in, he reached into his pocket, pulled out a small packet of candy, and said, "Fred, care for an M&M?"

As Jason got out of his cab at the port of Piraeus, the hot and humid day turned into a hot and humid rainstorm. It was raining hard and the water had the color of rust and was almost hot.

He had been warned that Tinos was going to be a difficult place to get to because of the important holy day tomorrow.

"The island is dominated by the Cathedral of the Virgin Mary," the cab driver had said. "They work all year toward this celebration."

Jason stood in line for three hours with a crowd of at least a thousand people. Six boats came and left, and he was still there. Then he saw a short, stocky man with a thin mustache take a couple and their child out of the line and, with authority, place them in a boat. Then he saw another man slip some money into the hand of the short, stocky clerk and get similar priority. Jason decided to do the same.

A man standing next to him on the boat hours later was blowing Turkish tobacco smoke casually, all of it wafting into Jason's face. The man flashed a smile of brown, tobacco-stained teeth. It seemed to Jason a shifty smile.

"Smoke?" he asked, offering Jason a filterless cigarette.

"No, thanks," Jason replied. *Was* he being followed?

"Are you going to Tinos for the Virgin Mary's day?"

"One might say so."

"Tinos is a sacred place," the man said. His face was as brown as his teeth, his fingernails were yellow-brown, and he had myriad wrinkles in every part of his skin, although he did not seem older than fifty.

Then, after a long silence he spoke again, as if to himself. "Yes, a place for miracles." He turned to Jason and said, "See for yourself," nodding his head in the direction of the pounding rain.

Jason looked out and saw the island's harbor, and people swarming over the quay. They were in Tinos.

The gigantic white cathedral looked more like a threat than a haven to the thousands of crippled and suffering that crowded the streets, weeping, moaning, and praying. As soon as they got off the boat, many walked slowly, while others fell to the ground and sank their faces in the muddy waters to kiss the soil blessed by the Virgin, then knelt and crawled on their knees the one and a half kilometers to the entrance of the holy church, only vaguely visible in the torrential rain.

It was a moving sight, and the thought flashed through Jason's mind, *How would these people react if they heard the story of Lael?*

Jason looked around. He saw that an old man had set up shop, selling umbrellas to the less faithful, and Jason hurried over to buy one. Many of the shopkeepers spoke English and he asked them how to get to the convent.

"Not within walking distance; five kilometers uphill climb," said one.

"But how else he going to get there on a day like this?" put in another.

"Why go up there at all?" a rosary seller asked. "All the nuns will be in prayer by now."

Jason thanked them all and started up the hill. He finally arrived, staggering and wet to his skin from both the rain and his own heavy perspiration. He was pale and panting when he knocked on the tiny wooden door that was painted with white lime, as was the rest of the building. He waited for long minutes in the unrelenting rain. Finally a small porthole in the door was opened and a pair of dark, curious eyes scrutinized him. He asked for Sister Eugenia and the porthole was shut in his face without a reply. Then he heard footsteps and this time the door was opened.

"I am the mother superior," said a woman in a black nun's habit. She had an accent, which Jason sensed was not Greek.

"Looking for Sister Eugenia," he gasped.

The mother superior looked at him from head to toe, hostilely, for he was an intruder in this convent. All men were intruders.

"Sister Eugenia is at Mass," she replied. There was no touch of sympathy in her inexpressive, disciplined voice as she asked, "Are you friend or relative?"

"Friend," he assured her, nodding his drenched head.

The nun pointed to a bench, also painted with white lime, on a small porch under a tin roof.

"You will have to wait for her right here," she said.

Jason thanked her and closed the umbrella. He needed nothing more than to sit down somewhere. He leaned back and wiped his forehead. The mother superior had already disappeared.

Jason's weary body and tired mind succumbed immediately to the sedative effect of the warm rain clattering on the roof of the little shelter as he slumped back on the wooden bench.

He didn't know how long he'd been sleeping when he was awakened by a gentle touch. He opened his eyes and saw a nun standing timidly in front of him.

"I am Sister Eugenia," she said.

About forty, she was quite pretty, her scrubbed face framed by a white coif and her petite body held erect. Her black habit seemed to give off a strange odor, which he could not identify. She had a nervous smile that revealed bad teeth. She spoke excellent English, but with a definite accent.

Jason told her about her father, and she sucked in her breath and made the sign of the cross, but said nothing. He did not tell her how her father had died, and he thought that since Lascaris was over ninety years old, she would assume that he'd died of natural causes.

Looking at this gentle woman, he could understand why her cousin had been reluctant to tell her of her father's death. If she had known in time, she would have wanted to come to his funeral, where she would have learned of the shocking way in which he'd died.

Jason was relieved that she asked no questions of him, but only bowed her head and closed her eyes for a few moments, as if in prayer. And then he identified the odor: camphor.

After a discreet silence, Jason cleared his throat and said, "The reason I am here, Sister Eugenia, is that your father and I were working on a book together when he died."

"A book?" she asked apprehensively.

"On the scrolls," Jason said. "The Ephesus scrolls."

Her bad teeth bit down on her lower lip. Then she gave a little laugh.

"Was he still talking about those old papyri? Of course you realize it was all fantasy. There were no scrolls . . . only in his imagination. He was very old, you know, and"—she tapped her head—"not quite right in his mind. Not crazy, you understand, just, how you say, senile."

"Sister Eugenia, I saw photographs of those scrolls. And read the translations. They were real. If not, how would you know they were on papyrus, not parchment? I'm not saying I necessarily believe what they said—just that they did exist."

She lowered her eyes guiltily. "All right. There were scrolls . . . those terrible things." Tears came into her eyes. "I wish we'd never had anything to do with them."

Jason urged gently, "Would you tell me what you know about them? Please? It is very important that I know. Two people have died because of them."

"I do not choose to speak of them!"

Jason sighed. "Sister Eugenia, I must tell you now that your father did not die a natural death. He was murdered."

She sucked in her breath, then gasped, "Oh, God in Heaven!"

"I'm very sorry."

"Because of the scrolls they murdered him? Who did this?"

"I don't know. That's why I'm investigating this. That's why I'm talking to you. I want to prevent more bloodshed."

She said nothing for a long moment. Then she looked around and said in a low voice, "All right. I will tell you what I know about them."

"Thank you." And he told her how much he already knew.

"I must warn you, some of the teachings in this, not just the part about Lael, are far from traditional."

"Like the Nag Hammadi scrolls? The Gnostic Gospels?"

She shook her head. "I do not know these things."

"They were found thirty-five years ago, but just recently came to light."

"You impress me," said Sister Eugenia. She was very pretty; only a suggestion of a mustache and her bad teeth kept her from being beautiful.

"Don't be impressed," Jason said. "I heard of them only recently, through a friend." He did not quite know how to proceed. He'd done much interviewing in his life, yet this was different. "The translator was a friend of yours, I understand."

"Yes," she said, and lowered her eyes. "Paul Krenski."

"I am curious as to why some of the translations sound more biblical than others."

She did not look up, but a faint smile came to her lips and she answered, "My friend Paul was young then, and he found the repetitions tiresome, but my father would demand them from time to time, so he put them in to please my father."

"And what about Mary Magdalene? For example," Jason ventured, "there are some references to Mary Lael being referred to as Mary of Magdala. You must understand that I am embarrassed about my ignorance of biblical history."

Sister Eugenia sat silently.

He was not sure she had understood him. "Sister Eugenia?" he prodded.

The silence continued.

Jason sensed that her reticence might be due to fear. "It seemed a bit extraordinary to me at the time, but I'm quite sure the Apostle John said that Lael was frequently referred to as 'she of Magdala,' and I've always been under the impression that Mary Magdalene was a woman of ill repute, as they say."

"There was a Mary of Magdala out of whom Jesus once cast seven devils . . ." she began.

Jason sat forward on the bench. "You mean . . . ?"

"This woman was beautiful, and she too had red hair."

"And Lael had red hair," Jason added.

"So she was *thought* to be the one they called Mary of Magdala."

Jason shook his head and smiled. "Sister, please, enough is enough. Are you trying to tell me that the one born the Messiah became a prostitute?"

"I am not trying to tell you *anything,* Mr. Van Cleve! You are the one who has come to me, prying!" She began to cry softly. "I only know what these scrolls *say* . . . and I should not be telling you anything at all."

He gently put his hand on her shoulder, and she blew her nose on an un-nunlike embroidered handkerchief that she had tucked into her sleeve.

"Mr. Van Cleve, John does *not* say that Mary Lael ever became Mary, the Magdalene. What he says is that for some reason she was mistaken for her—*mistaken* for a sinful woman from Magdala, and that she encouraged this misconception even to the point of almost being stoned by the Scribes and the Pharisees. It was then that Jesus stepped forward so authoritatively and commanded, 'Let him who is without sin cast the first stone.'"

"I thought that was the story of the adulterous wife," said Jason.

"Not in the Ephesus version."

"And Lael continued in the role of Mary Magdalene?"

Sister Eugenia nodded. "According to the scrolls, Jesus asked why she chose to allow this mistake to soil her reputation, and she explained that many of his followers were of humble, poor, and low station, and so would find her presence as his constant companion easier to understand if they continued to think that she was the grateful woman from Magdala out of whom Jesus had once cast seven devils. After all, Lael was an unmarried woman close to thirty years of age. That in itself cast suspicion on any woman, so it was a natural assumption that was easier to go along with than to refute, especially as it was unwise to reveal her true identity."

Jason said, "There is a poem in the Gnostic chronicles—I have it here—of a divine female power making declarations that might fit . . ." Jason took out his notebook and leafed to a page and recited:

> "'For I am the first and the last,
> I am the honored one and the scorned one,

I am the whore and the holy one.
I am the wife and the virgin . . .
I am the barren one, and many are her sons . . .
I am the silence that is incomprehensible . . .
I am the utterance of my name.'"

They sat for a moment, then Jason said, "That seems to make more sense to me now." Then he looked up at her, and said, "I must ask you something."

The nun stiffened. "You have asked me a great deal already." She made as if to leave. "I have told you too much."

"Sister Eugenia, do you believe in these scrolls? Do you believe they are authentic?"

"It is unfair of you to ask me that. All I can say is that I believed in my father . . . and I believed in Paul . . . and I believe in Jesus Christ."

"I'm sorry, I know this is an indiscreet question, but are we to believe that there was a relationship between Mary Lael and Jesus that might have been beyond that of brother and sister?"

"My opinions are of no value. I am no great biblical scholar."

"There is a passage in the Gnostic Gospels—"

"I have already told you, I do not know that book."

"But I was only wondering if this might resemble some of the ideas expressed in the scrolls," Jason explained. "It is the so-called Gospel of Philip, one of fifty-two scrolls found at Nag Hammadi, and I have made a note of some of it." He leafed through his notebook, then quoted:

"'The companion of the Savior is Mary Magdalene. But Christ loved her more than all the disciples and used to kiss her often on her mouth. The rest of the disciples were offended and said to him, 'Why do you love her more than all of us?' The Saviour answered and said to them, 'Why do I not love you as I love her?'"

Jason looked up at Sister Eugenia. Finally she said, "We will speak no more on that subject."

"I'm sorry if I have offended you," said Jason. Then, to change the subject he asked, "What ever happened to your friend Paul? Do you ever hear from him?"

"He went back to America. He phones me sometimes."

"When was the last time you spoke to your father?"

"Last Tuesday. He called to tell me he'd met you and was going to turn all his information over to you. I told him his life would be in danger, but he said he no longer cared. It was more important that the world should know about his scrolls."

"I'm sorry, Sister, he was killed that very night. We must stop them from killing anyone else." Then he asked, "Do the originals still exist?"

She nodded and whispered: "Yes, they still exist."

His heart gave a thump. "Would you know where? Could you tell me about them?"

She lowered her voice even more and said, "All through my father's life he was tortured by those blasphemous scrolls, and I have inherited his curse. He brought me to the Church and offered me, perhaps as a sacrifice, to atone for his failure to rid himself of his intellectual rationalizing over the heresy. First he went to Mount Athos to become a monk, hoping to strengthen his faith in the True Church. He entered the secluded monastery of Vatopedi. Finally he showed the scrolls to Abbot Constantine, hoping to be given an explanation that would allay his doubts once and for all. The abbot denounced them as blasphemy, confiscated them, and expelled my father. When he came home, my father was sick and shaken, convinced by the reaction of Abbot Constantine that he was headed for Hell. That was when he begged me to enter the Church as a nun. I did not have the vocation, but I could not refuse my father. I have since felt that he probably insisted on it for my own safety, thinking that I would not be accused of conspiracy in the blasphemy of the scrolls if I embraced the Church as a nun."

"You must have loved your father very much," Jason said.

"I shared much of his grief and much of his guilt over his findings. Paul and I discussed the translations. We—all of us who believe the teachings of the Church without question—do not quite see some things as Paul did. He was a Christian, but he did not belong to any particular church, as I understand is common in America. Paul could look at things like the scrolls with a clear conscience and an open mind; my father and I could not. Do you understand what I mean?"

Jason felt a constriction in his throat and nodded. He felt badly about his lack of trust in Nestor Lascaris. After the remarks made by Lascaris's nephew in Istanbul, Jason had expected Sister Eugenia to be hysterically evasive, but she had told her story in the straightforward manner characteristic of her father.

Jason delivered the message from her cousin, that her father had been given a good funeral.

Sister Eugenia thanked him and said, "Dominic is coarse and gruff, but he has a good heart. I will write to thank him for his kindness to my father."

"It's been a privilege to meet you and talk with you, Sister," said Jason in parting. "I was much impressed by your father, and perhaps one day we will find some . . . some justification, so that his cross and yours will have meaning and will not have been in vain."

"God bless you, Mr. Van Cleve. I will light a candle for you."

"Better make it two," Jason said as he took her hand.

As Jason left the convent, he noticed the mother superior watching him from the window of an alcove next to the shelter where Jason and Sister Eugenia had been talking. Her mouth was a hard slit and her eyes flinty as she turned and headed for Sister Eugenia's cell. Her footsteps echoed threateningly from the convent walls as she fiddled nervously with the thin rope that was tied around her waist.

How much had she heard of Sister Eugenia's conversation? Certainly Sister Eugenia would be in no danger in as sacred a place as this.

Yet when he started out into the dark storm, down the hill, his umbrella opened against the driving rain, he felt a terrible sense of foreboding and fear for the good woman he had just left.

8

IT WAS a hot and sticky Athens afternoon when he returned from Tinos, rain-wrinkled and mud-spattered. He got in a cab and started to direct the driver to take him to the Hilton—God, how good a hot bath would feel. Then he remembered Yanni Elias.

He looked in his little address book. Rather than wrestle with the difficult names, he showed the driver the address and telephone number, as well as his own name.

"Parakalo," Jason said. "You stop somewhere, you call, see if he is there and will see me . . . *efharisto."*

They stopped at a cafe and Jason waited while the driver went in and called. Ten minutes later he came back. He shook his head and his finger at the black book.

"He got new place now," said the cabby. "He glad to see you . . . very glad."

It was dusk when they got to a poor, rundown neighborhood. Jason told the cab driver to wait after they pulled up in front of a little house. In the street, several noisy children were playing at *balla*—soccer.

Jason saw a man, clad only in shorts, lying on a canvas cot in the yard under a naked lightbulb strung from a grape arbor, so Jason went in the garden gate. It had a bell on it that tinkled as he opened it, and the man, who had been asleep with a tape recorder in his hand, sat up.

"Van Cleve?" said a reedy voice. "That you?"

Jason walked over to the cot. It was a terrible shock to him when the man extended his hand. Unquestionably this was Yanni Elias, but he was a mummy of the vigorous, vital man he'd met some twelve years ago. Blind, feeble, wrinkled as a raisin, and skinny as a sideshow thin man, he struggled to get up, a dying man, then fell back.

"Jason? *Yassou!*"

"*Yassou*, Yanni!" said Jason. "How great to see you! How . . . how are you?"

Elias sighed, but with no self-pity. "Ah, you know, friend Jason, the mind is fine . . . it's the body. But you, Jason, you are really all right? How good of you to come. Here you catch me napping and recording my memoirs. And I have just got to Clara and Benito. Old Musso wasn't a bad sort actually— a fascist bully, of course, but always considerate of the lower folk, and he considered us journalists the lowest of folk, I assure you. Look here, I'm being rude. I'm drinking my *ypovrihio*—my submarine." He pointed to a glass of water with thick vanilla candy submerged in it, next to his tape recorder. "Have some, Jason?"

"No, thanks, Yanni, I have no time." But he sat down on the edge of the cot.

Yanni Elias gave a faint chuckle. "You think *you* have no time, my friend! My doctor has told me my days are numbered. I have maybe a month."

Jason gave a low whistle of sympathy.

"Maybe if I refuse to pay his fee, he will extend my time until I do. But what brings you to Athens?"

Next door was an open-air movie in a large garden filled with sunflowers and fragrant jasmine and equipped with wicker chairs. Young people ate *stragalia*—popcorn—and drank cola as they watched the movie. Over the dialogue of *Butch Cassidy and the Sundance Kid*, Jason filled in his friend about the past few years. He started to tell him about the scrolls, but hesitated; the man was so obviously sick.

"I'm thinking of writing something about Mount Athos," Jason said.

"You, a writer on religious matters?" Yanni said with surprise.

"Not exactly," Jason smiled. "This Constantine, what do you know about him?"

Yanni snorted. "What do I know of Constantine? Everything. Well, everything and nothing, as they say. Everything except the mystery of why this man, a very astute, worldly man, mind you, would gracefully and voluntarily give up his leadership of the Church, and retreat to Mount Athos to live in seclusion as the abbot of a monastery, never to be seen by anyone but the monks. For what reason?"

"Then he really was a powerful force in the Church?" Jason asked.

"The most powerful man in the Greek Orthodox Church. But then there is the Vatican. If only people knew the inside workings of these two powerful churches, these two pious, Mafia-styled operations, locked in mortal rivalry. What would Jesus think if he came back and saw the things that are being done in His name? Sweet, romantic Jesus . . ."

"Did you ever meet Constantine, Yanni?"

"Did you ever meet the Pope, Jason? One does not 'meet' them, Jason. Important people are 'granted audience,' but men like ourselves—writers, journalists—we are granted press releases. Surely you know how much to believe of press releases, my friend."

"When he stepped down, wasn't that a big story, Yanni? Didn't the press releases give some explanation?"

"That was the most interesting part, Jason. It should have been a big story. It should have been a stop-the-presses kind of story, but it wasn't. The releases gave no reasons, just that Constantine's job had been filled by another with no more fanfare than if you or I were replaced. It was not known for some time where Constantine was. That leaked out later."

"Any ideas, Yanni, any theories, hunches?"

He began to cough. "Who knows exactly what goes on with Constantine? I wish I did. It would make a good chapter for my memoirs. Some scandal, perhaps. Blackmail? Who knows? It would only be a guess, Jason . . . that is why I can't use it. I want this book to be a best-seller. The money is to go to my niece. Dying is not cheap."

"You mention scandal. What kind of scandal could touch a man who had gone that far?"

"As with any politician, the follies of youth may surface at any time—an illegitimate child, anything like that—maybe he stole from the poor box when he was nine years old. Maybe . . . maybe . . . you see? It is silence that arouses the curiosity, that spawns such ideas. It might have been something as mundane as his doctor telling him to slow down."

"But that would be a valid reason, no cause for secrecy?"

"Unless he was dying of advanced tertiary syphilis or a violent psychosis."

Jason laughed. "You're right, Yanni—the mind is as sharp as ever!"

"Not really, Jason, but it's nice to hear you say so."

The taxi driver was honking.

Jason took the man's skeletal hand. "I'd best go, Yanni. Courage, my friend. I'll think of you often. Maybe I'll even pray for you."

Yanni smiled wanly. "Don't do anything rash, my atheist friend."

"Agnostic, please."

Jason got up, started to go, and then, on an impulse, said, "Speaking of that sort of thing, did you ever hear any talk about some scrolls—you know, sort of like the Dead Sea Scrolls or the Gnostic Gospels—only really heretical? Crazy stuff, the Messiah being a woman."

"You mean," Elias asked, lowering his voice, "the Ephesus scrolls?"

"So you have heard of them!"

Yanni's blind eyes stared off into space, into the past. "Some time ago they were brought to me by a man named Paul Krenski. Not the scrolls *in toto,* but enough to get an idea of the contents. He said he'd translated the work for a man in Izmir and made certain copies for himself. He wanted me to evaluate their authenticity, which, of course, I could not do, certainly not from a copy, although I had to admit the Aramaic samples that he showed me seemed valid and his translations seemed close enough."

"And what was your opinion of the story? Doesn't it sound pretty crazy?"

"Unusual, perhaps—but then, isn't the story of Jesus of Nazareth a bit unusual?" Yanni shook his head. "No, I don't think Krenski was crazy, either."

"What ever happened to him?"

"He said he was going to Rome, going to the Vatican, see if anyone there could help him. I agreed that it would probably be there that archives might be found to lend credence to the story. I've never heard from him since, but then, I never really expected to."

"So where do you think the scrolls—the originals—might be?"

"I could make an educated guess. Constantine would know . . . and the Vatican might know. But I doubt it."

"Somehow you've just made the incredible sound possible, Yanni."

"History, Jason—the study of the history of human misconceptions, mythology, and superstitions—can make the incredible sound credible. God as a woman, a new idea? Hah! It's been around for a long, long time, down through the ages to images from an excavation in southwest Turkey dating from 7,000 B.C., when the goddess was the dominant deity and males were only consorts depicted in animal forms like the pig and the bull. The original supreme deity was the bountiful Earth Goddess. More than a fertility idol, she was a metaphysical symbol, the personification of the power of space, time, and matter. Everything—and this is important—*everything, including God,* was her child."

"And what happened to the idea of God as a woman?"

"The era seemed to have ended around the late fifteenth century B.C., which just happens to coincide with the volcano eruption on the island of Thera in the Aegean Sea, which destroyed the Minoan civilization. With the dawn of the Iron Age, exit the goddesses and enter your—what's the word, macho?—thunder-hurling warrior gods."

"But what of the goddess in modern times?"

"Believe me, Jason, I have thought much on the subject. Our modern concept of God, in my opinion, is really just the cosmology of the goddess Mother transformed by those patriarchal warriors. Christianity has kept a lot of the Greek mythological symbolism in its rites. Take the Eleusinian ritual of

117

initiation. Dionysus, the god of bread and wine, was born of Persephone, conceived by her father, Zeus, disguised as a snake. Now match that with the Christian version of God, who, in the form of a dove, conceived God the Son, who died and was resurrected and is present, symbolically, in the bread and wine of the Mass. And for a final irony, friend Jason, how about the fact that one of the most celebrated temples to the great goddess stood at Ephesus, where, in 431 A.D., the dogma of Mary as Mother of God was first proclaimed by special council. There's a book you should read, Jason, by Merlin Stone, called *When God Was a Woman*. It should—"

"Yanni! I have so much to learn and you have so much to tell me!"

"But the gods, whoever they are—Zeus, Athena, Jehovah, Mary, Joseph, Jesus . . . Lael?—they have seen fit to make this our last meeting. Envy me, dear Jason. Shortly I'll know all the answers that you now seek so fervently."

Jason clasped the older man's hand warmly in both of his, tears in his eyes.

The cab's horn blew again, this time more imperatively.

Jason gripped his friend's shoulders.

"Yassou, Yanni . . . *efharisto."*

"Goodbye, Jason . . . God bless you. I shan't see you again in this life, but I look forward to seeing you in the next."

Jason went out to the cab.

The driver wailed, "Mister, I sorry. Dinner waiting. My wife . . . she get mad, understand?"

But Jason was thinking about his dying friend, and only nodded.

It was still hot and very late when Jason returned to the Athens Hilton.

"She's waiting in your room, sir," said a cadaverous room clerk with a pencil-thin mustache, as he handed Jason the key.

"She?" Jason looked quizzical.

"Why, Mrs. Van Cleve, sir."

Forty years ago he'd first heard a person called that—his grandmother. Then "Mrs. Van Cleve" gradually became his mother. Then the title was bestowed on his wife, Beth. But now Beth was gone, as were his mother and his grandmother. There was no Mrs. Van Cleve in his life now, and he felt a brief pang, a recurrence of the clutching pain of Beth's death that dwelled in his chest and that had lain dormant these past few days.

"And . . . you say she's up there?"

"Yes, sir. Hasn't been there long . . . fifteen, twenty minutes."

Going up in the elevator, he thought: *Is this a trap? A prostitute? Or . . . could it be Tay?*

Nevertheless, he approached his room warily. He inserted his key as quietly as possible, quickly opened the door, and ducked back.

"Jason?"

He stepped into the room.

"Taylor!"

She was lying on the bed in a shantung skirt with a pongee blouse, her shoes off and her jacket hung on the back of a chair. She had been reading Jason's guidebooks.

She got up with an embarrassed laugh, wiggled her feet into her shoes, and said, "Nothing like making myself at home. Surprised to see me?"

"What are you doing here?" He frowned. "I mean, yes, I am glad to see you, but dammit, the risk!"

She looked so beautiful, even with her streaked brown-blonde hair tousled. She came nearer and he thought again that she always smelled as though her clothes had been freshly ironed.

"I came here to beg you to stop this witch-hunt or God-hunt or whatever it is." Her voice had a tone that Jason hadn't heard in it before, more than her usual motherly concern. Was it fear?

She went on, "Nestor Lascaris, dead. Phillips Taylor, dead. I can't help worrying about you, Jason."

"Who can be doing this? Who is behind it?"

"What does it matter?" she cut in. "The important thing is that this is much too dangerous and I want you—*please*—to give it up!"

"I can't quit now. Whoever is doing the killing isn't going to stop with Phillips Taylor and Lascaris."

"That's just what I mean!"

"But don't you see? I've got to keep going, to bring them out in the open. I'm probably high on their hit list, I know that. And if you are seen with me, you will be too. I think the only reason we're still alive is that they don't know where the original scrolls are and they think I'm on the track."

"And are you?"

"Yes." He told her about his interviews with Sister Eugenia and Yanni Elias.

"So you're off to Mount Athos—and more risking of your life?" She pulled away from him and walked across the room. "Jason, I have to tell you something . . ."

"Yes?" he said.

For a terrible moment she started to blurt out that Jonny had been kidnapped. But she knew it could result in disaster— destroy her chances of ever seeing Jonny again. She forced herself to say calmly, "Whoever they are, they mean business. Doesn't the death of two men tell you anything? I wish to heaven you'd listen to me. Forget it! Please!"

There was something strange about her tone. Her usual serenity had been replaced by tension. Had somebody already threatened her? "Are you all right?" he asked.

"Of course I'm all right. Just . . . just worried about this messy business."

"Taylor, I'm very sorry to have involved you in 'this messy business,' as you put it. That's why I wish you hadn't come here. Much as I love to be with you, I don't want to involve you further," Jason said. "And as for the deaths of two men— that's *why* I must get to the bottom of this."

Taylor frowned and looked away.

Jason sat down on the bed. "Who stands to lose the most if the story gets out?" he mused. "The Church. All the Christian churches, but especially the Roman Catholic Church. I'm beginning to wonder whether the people behind all this might not be in the Vatican itself."

"Don't you think that's pretty farfetched?" she asked as she walked to the bureau and took a brush from her purse. She could feel her heart pounding as she brushed her hair to cover her shock. The Vatican? Whom had she told about Jason and the scrolls? Father Bartolomeo! And where was he? At the

Vatican! But how ridiculous! When John had left her, who had come to her aid, pulled her out of her depression? Who had arranged for her son to have adequate schooling? Who'd been her most reliable friend in these last few lonely years? She couldn't conceive of his kidnapping her child!

Jason broke in on her thoughts: "Let's forget about it all for now, Tay, and get something to eat. I'm starved."

She looked lovely as she smiled sadly at him in the mirror and nodded, but she had no appetite.

Suddenly, the lights began to flicker, then went out. They looked out the windows and could see no lights anywhere in the city, except those of flashlights or candles being lit.

"What do we do now?" asked Jason as he rummaged through his pockets in search of matches.

"I think I have an idea," Taylor said in her low voice.

Jason lit a match and held it up to see her face. "Yes?" he said.

"We could have a picnic."

He held the match up for an instant longer to see if she was kidding.

She was not.

Half an hour later they had a bottle of wine, some cold chicken, and a wedge of cheese in a basket, thanks to the concierge.

"Have a good time, Mr. and Mrs. Van Cleve," the man had said as they left the lobby, now illuminated by the glow of large candles.

Athens was in total blackout, the only illumination coming from automobile headlights and the moon. Straight ahead of them the Parthenon's pillars glowed in the lunar rays. It looked more beautiful than when lit, as it usually was, by powerful arc lights.

"Lady, isn't that something?" said Jason. "You know, I once saw the Taj Mahal, but alone. One shouldn't look at this, or the Taj, alone."

"It is staggering," breathed Taylor as she slipped her arm through Jason's. "In this light you can barely see the scaffolding. In fact, the scaffolds seem somehow to add something . . . magical."

Jason bantered, "What you're trying to say is, the less light there is, the more mystery and magic and beauty remain."

There was a frown in her voice as she said, "Oh, Jason, can't we even look at the Parthenon without sly allusions to those damned scrolls?"

"I hadn't thought of it that way, Tay...but the analogy is there, isn't it?"

They walked the rest of the way to Filopapou Hill in silence. There amid the pine trees they came upon some marble ruins. Taylor put the food on top of an Ionic capital that was broken and tipped sideways, forming a flat surface.

"You are clever," Jason said as he sat on a shard of another column.

"Talent," she said. "Pure and simple."

"Incredible," Jason said as he looked at the scene in front of him. The Acropolis was no more than half a mile away, and every miraculous detail of the Parthenon could be seen in the moonlight.

"Forgive me, Jason. I'm sorry I jumped on your remark back there. I'm just...just nervous these days."

"You sure you haven't been threatened by one of these weirdos?" he asked.

She shook her head emphatically. Too emphatically.

"What is it, then?"

Oh, God, she wanted so much to tell him. "I'm just nervous about all this. For your safety and mine. And now Athos. What makes you so sure that this Constantine has them?"

"I'm not sure. Not at all. But from what Yanni Elias told me, it's my only lead. Constantine was the strong man in the struggle for the leadership of the Orthodox Church—very ambitious, very shrewd. But Elias said he could give me no reason for Constantine's leaving the heavy politics he was involved in to retire and go into seclusion as the abbot of a remote monastery on Mount Athos. Yanni says it's a mystery, and I just think it might be worth investigating."

"Did Elias know about the scrolls?"

"Yes, and if he is right about Constantine, then it is possible that Constantine could have the scrolls locked away up there...waiting for the moment to strike back at the Vatican for the pressure it brought to bear in ruining his career."

"Are you saying that the Orthodox Church could blackmail the Roman Catholic Church with the use of such documents?"

"I'm only saying that Elias made it clear to me that in the Church, as elsewhere, there is often a power struggle. What I'm also saying is that I believe the scrolls may be up there somewhere." Jason turned and looked squarely at Taylor. "And I'm going up there and try to get the rest of the story."

"Want me to take you up there?"

"Females are not allowed on the Mount Athos peninsula," Jason said. "Not even female animals."

"I could take you to Thessaloniki and then as far as Ouranopolis," she offered. "I think women can go that far." She looked up at him. "Please? If you're being followed, they know by now that I'm in this with you, and they'll have two to contend with instead of just one."

"I'm grateful I found you, Taylor," he said. "I'm even grateful to the late Phillips Taylor, or whatever his name was, God rest his miserable soul in the turf club." He kissed her gently on her lips. "But I can't let you take any more chances. Much as I hate to leave you, I'd better fly."

She nodded in agreement, knowing it would be useless to argue with him about it.

And as they walked back to the hotel, the lights came on all over the city and some of the magic disappeared with the light.

They went up to the room and made love, but, unlike before, there was a feeling of tension, even desperation about it.

And afterward, Taylor lay there in the dark, thinking. There had been no message for Taylor when they got back to the hotel that night, and she felt both relief and foreboding. She wondered how much longer she could hold it all in, how much longer before she would crack and tell Jason the truth . . . tell him she'd been paying for her son's life by informing on Jason, tell him that all her generous offers were not motivated solely by love for him, but also by love for her son, her only child. Would Jason understand? Surely he would understand; he was still suffering from the grief of having lost his wife. How solicitous he had been, how concerned for her welfare. And how base it was to use this fine man to get her own son back.

But how could she tell him now, without jeopardizing Jonny? What would he think of her if she told him, now, that she'd been holding out on him—even to the extent of letting him go to his death! But she'd tried to warn him. She *had* tried to get him to abandon this lethal project. But it was not the same thing, she knew. It was not the same thing as telling him about her son's kidnapping, about the voice on the phone that gave her instructions. It was not the same thing as telling him the truth . . . the whole truth.

The first glint of dawn found Taylor still awake and waiting for Jason to finally open his eyes. When he began to move about fitfully, she pretended to be asleep, then gave a stellar performance of awakening from a good night's sleep . . . smiling, yawning, stretching . . .

"You're so lovely when you're asleep," he said when she opened her eyes.

9

_____

IT WAS early morning when Lieutenant Andrea di Grazia hurried into the police station just off the Piazza Novona. A young officer jumped up eagerly to open the double doors for him; di Grazia was a bit of a god around here these days. *"Buon giorno!"*

Andrea had only been on the Italian police force for thirteen months, and he was barely twenty-six years old, but he was already being considered for promotion from lieutenant to captain because of his record. The most outstanding exploit on that record was the brilliant way he had handled a plane hijacking at the Rome airport a month ago. The hijacker had been a lunatic from the Middle East, demanding a million dollars and an audience with the Pope . . . or else he'd pull the pin on his grenade and blow people on the plane to kingdom come. Andrea had commandeered a cardinal's cassock, wriggled into it as the police car screamed its way to the airport, and boarded the DC-10. Calmly he had walked down the plane's long aisle with a beatific smile on his face, telling everyone to be calm.

As he approached the wild-eyed fanatic brandishing the grenade, he said, "My son, they tell me you wish to see His Holiness. I have the authority to grant that wish. Kneel, and I shall bless you so that you will be worthy of an audience with him."

The man hesitated. For a terrible moment he studied di Grazia, wondering if this was a trap.

"Kneel, my son," said di Grazia in a soothing, clerical voice.

The man knelt, still clutching the grenade. Andrea held out his hand as though to bless the penitent, then dealt the terrorist a slamming karate chop across the base of the neck, dropping him to the carpet, but not before the man had pulled the pin on the grenade. The policeman scooped it up, lunged for the open door, and hurled it out where it exploded harmlessly on the tarmac.

Andrea, a good-looking and likable Milanese, had had several other successes, though none quite as sensational as that. Therefore, his superiors had picked him for the case of the kidnapped American boy, Jonny Phillips. He had gone immediately to the residence of the Thomas Hudsons, where the boy had been living, and afterward reported to his superior officer.

"It doesn't make sense," di Grazia said to the captain with the waxed brigadier-style mustache. "I assumed it would be the standard kidnapping, with ransom demands or some sort of political demands—the kind you Romans invented and still hold the patent on." He shot a sly look at the captain, who chose to laugh goodnaturedly and accept it as a backhanded compliment.

"Thank you," he said mockingly. "We Romans have had many other ideas which you of Lombardy have been quick to steal. That is why we must have patents."

"Very true, Captain. But wait until you hear all of this. The boy's aunt says they have received only one phone call, and it was *not* a threat or demand for ransom."

"Then what is it they want?" the captain demanded, looking at Andrea seriously for the first time.

Andrea di Grazia finally realized what it was about the captain that had always intrigued him; he had a face whose features seemed not quite to go with one another, like one of the portraits done by a police artist of a suspect, based upon conflicting descriptions by eyewitnesses.

"That's just it! Apparently nothing. They simply told Mrs. Hudson not to call the police or the newspapers or the boy's mother, and that he would be returned in a few days unharmed."

"But sexually molested."

Andrea shook his head emphatically. "I don't think so. I didn't get those vibrations. The aunt said they assured her repeatedly that the child would not be harmed in *any* way."

"You've called the mother?"

"She lives in Istanbul. Doesn't answer the phone."

"The father?"

"Lives in California. Can't locate him, so presumably neither can the kidnappers. They're divorced."

"And what if the father is the kidnapper?"

"I asked Mrs. Hudson that. She said the father does not pay support money, although he's well able to do so. He has not called to talk to his son, although he does know where he is. He forgets the child's birthdays, and has in no way exhibited the kind of interest that would make *him* a likely suspect."

"Rich?"

"The father may have money. Mrs. Hudson's evaluation of him may be colored by the fact that she is the sister of the mother, but she was quite calm and not in the least vindictive when she said simply, 'John's a born playboy. I doubt that he has anything left of his inheritance.'"

"And what of the mother?"

"No big money there. Mrs. Hudson said her sister asked nothing for herself, but only child support for the son. She had been a vice-consul for the United States, but now she is writing a book."

"How did they get the boy?"

"His aunt says he was playing soccer with her son in the front yard. A car—a blue pickup truck, they didn't get the license—pulled up. A man dressed in jeans got out, came up to the Hudson boy, and asked for the Phillips boy. Apparently he did not know either one, right? Then the cousin, the Hudson boy, heard them talking in English, but he wasn't paying any attention, so he couldn't remember what was said. But he does know they were speaking in English, and the name 'Father Bartolomeo' was mentioned. The Phillips boy said he'd be back in a few minutes—he had to see a friend. He waved good-bye to his cousin as they drove away, and that's it."

"Isn't there a cardinal by that name?"

"There is at least one. Where do you think I got the cassock so that I could bless the hijacker last month?" Andrea said with a grin. Then he leaned over toward the telephone on the captain's desk and asked, "May I?"

The captain's eyes locked with di Grazia's as he telephoned the Vatican. Then Andrea jammed the phone back into the cradle.

"Wonderful," he said, shaking his head. "The good father is in Paris with the Pope."

"Vive le Pape!" The shouts rang out over and over. *"Vive le Pape!"*

The Parisian crowds lined the curbs, cheering the Pope's massive black sharklike limousine with the papal seal on the doors, flanked by policemen on motorcycles and guarded by security men by the dozens at every block; there would be no recurrence of the papal shooting of 1981.

It was a warm afternoon, and Paris was living up to her reputation as a belle among cities, alluring and alive.

The Pope was here on the occasion of the naming of the new Archbishop of Paris, Monsieur Jean-Marie Lustiger. It was somewhat unusual, this appointment, since Lustiger's parents were Polish Jews who had come to Paris early in the century and who had died at Auschwitz. In his opening remarks, the Pope had said, "We see no contradiction at all to be of Jewish birth and to become a Catholic. After all, Jesus Chirst was the King of the Jews."

He then went on to make a stirring address on the state of the Church, with regard to the condition of the world's morality:

"Our conclusion, then, is that religion is necessary to morality. Even your agnostic Renan affirmed this in 1866, when he said, 'Let us enjoy the liberty of the sons of God, but let us take care lest we become accomplices in the diminution of virtue which would menace society if Christianity were to grow weak. What would we do without it? If Rationalism wishes to govern the world without regard to the religious needs of the soul, the experience of the French Revolution is there to teach us the consequences of such a blunder.'"

The audience in the cathedral was hushed and awed as he ended with:

"At any moment a comet may come too close to the earth and set our little globe turning topsy-turvy in a hectic course, or choke its men and fleas with fumes or heat. Or a fragment of the smiling sun may slip off tangentially—as some think our planet did a few astronomic moments ago—and fall upon us in a wild embrace, ending all grief and pain. We accept these possibilities in our stride, and retort to the cosmos in the words of Pascal: 'When the universe has crushed him, man will still be nobler than that which kills him, because he knows that he is dying, and of its victory the universe knows nothing.'"

He was not the greatest orator Bartolomeo had ever heard, yet the force and energy and sincerity made him most effective.

Now, as the gentle but vital man in full papal regalia of white brocade and satin, with a little white and gold cape, waved to the people from inside the car as it edged its way past the throngs that almost blocked the Pont from the Ile de la Cité, he said to Bartolomeo, who was in front next to the driver, looking back at the magnificent Notre Dame, "Cardinal Bartolomeo, how do you think it went? We wanted it to turn out well. Was it—to use your favorite phrase—'life-enhancing'?"

"Holiness, it was magnificent! And yes, it was definitely life-enhancing." And he meant it; he felt great admiration for this man, not only because he was the Pope, for there had been other Popes about whom he had not felt this way, but out of genuine love.

"Thank you, good friend. I respect your opinion. Well, when we get to the hotel, give me fifteen minutes alone and then come to my suite, please. I've had something on my mind to tell you, but these last few weeks have been so rushed and crowded."

"May I dare to suggest that His Holiness slow the pace a bit?"

The Pope smiled ruefully, never stopping his gentle waving to the crowd. "One of these days, Your Eminence, one of these days."

Later, in a sumptuous, heavily guarded suite at the Plaza

Athené, the Pope greeted Bartolomeo, who was still in his white robe, with the cardinal's crimson sash and red biretta. The Pope was now dressed in a long purple dressing gown, but he still wore the white cap of office.

A little altar had been set up at one end of the room, with two large, lighted candles and a crucifix above it. The French doors were open to the Avenue Montaigne's traffic noises, which purred below in an unobtrusive way, but on the balcony Bartolomeo could see the backs of the security guards with their automatic rifles.

The Pope's secretary poured the cardinal a cup of tea from a large silver pot, then excused himself. The Pope, holding a cup in his hand, sat down on the gold sofa and patted the space beside him.

"What I wanted to talk to you about is that we are worried, very worried about the scourge of drug abuse throughout the world. Of course, we have long known that New York is infested with the vermin who spread the evil—who make drugs seem romantic and desirable. Now, there are some 408 parishes in the New York archdiocese. I thank that with some really vigorous program, we could make inroads. We might consider—depending upon our ever-present accursed budget—opening halfway houses for addicts who are trying—how do they say?—to kick the habit."

"And how would you accomplish this, Your Holiness?" Bartolomeo asked thoughtfully. "By concentrating on the individuals and their families?"

"Exactly," said the Pope. "Individual is the word. Not these big impersonal state programs that haven't worked. I would like Your Eminence to go over there and see what you can do."

"But . . . how, Your Holiness? In what capacity?"

"For some weeks now, you have been an archbishop. You will be the Archbishop of New York."

Bartolomeo's jaw dropped. "But I am a cardinal deacon, Holiness!"

"You have been an archbishop"—smiling, he tapped his chest—"as we say, *in pectore*. We will make it official as soon as possible, and then off you go to New York to tend my ailing flock. I have long admired your efficiency, honesty, and loyalty."

Bartolomeo knelt briefly and kissed the papal ring.

"I shall not disappoint Your Holiness." He thought of how proud his parents would have been, of how God had blessed him. He would encounter resentment, he knew, because of his abrupt appointment, but no matter. He felt a great exaltation and gratitude.

"You will do splendidly, Your Eminence. You have a *simpatía*, as the Spanish say, that is irresistible. You wear life easily, like a loose garment. Also, I understand that you have many friends and connections there. I should have sent you there a long time ago. You were born in Brooklyn, yes?"

"I am deeply grateful to Your Holiness. And yes, I was born there."

"Americans understand Americans best," the Pope said.

"I suppose so," Cardinal Bartolomeo agreed.

He paused for a moment, then thought, *Yes, now is the time*.

"Your Holiness, speaking of Americans, before we prepare to return to Rome, one delicate matter, if I have your permission to occupy your valuable time . . ."

The Pope nodded. "Yes, of course."

Cardinal Bartolomeo sighed, "How to begin? I have a friend, an American woman named Taylor Phillips, who lives in Istanbul. The details of how she became involved in this matter are not quite clear to me, but has Your Holiness ever heard of some lost papyri, a hoax involving some heretical scrolls purportedly found at the site of the Virgin Mary's house in Ephesus?"

The Pope shook his head. "Over the years I have heard of many false writings about the origin of the Christian faith, but none from Ephesus that I can recall. What is the premise of these scrolls?"

Bartolomeo, with apologies and hesitations, told him about the story of Lael.

The pontiff smiled. "Well, they say that if one is determined to tell a lie, it is best to tell a big one. The Messiah, a woman! That, I must say, is an Olympian and magnificent lie." He thought for several moments, then he said enigmatically, "Do you read Wittgenstein? I find him hard to understand sometimes, but he says, 'The point of all philosophical discussion is to show the fly the way out of the fly bottle.' This scroll story is clearly a hoax, but to tell you the truth, I would very much like to see these scrolls, or a translation of them. If it is an ancient hoax, not a modern one, it would have great value, especially to scholars. For example, why would anyone perpetrate such a hoax, and at what point in Christian history?"

"Your Holiness, I cannot say, but my friend is not uneducated in these matters, and she says it is a convincing forgery indeed, executed by experts, whenever it might have been done."

"Then pursue this," mused the Pope. "To a conclusion."

Bartolomeo knew that the Pope did not make idle requests. Though his "suggestion" had been made offhandedly, in a week he would be expecting a full written report—and it would be ready. That, Barto knew, was one of the reasons the Pope valued him so highly.

"I should like to see them. If the Turin shroud is proven to be either authentic or a fake, we should like to be the first to know. So with the scrolls."

"Would Your Holiness . . . would you suppress these scrolls if they are found to be authentic?"

"I like to think that I would not—but who knows? In the present world, where the people have lost their confidence in the politicians, and in their everyday lives, where romantics are doomed and saints assassinated, people have little left except their faith in the Church. Faith has survived every major disaster. Perhaps these scrolls would not be as damaging as a third world war, but they could certainly weaken the faith, hoax or not."

Bartolomeo was reflecting on this when the Pope's active mind jumped ahead, bringing up some historical information and applying it to the situation.

"In olden times there was a clan of fanatics called the Guardians of the Faith in Our Lord. They would have killed to suppress such a story as the one you've just told me. But they, and similar groups, have been condemned by the Church for many centuries. Originally, they were simply good Christians, intent upon keeping false versions of Jesus' life and Resurrection from being circulated. Soon they clashed with the writings of the Apostles, but their struggle was kept secret so as not to shake the faith of the new Christians. The Guardians branched out. Some were rejected and expelled, but one later branch bore fruit: a secret group, always headed by three men, always operating within the Church, almost always appointing members whose own families had been connected with the Guardians in the past, in order to maintain the secrecy. Father to son, or grandfather to grandson. Oh, yes, Bartolomeo, as you know, we clerics have not always been celibate. Remember that even our first Pope, Peter, was a married man, and several Popes since have been married."

"Including Clement the Fourth, around the end of the thirteenth century," said Bartolomeo, "who had two daughters."

"And, of course, hundreds of cardinals were married," continued the Pope. "The crackdown on marriage began in the eleventh and twelfth centuries, although the constitution of the French revolution did allow clerical marriage. But in more modern times, when the Guardians had to observe the vows of celibacy, they had to recruit their followers from outside their families."

"Were they really all that powerful," asked Bartolomeo. "These guardians?"

"For a time, they were very influential," the Pope replied, "often driving the Church into unforgivable mistakes, such as condemning Galileo. Have you seen the Galileo letters in our secret archives?"

Bartolomeo felt remiss, a boy who had failed to do his homework. "No, Your Holiness, I confess I have not."

"Very interesting. In a letter in 1633, Galileo wrote to the papal office of the Inquisition to plead his innocence to charges of heresy. Galileo, of course, had supported the Polish astronomer Copernicus, who, contrary to the prevailing belief, had declared that the earth revolved around the sun and not vice versa. A most moving letter, and the Pope was inclined to absolve him, but it was the Guardians who persuaded him to pursue the matter and bring Galileo to a shameful trial and prison."

"So these Guardians were important factors in the Inquisition?"

"They fanned the flames of the Spanish Inquisition and similar matters. But eventually they became outlaws, for the Church could not condone their extreme methods."

"And so they were banned, Your Holiness?"

"Yes. It became clear that they were not only operating outside the interests of the Church, but were also showing signs of conspiring to seize complete power of the Church. One incident that created real trouble was the discovery that certain heretical writings had fallen into their hands and instead of delivering them to the Vatican for proper scrutiny and evaluation, they were held as a powerful weapon to be used against the Church when they so chose. Of course, the priesthood today is much more progressive. All that is needed to fight such persuasive and devilish heresy is *reason*. There is no room or need for Guardians today."

Why is he telling me all this now, Barto thought. *Does he suspect a resurgence of new fanatics, new Guardians, in the Vatican? He never says things without a reason.* But Barto knew better than to query him directly about the matter. He would be told whenever His Holiness decided to tell him, so he merely said, "Your Holiness is wise."

The secretary came back into the room. "Your Holiness must excuse me, but we must prepare to return to Rome."

The Pope gave an exaggerated sigh and patted his new archbishop on the shoulder.

"Your Eminence, we come to 'gay Paree,' and what do we see of her? The inside of a cathedral and a hotel room! Not even the Mona Lisa! What we gave up when we elected to put on the cloth, eh, Archbishop Bartolomeo?"

Jason and Taylor were having breakfast at the Byzantine Cafe in the hotel when a bellboy went by, paging Mrs. Phillips.

"Excuse me, darling," Taylor said. "Probably my sister."

"Of course," said Jason, and, as he watched her go, he wondered about the look that came to her eyes when she'd heard the boy call her name.

Taylor went to the phone booth, her heart pounding, her

palms wet. She did as she had been instructed; she waited for "them" to speak first. The silence was almost as loud as the beating of her heart. Finally she realized that the rules could not apply in a public phone booth, for how could they know when she had been reached and was on the line? Very quietly she said, "This is Mrs. Phillips."

The voice from Rome said, "Thank you, Mrs. Phillips, I'm glad to see that you have the intelligence to know when to bend the rules. I was getting a little worried and was about to ring off and try again with further instructions—which might have proven embarrassing. Now, Mrs. Phillips, you have been doing well—very well. Most commendably accurate information. We are happy to say that our contact has arrived in Athens and is ready to back you up."

"But . . . but you said he'd *replace* me!" Taylor protested.

"Exactly what I said," the man replied. "But we think it would be in everybody's best interests if you stuck with Mr. Van Cleve. Where is he going now?"

"Thessaloniki," she said. "Salonika."

"Thessaloniki? Why?"

"To get to Mount Athos."

"Why Mount Athos?"

"He believes the scrolls are there."

"In which monastery?"

"I don't know."

"Does he?"

"I don't know."

"Try to find out. Meanwhile, your son will be delivered to you in Thessaloniki."

"And then we are both free?"

"As far as we are concerned, there's where your journey and your job come to an end. Even if we wanted you to, there is no way you could enter the no-woman's-land of Mount Athos."

"I see," said Taylor with relief.

"However, we will count on your powers of persuasion, which seem to be considerable, to persuade Van Cleve to *drive* to Thessaloniki rather than fly. He has relied on you to be his chauffeur up to now, so we see no problem with that."

"When will Jonny . . . ?"

"One moment, Mrs. Phillips! We'll get to that. First, we have one more thing. Take your time driving up there. Take the longest route. We have certain things we have to take care of. Now, about Jonny. Yes, Thessaloniki . . . here we are . . . yes, the Macedonia Palace, that should do nicely. We will expect you to stay at the Macedonia Palace Hotel and wait for your son there. You will be contacted there. Now remember, do take your time driving up. Understand?"

"Yes," Taylor replied.

"Very good." The line went dead.

When Taylor returned to the table, Jason asked, "How is he?"

For one panicky moment she could not think how he would know whom she'd been talking to. Then she realized that Jason meant the boy.

"He's all right, thank you," she said. "Just a minor infection. My sister's sure he'll be all right."

"Good news," Jason said.

"However," she said, "I do have some bad news. As I passed the desk, I checked with the concierge, and all the Olympic flights are booked solid for the next two days. There's a fair coming up—the Thessaloniki Trade Fair."

"Another airline?"

"No other airline," Taylor replied. "We can drive up. And I just thought of a friend, a man who can act as a guide for you. Andoni. You'll like Andoni. He once helped me with some research. Not very bright, but he does know the area and the monasteries. He's an excellent guide." As she spoke, she wondered how she could sound so convincing. But what could she do? She had to go along with this, if she hoped to get Jonny back.

And Jason was disquieted by her sudden false air of enthusiasm. Something was very wrong.

In his Rome office, Tobin concluded a brief conversation with Instanbul.

"Good work, Melnick. You've done well so far, very well. Now we want you to proceed to Thessaloniki. Stay at the

Macedonia Palace. That is where the lady will be staying. Keep her under strict surveillance, but nothing should be done as yet. I will call you shortly—or you call me, if there is anything to report."

Tobin hung up and called the Hilton Hotel in Athens again, but this time he did not speak to Mrs. Phillips.

Not long afterward, a smallish, dapper man removed the folded handkerchief from his breast pocket and tapped the end of his moist nose carefully as he went to the desk of the Athens Hilton and asked the concierge, "Any messages?"

"Oh, yessir, this came for you. I rang your room, but you were out."

"Probably in the shower," said McCue, taking the note. "Thank you."

He walked away as he read the message, then turned and went back to the desk. "Is there a travel agency around?" he asked.

"I'll be glad to help you if I can, sir," the concierge offered.

"Can you get me on a flight to Thess...Thess..."

"Thessaloniki?" The clerk shook his head. "Sorry, sir, all booked."

The small man pulled out a large bill and held it out.

"There just might be a cancellation," said the clerk, picking up the phone.

"Why haven't they killed me?" Jason said, as they lay together in the dark. "It would be so simple for them just to kill me. Why?"

It was two-thirty in the morning and they were in Thessaloniki. Although tired after the six-hour drive, neither had slept. They had made love and lay in each other's arms, preoccupied with their thoughts.

"They obviously don't choose to," said Taylor. "Thank God."

"At this particular time they don't choose to," he said. "That means they *want* me to pursue this business. They *want* me to find the scrolls! That makes some sense, doesn't it? It's just possible that they, whoever they are, don't know exactly where the scrolls are, and I'm doing their legwork for them. The moment I find them, I'm dead. Then they take the scrolls and burn them . . . or whatever . . ."

"That's why I say quit, darling. Quit!"

He shook his head in the dark. "There was a time, back in Izmir, when I guess I had that option. No longer. They don't want me wandering around with all this information ready to blab to all the world. I'm safe as long as I stay on the story. If I were to abandon the search—bam!—they'd nail me." He gave a rueful laugh. "That's the Catch-22—as long as I follow the clues, stay on the treasure hunt, I'm fine. It's just when I win and find the treasure that I'm in deep trouble."

He was ready to throw back the bedclothes and get started on the hunt, but Taylor was asleep. He thought he'd better get a little sleep himself. He wondered that Taylor could sleep so soundly under the circumstances, not knowing the night of anguish she'd endured in addition to the constant anxiety for her son and the physical stress of all the driving. But he soon succumbed and slept for a few hours himself.

It was not yet dawn when Jason awoke. He shook Taylor gently and whispered, "Time, darling."

"Jason, it's still dark," she murmured as she turned over and prepared to go back to sleep.

"Ouranopolis is a good ways from here. Your friend Andoni will be waiting."

"Okay," she said, wide awake now as the name Andoni reminded her of her mission.

"Why don't you just stay in bed? You're exhausted, and I can find my way to Andoni's place."

"No, no, I'll drive you. This way I'll have the car. You might be gone a couple of days."

As she got dressed, she realized Jason was right; he had to keep going. To stop now would be tantamount to repeating the fate of Lascaris and Phillips Taylor and who knew who else? Maybe even that poor innocent man, Elias, whom she had put the finger on. But no, he was such an old man. But then, Lascaris was an old man too! Oh, God!

Her torturous thoughts caused her to look pensive, and Jason said, "You all right?"

"I was just thinking, Jason, that maybe when you get back, you'll get to meet Jonny."

"You didn't tell me," he said. "He's coming home?"

Should she tell Jason about the kidnapping now, and trust his assessment of the situation? No, he had enough to worry about, and anyway it would soon be over. They had promised that Jonny would be delivered to the Macedonia Palace; he might even be there when she got back.

"Yes," she said, then added uncertainly, "I think he's coming home soon . . . very soon."

The thought came to Jason, *Could they have threatened her son in some way?* That would explain all kinds of things. But if she hadn't told him . . . no, she surely would have told him. Best not to mention it. It wouldn't do to put such a thought in her mind.

It was seven-thirty in the morning, and Jason stood quietly where he had gotten out of the car when Taylor drove off to return to Salonika. In his pocket he felt the pistol that she had insisted he take.

"If you take it, I'll bet you won't need it. If you don't— I'll bet you will."

"There's female logic at its absolute finest." He grinned.

As he stood looking at the spot where the car and Taylor had disappeared, he felt overwhelmed by his task, by his efforts to make some sense of this strange situation he'd got himself into. And something was still very wrong with his relationship with Taylor. It had started off so beautifully . . . but maybe it was for the best; who wanted another relationship that could turn out painfully? He turned and walked toward the *taverna*.

As he approached, a great bearded giant of a man came out of the Pegasus Taverna and threw a bucket of water into the street. He fit Taylor's description, and Jason followed him as he went back into the *taverna*. The man did not notice Jason, and when he reentered the *taverna*, he closed the door.

Jason stopped and once again looked back toward Salonika. Taylor had been anxious to get back to the hotel, and hadn't wanted to say hello to Andoni, her old friend. Jason could not

139

shake the feeling that something was going on that Taylor hadn't told him. Then he pushed the door and it creaked open. He stepped in. The house was dark, ominously dark. Was this a trap? Was Andoni yet another one of them? Had Taylor unwittingly led him to an assassin?

His foot came down on something soft. With a yelp and then a snarl, a black dog exploded to life and fled.

"Andoni?" Jason called out tentatively.

He could hear a gruff voice singing boisterously from another room.

"Andoni!" he called again, but the voice went on and Jason walked toward the sound. Opening another door, Jason smelled hot olive oil and garlic, and saw the oil lamp that illuminated the kitchen. He could see the big man standing in front of a large wood stove. There was no one else in the room except a yellow-striped cat, asleep under the stove. In the confined space, the man, who was about sixty, looked even more powerful than he had outside. He sang lustily as he stirred several small fish in the pan of oil.

"Are you Andoni?"

The bearded man turned around, unstartled.

"Breakfast won't be ready for a while. Have some ouzo?"

"A little early for me," said Jason.

Andoni poured anyway, from an unlabeled bottle into two cloudy glasses.

"You friend of Mrs. Phillips, I know. You Professor Hoover, no?" He clapped Jason on the shoulder.

He speared a tiny fish with a fork. "Have a *marida*—eat bones and all! Good! Good!"

He extended the fork to Jason's mouth. The fish was soggy with olive oil, but fresh and tasty.

"So you want I should take you to Vatopedi." He shook his head. "Dangerous. It can be outrageous."

"The guidebook I've been reading says, quote, it is peaceful and the monks have little, but are very hospitable, unquote," Jason replied.

"Hah! Guidebooks not right. Lots of trouble. Bands of outlaws hide in the hills. Some monasteries afraid even to let stranger pass."

"But surely . . . why, those monasteries are like fortresses!"

"And like fortress, they careful who come in. You got papers?"

"Papers? What kind of papers? I have my visa, my passport—"

"Sure, but extra papers . . . important papers they give you at Athens . . . special papers to let you travel on Mount Athos."

"I'm afraid I don't have any special papers, just my—"

"Maybe they decide not to let you go." He shrugged and shook his head. "Make no difference either way."

Jason hesitated. "Perhaps I should look for another guide if you aren't willing to take me."

Andoni shrugged again, shaking his head. "Anyone else tell you same thing, boss."

Jason extracted two thousand drachmas and put them on the table.

"And the same when we get back."

Andoni's face broke into a grin, and he pulled at his beard. "On other hand, this outrageous sum of money. I get you papers. We go, boss, we go."

He poured himself another glass of ouzo.

"When?" asked Jason.

"Soon, now." He pointed to the glass with a hurt look. "My friends, they drink with me. Drink, boss, drink!"

Jason took a cautious sip. "That's . . . that's slow poison," he gasped.

"Yes," roared Andoni happily. "Very good slow poison for people not in hurry to die!" He hesitated for a moment, then said, "You sure you want to go to Vatopedi?"

"Yes," said Jason.

"Okay," said Andoni with a doubtful nod of his head.

There was a donkey in the backyard, along with two chickens, and after Andoni had cleaned up the kitchen, he packed the animal with some tins of food and a bottle of ouzo. Then he fed the chickens and, leaving the taverna unlocked, started for the boat landing.

Jason, carrying his gear, walked alongside the big Greek. He did not see a small man who kept dabbing at his runny nose, sitting in a car that now moved forward slowly about a hundred yards behind them.

• • •

Once out of Ouranopolis, Taylor drove as fast as conditions would permit in order to make up for the time she'd spent in bringing Jason to Andoni's. She wanted to be waiting for Jonny when they brought him to the hotel. She had done her duty, had followed instructions to the letter, stalling for time as she drove Jason up from Athens. She had not once given away her secret—not to Jason, not to the police. They could not ask for more.

There had been a few moments back on the narrow strip out of Ouranopolis, when the fog was thick and she'd had her headlights on, that she'd seen headlights behind her and she'd thought she was being followed, but now she hadn't seen any sign of anyone following since Ierissos.

She thought of Jason. Was he still being followed? But who would dare to harm him on the holy mountain, surrounded as he would be by men who were devoting their lives to God? It was incomprehensible to her that such men could commit cold-blooded murders like that ghastly mutilation of Lascaris. And as for Jason's notion that the Vatican could be involved in anything like that—impossible!

She made good time crossing the Chalkidiki peninsula, and as she reached the outskirts of Thessaloniki, she wondered if she should buy a gift for Jonny. But no, when he returned, they could go shopping together and she could get him whatever he liked.

And when Jason returned . . . but would he? Even if he found what he was looking for and got away with it, would he not fly directly back to the United States? Why had she assumed he'd want to meet Jonny? Would they like each other if they did meet? It warmed her to think so. She truly loved this man.

When she arrived back at the hotel in Thessaloniki, she asked the room clerk anxiously, "Any messages?"

The clerk shook his head.

"No one's been here?"

"No one, madame. I'm sorry."

Taylor thanked him and went to her room. More waiting. How much longer . . . how much longer? She went into her room, locked the door, and flung herself facedown on the bed and cried.

Finally, she got up and stood looking out of the window. Had they reneged completely? Or was Jonny, perhaps, on his way? Why had no one tried to contact her? But maybe they had—yes, of course they had; it was illogical of her to suppose they would leave a message with the concierge. She could only sit in her room and wait.

Or if she did phone Father Bartolomeo, who would know? She had to talk to someone. She could no longer keep this bottled up inside her.

She picked up the phone...then put it down. Supposing the outgoing calls were being monitored? She'd be jeopardizing Jonny's safety. She put down the receiver slowly. She paced the room, then walked back to the telephone and snatched it up.

She gave the number in Rome. She had second thoughts while she listened to the distant hums and clicks. She forced herself to hang on, and in a moment the voice of Antonio, Father Bartolomeo's secretary, said in Italian, "*Si, Signora.* His Eminence just came in the office."

"My dear child, what luck! I've just this moment returned from Paris, and—"

"Father, I'm so terribly worried. I must tell you..." Taylor's voice broke, but she held back the tears. "I have promised not to tell you, or anyone...but...it's Jonny..."

"Tell me, Taylor," he said firmly as he sat down at his desk. "Tell me everything."

As calmly as she could, Taylor told her story—all that had happened, and how and why. "And now, Father, they still haven't returned Jonny, and I simply cannot take any more of this!"

Father Bartolomeo said quietly, "You poor girl. Now listen to me carefully. You stay there and let me get to work at this end. If they release Jonny and he does join you there, call me. Otherwise, leave it all to me. Continue to follow any instructions you may receive. I will get back to you."

When he hung up, the cardinal tried to sort out the facts and recent events. Suddenly there flashed through his mind what the Pope had said in Paris about the group called the Guardians, those religious fanatics of another age. Could it be that the organization was not extinct, as His Holiness would like to believe? But how was the connection made between them and Taylor's boy? With whom had he talked recently about Taylor? Patrick. *Patrick!* And whom had he told about Taylor's son, mentioning the aunt's name? And whom had he told about Taylor's involvement with the Ephesus scrolls? Patrick! It was just too monstrous to contemplate. There wasn't anyone alive whom he'd known longer than Patrick!

Archbishop (*in pectore*) Bartolomeo sat momentarily stunned, at his desk. Now, what to do about all this? Idly he riffled through the dozen or so telephone messages that had accumulated in his absence. What *could* he do? Cardinals were expected to be able to work miracles, but after all, he was just an ordinary man under his robes. He had even *promised* miracles, telling Taylor not to worry. Let the archbishop handle it! The great archbishop, whose big mouth and lack of judgment of his fellow man had got her son kidnapped in the first place.

Then a name on one message caught his eye. Rozmyslowski. Not an easy name to overlook. Al had been a close wartime friend, a fellow American, and they frequently got together for dinner and reminiscences when he was in Rome.

Al! That was it! He was a man of action—a hotshot pilot, a reliable, resourceful man. Right now he might be a godsend!

Father Bartolomeo telephoned the number and asked for Al Rozmyslowski.

"Al! Where *are* you?"

"Right here at the Excelsior, Barto, just passing through. Can we get together for a little bull session, old buddy?"

"Of course. Al, listen, I've got a pressing problem. You still flying?"

"Sure, Padre. It's the only thing I really like to do."

"Al, how soon can you get over here?"

An hour later, Father Bartolomeo said, "The Lord *does* work in mysterious ways," shaking his head incredulously as Al was about to leave.

"Don't you worry, Padre. I can take care of my end. And from what you've told me, I'd put my money on that Guardians outfit. Hate to say it, but your old friend Patrick sounds like the fink, if not the actual kidnapper."

When Al had gone, the cardinal thought about Patrick. He recalled Patrick once telling him about a visitation from Jesus. When Bartolomeo had said, "It was just a dream, Georgie," Patrick had turned very red and said fiercely, "No! He came to me, I swear it!" Then he insisted that he'd been told always to protect His name and the Faith at any cost. And for years Bartolomeo wondered why Jesus had never come to *him*.

Could Patrick Cardinal Furst really be involved in such a thing as kidnapping? How naïve of Bartolomeo to have divulged all he knew of Taylor and her son to Patrick! But Patrick . . . Georgie . . . was *that* the key? Did Patrick still identify with those old George Raft roles? But why not? Patrick, the scholarly historian, could have a Walter Mitty-type outlet for his aggressions in just such an outfit as the Pope had described. And his justification for his acts would naturally come from the very history of the Church itself. The only recollection Barto had of George Raft was one of a pensive man, silently tossing a coin. Was Patrick that quiet man, tossing coins and deciding the fate of— No, no, it could not be that simple. But Barto had a feeling that it might not be far wrong.

He paced up and down the room. He stared up at the small crucifix on the wall.

Guidance, please, Lord, *guidance!* he beseeched silently, but nothing came to him.

He went to the desk, picked up his Vatican directory, and looked up the telephone number of Patrick's apartment. He lifted the phone and started to dial. Then, as though an unseen hand were pushing down on his, he hung up. He hesitated a moment, then went quickly into his bedroom. He got out of his cardinal's robes and into slacks and a beige turtleneck sweater. Then he went out of his apartment and down the stairs to the basement garage. His Fiat was next to two other cars that belonged to clerics who also lived in the building, all with the distinctive SVC to be found on all Vatican license plates.

In five minutes he was at Patrick's quarters, although the evening traffic on the Via Veneto was especially hectic. He parked across from the elegant apartment on Del Sarto Street and walked across the street to where the uniformed doorman stood.

"Cardinal Patricio," he said.

"And your name, sir?" The doorman's hand went to the brass phone that connected the lobby to the apartments.

Bartolomeo had the feeling, for some reason, that if he was announced, Patrick might not see him, might pretend not to be in, so he said for the first time in his life:

"I am Archbishop Bartolomeo, but you needn't announce me. I am expected."

The man dipped his head slightly and said, "Yes, Your Reverence," and quickly opened the door.

Bartolomeo took the elevator to the third floor, saying to himself, "Archbishop Bartolomeo... my, my, you've come a long way from Brooklyn, kid." And then he thought of the reason for his coming, and, as he went down the carpeted hall to Patrick's apartment, he thought how far apart he and old "Georgie" had drifted, although they had started out together in the same community and ended up together here in the Vatican.

He rang the bell, and in a moment the door opened. Patrick stood there, his handsome face framed by a round, white Della Robbia bas-relief of the Crucifixion on the wall of the foyer behind him. The cardinal's mouth opened in surprise, and he glanced furtively toward the living room. Bartolomeo could see two male figures with their backs to him, sitting on a red velvet sofa under a large painting by Rouault of Christ's head. Then Patrick's face spread into a charming smile.

"Barto!" he exclaimed. "What a pleasant surprise! Rumors are flying that you are to be our newest archbishop!"

"Patrick, I came to talk to you about something far more serious!"

Patrick's smile faded when he saw the scowl on Barto's face—and heard himself addressed as Patrick rather than as "Georgie."

"What is it, Barto?"

The smile, the greeting, the look of genuine concern on Patrick's face disarmed Cardinal Bartolomeo for a moment, but he went on.

"What do you know about the Guardians?" he asked.

"The Guardians?" Patrick wrinkled his brow.

"Yes, the Guardians." And Father Bartolomeo knew that

Patrick's query had been phony, for few would be in a postion to know more about any historic organization connected in any way to the Vatican than his old friend Patrick.

"Only what everyone knows, that they are—"

"*Were* is the verb of choice here, Georgie, remember?"

"Right. They were—"

"Georgie, when I told you about Taylor Phillips, her son, and the scrolls, whom did you tell about our talk?"

"Why?" He hesitated. "I can't remember. Why is it important?"

"Please think," Father Bartolomeo said.

"Barto," said Father Patricio, "what on earth is going on here?"

"Think!" Bartolomeo said. He took Patrick by the upper arm in a steel grip and backed him through a swinging door into the kitchenette, across that room, and pushed him hard up against the refrigerator.

"Think!"

"Barto!" Patrick hissed in a hoarse whisper, alarmed by the other's ferocity. "I have guests!"

"Whose brilliant idea was it to kidnap the boy?"

"What boy? What are you talking about?"

"You know!" Bartolomeo growled. "*You know!*"

Patrick hesitated. "Let me get rid of . . ." he jerked his head toward the living room.

Bartolomeo released his grip.

Patrick, rubbing his arm, went back into the living room, closing the kitchen door behind him.

"Gentlemen," Father Bartolomeo heard him say apologetically. "Something has come up. Let us continue this matter, if you will, in my office. Nine tomorrow, please."

Bartolomeo opened the door a crack. He could see the two men as they rose to leave. He could not see them well, but again the Pope's words came to him as he watched Patrick ushering them to the front door; didn't the Guardians operate with three men? Could they all be part of this monstrous kidnapping?

The men muttered good night to Patrick and left. Bartolomeo came out of the kitchenette when he heard the door close.

"Now just what is this all about?" demanded Patrick haughtily as he stood by a large wooden statue of Mary. "The serpent of hate appears to be in your bosom!"

Bartolomeo grabbed him by the shoulders and shook him hard. "Don't use that tone with me! Where the hell is the boy being held?"

"I told you, I know nothing of a boy! Kidnapping? What kind of accusation is this?" Patrick jammed the tips of his fingers hard on Barto's chest with indignation.

When Patrick's fingers touched him, Bartolomeo was instantly back in the streets of Brooklyn. Without thinking, just a reflex action, he shot out a left jab and almost simultaneously, a right cross to Patrick's face, shouting, "Don't you touch me, you damned kidnapping . . . Guardian!" For a moment Bartolomeo looked down at his still-clenched fists in horror and shame.

Back against the wall, Patrick put his hand in amazement to the trickle of blood at one corner of his mouth. "Where in the world," he panted, "did you get that idea? Of course I haven't kidnapped . . . what boy? The Phillips boy? I've never even seen him! Never heard of him till you told me about him!"

"Liar!" said Barto.

Patrick suddenly leaped forward and swung his fist. Barto ducked under it, slamming a left into Patrick's stomach as he did.

Patrick doubled over for a moment, then snapped out with an uppercut that caught Bartolomeo under the chin. The archbishop fell back against the wooden statue of the Virgin, grasped for it, and they both toppled over to the floor.

Bartolomeo shook his head, pushed the statue off him, lunged for Patrick's legs, and jerked him off his feet. Patrick's head hit the wall as he fell, and he lay there dazed. Bartolomeo crawled to him, grabbed him by the shoulders, and shook him.

"Where is the boy?"

"I don't know!"

"But you *are* a Guardian! Yes or no?"

Patrick nodded.

"And the boy?"

"Barto!" Patrick gasped. "I swear to you in the name of the

Savior, I don't know about any kidnapping!"

Bartolomeo relaxed his grip and said, ruefully and ashamed, "Look at us, Georgie! Men of the cloth, fighting like street brawlers. Ridiculous! I must believe you. We've known each other too long. I'm sorry, Patrick, truly sorry. Now what can you tell me of this . . . this conspiracy?"

Patrick dragged the back of his fingers across his bruised mouth. "*You* call it conspiracy! We of the Guardians call it faith and zeal and a burning desire to purge the Church of anyone who would lessen it in the eyes of the world."

"Bravo, a noble speech! And is the kidnapping of a young boy one of your nobler acts? I understand that at least two people have been murdered. Isn't that a rather fanatic distortion of religious zeal? Positively medieval! So the Pope was right—the Guardians *do* still exist. Very much so."

Patrick said nothing, but his eyes lowered.

"Patrick, we are running out of time! Where do we start to find the boy?"

"I don't know, Barto . . . let me think . . . give me time . . ." His mind was in turmoil. Two people killed? So Tobin had lied! He'd never liked or trusted the man—an evil, power-lusting maniac in cardinal's clothing. How was it possible that such a noble, God-inspired institution as the Guardians had gotten so far out of hand? Or had it always been thus, and had he been too much of a zealot himself to see it? Had he been duped unwittingly all along? Was a hunger for power the real motivation of the Guardians, and was violence their method, rather than faith and vigilance? Then to his friend he finally said, "I have killed no one, Barto. Kidnapped no one. I will help you. I told someone—unaware, so help me—of any possible consequences to your friend or her son. It had to do with surveillance on this man who is bent on exposing the Ephesus scrolls."

"Whom did you tell?"

"Tobin."

"Tobin!" Bartolomeo nodded. "Tobin, of course. How he rose to become a cardinal, I'll never know. Tobin!"

"I never truly liked or trusted him either." He seemed to see him now, clearly, for the first time, as the evil man he was. "Tertius is also involved, but he is nothing but Tobin's puppet."

"And where would they have taken the boy?"

Patrick thought for a moment. "A likely spot might be Tobin's summer place—his house in Calese."

"Let's go, then—straight to Tobin, and confront him and demand the release of the boy."

Father Patricio shook his head. "That would be foolish. He would only deny it and move the child to another location. Or even kill the boy. Yes, I believe now that he is ruthless enough to kill the boy." Patrick shuddered, then said, "Instead, let us go to the house and, if the child is there, free him ourselves."

"Better still, let's call the police. I have a young friend on the force, Andrea di Grazia, who—"

"Barto! The police? Never! Think of the implications! The police find a boy kidnapped by a *cardinal!* Think of the damage to the Church, the reflection on the Pope, on all of us!"

"You're right."

"The two of us can free him. How much protection do they need to contain a boy . . . how old, would you say?"

"Eight, nine. You're right. We have no choice. Do you want to go in my car?"

"No, you follow me. We might need both cars for the getaway."

"Georgie, you sound like a gangster."

"Well, Barto, you always said I looked like one."

"Before we go, I've got to call the boy's mother."

As he was waiting for the call to go through, he kept thinking, *Answer, answer, answer, sweet Taylor.* For if she didn't, it might mean that someone had gotten to her. She knew far too much now to be allowed to stay alive. And then his heart gave a skip as he heard her voice: "Oh, Father . . ."

"I've no time to talk, but there's a pilot friend of mine who will be there soon to help you. Taylor, I want you to clear out of that room they've set you up in. Not out of the hotel. Just tell the manager you want a different room. My friend will ask for you by your maiden name. No one else is to know where you are, understand? Of course, you are being watched, but this may slow them down a bit. And don't worry, my dear, I'll get Jonny."

"Oh, Father, I'm so grateful. But don't you think it might be better if I went to another hotel?"

"No, Taylor, dear. You couldn't gain anything by it. If you walked out, you'd only be followed. This way, as long as they think they know where you are, it could be much more confusing for them, since there will be nothing to indicate that you are no longer still in the room they reserved for you. Do as I say, my dear, and be careful. My friend will be there soon. His name is Al, a good man, a very good man. I must go now. Goodbye, child, and God be with you."

Taylor immediately arranged to have her things moved to another room. She re-registered, using her maiden name. Once settled, the respite that had come with the activity, the sense of doing something subsided, and once again she was left with her doubts.

How could Father Bartolomeo be so sure he could get Jonny? Was the Vatican really involved in this? Now that she had moved, how could Jason find her when he returned? Would he ever return? Would he be a good father for Jonny? How little she knew about him, really. But then, even her own sister—how could she have let this terrible thing happen to Jonny? But she had to stop this doubting and fretting. She had to trust someone. It was the waiting, the inactivity that made her feel so helpless, so vulnerable, so alone.

10

ANDREA DI GRAZIA, pacing in his office at the police station, was frustrated and angry. He took pride in his work and considered himself a better-than-average detective, and yet this Phillips boy's kidnapping defied his powers of deduction. How many sleepless hours or days had he been on this case? He'd lost track.

Furthermore, he couldn't reach anyone at the mother's house, and no one seemed to know where she was. And Father Bartolomeo's phone had been busy for half an hour. Andrea felt in his bones that somehow the cardinal could shed some light on the situation. Why had the mother not contacted the Roman police? Obviously the kidnappers had told her not to, or they would kill the boy. To whom, then, would she turn for help and advice? Who else but her old family friend, the eminent churchman?

He could have had the operator cut in on the cardinal's conversation, but he felt he might do better in person.

"Lori, I hate to do this to you," he said to his aide, an older sergeant, "but can you stick around tonight? I might be needing some help."

"Sure, Lieutenant," said Lori.

"How's that girl of yours?" Andrea asked as he put on his hat.

"Incantevole," the sergeant grinned. "Fantastic!"

"Tell you what. Take tomorrow off and spend it with her."

"Grazie, Andrea. *Grazie."*

Andrea came out of the brightly lit police station and stepped out into grimy Banducci Street. A police car was parked there with two officers in it, its motor running.

"Want a lift, Lieutenant, sir?" asked the driver.

For a moment Andrea thought of taking a squad car, but why? He was only going to call on Father Bartolomeo, who was, although the lieutenant knew him only slightly, a good man, an honest man. No danger. Still, Rome at night...

"No, thanks, Leonardo, you'd be wasting your time."

"Ah, a girl, sir?"

"A girl?" Andrea thought for a second of Maria Freitas, a Brazilian student at the university whom he'd been seeing lately. They were a date away from *la grande,* "the biggy" as she referred to it, when they would go to bed together. But both were shy and holding off because both knew, without even coming close to saying it, that this could be the real thing—engagement, marriage, babies, all the rest. He'd told her he'd see her tonight—and, by God he would, after talking to Father Bartolomeo.

"How did you guess?" he said with his good, boyish grin. *"Buona sera!"*

He walked to his gray Fiat, which was parked down the block, and got in. He drove quickly through the winding streets to Father Bartolomeo's apartment, and went to the door. Father Antonio, the young secretary, spoke to him over the intercom:

"Lieutenant, I'm sorry, the archbishop is not in right now. I just arrived here a few moments ago to pick up some papers and found a note saying he'd gone to Cardinal Patricio's."

"And where is that?"

After he got the address on Del Sarto Street, Andrea sped across town. As he pulled up to the apartment house, he saw two men coming hurriedly out of the front door. They were both dressed in mufti, but even in this dim light, Andrea recognized the leonine mane and slight limp. That would be Father Bartolomeo. The other...he didn't know...probably Cardinal Patricio. Where were they headed in such urgency?

As they crossed the street, he thought of calling out to stop them, to question them. But his policeman's instinct was telling him, *Follow them. You'll get the answers . . . maybe better answers.*

The cypress trees were like two rows of huge greenish-black soldiers marching up to the villa in the moonlight. The big rundown house in Calese, white in the moonlight, had twenty rooms, and from the road, all of them appeared to be darkened.

The two cars approached slowly, with their lights off. Patrick parked a hundred yards away, and Bartolomeo glided his Fiat into a copse and stopped fifty feet from the other car. Silently they got out, leaving the doors open to avoid making any noise. Then they took advantage of the moon's drifting partially behind some clouds to run down the long dirt driveway, hugging the muted moon shadows cast by the cypresses.

As they drew nearer to the house, they could see one dimly lit room. Crouching, they crept up to the French doors. Bartolomeo peered in and saw two men seated on a couch in front of a flickering television set. Each had a glass of wine in his hand, and a fat bottle of Chianti was on the table. They appeared heavy-lidded, and one stretched and yawned. Patrick looked in at them over Bartolomeo's shoulder and whispered, "Guards posing as servants!"

"How do you know?"

"They must be. He only has one servant, the Sicilian housekeeper, Nina. There are only three bedrooms, all on the second floor—Nina's, Tobin's, and the guest room."

"Would Tobin be here tonight?"

Patrick shook his head. "His car's not here."

"So the boy would be in the guest room?"

"Probably. Follow me."

They crouched and, hugging the walls of the house, made their way through the flowerbeds to a low window fifty feet away from where the guards were. Patrick pointed to the window. Bartolomeo, the sleeve of his sweater pulled down over his knuckles, gave one sharp rap on the glass. The pane broke and they waited, holding their breaths. No sound after the tinkling glass. Bartolomeo reached his hand in, turned the catch, and pushed the window in. He stepped over the sill, and Patrick followed. They were in some sort of a pantry, and Patrick pushed open a swinging door into what, in the gloom, looked like the dining room with a refectory table in the center. Patrick went stealthily to the staircase. They could see the living room now, and though the guards were out of view, they could see the dancing white light of the television set, and a hand reaching out for the wine bottle.

Up the winding staircase they crept. It was solid mahogany and carpeted, and made no sound under their careful footsteps. But upstairs, the bare parquetry of the old floor creaked and squeaked as they stepped out on it.

Instantly the door at the end of the hall was unbolted and thrown open. A large figure stepped out and snapped on a flashlight. Patrick and Bartolomeo squeezed beside a huge, ornate chest of drawers, crouched down, and pressed against the wall. The ray of light pierced the dark and flickered here and there. The footsteps came slowly down the hall as the intensity of the light increased.

Suddenly a black and white cat leaped down from the chest of drawers where it had been sleeping. The cat stood for a moment directly in front of Patrick and Bartolomeo as the light focused upon it and a powerful-looking woman bent down to pick it up. She wore a white blouse over her husky breasts and light glinted off a heavy silver chain and crucifix as it dangled in front of the cat while she was bending over—less than three feet from the priests. She murmured gutturally to the cat in Sicilian dialect as she stroked it and carried it back to the room.

After he heard the door being bolted, Bartolomeo let out a long sigh of relief.

"That room is adjacent to the guest room," breathed Patrick, "and connected to it."

"I noticed that the window to that next room is slightly open. I'll try to get to it. You go back down and keep an eye on those guards."

Bartolomeo saw that the door to the room on the other side of the one they suspected Jonny to be in was standing slightly open. That could be Tobin's. Carefully he lowered his body to the floor. Dividing his weight between his hands and his knees, he crawled across the distance and made it with only one slight creak.

Inside the bedroom, he stood up and went across the carpet to the window. It was open and he looked down. About five feet below the sill ran a foot-wide ledge and metal rain gutter. He stepped out of the window and positioned his feet on the ledge, holding on to the sill.

He held his breath and felt a tightening in his gut as he forced himself not to look down. The ledge felt shaky under his feet, but it held. About seven feet away was another window. Hanging on to the shutter with his left hand, he shuffled his feet down the ledge, his belly pressed tight and scraping across the plaster wall of the house, his right arm extended toward the next window. There was a bad moment when he had to let go of one shutter for several shuffling steps until he felt his fingers grasp the next one. He repeated the maneuver on the second window and then he came to the one he wanted.

It was partially opened. He stared into the gloom inside.

"Jonny?" he whispered. "Jonny Phillips?"

He heard someone sit up in bed, but he couldn't see far enough into the room to tell who it was.

"Who is it?" came a sleepy young voice.

"Bartolomeo . . . Father Bartolomeo. Don't make a sound."

Pushing with his toes on the ledge, he eased the window up. He grasped the sill and was about to boost himself up and into the room when suddenly the beam of a flashlight burst into his eyes. Dimly he saw the great ugly face of the woman before him, smelled her fetid body odor, and heard her Sicilian oath. At the same time he felt the ledge and drain give way under his feet. He clung to the windowsill with desperate fingers, but now the woman was beating on his hands with the flashlight. He let go with his right hand, shot it up, and grabbed her heavy silver necklace by the crucifix and jerked her head down, pinning it to the sill. Then, holding her more or less immobile, he managed to sling one of his legs over the sill. She dropped the flashlight and her hands grabbed him by the neck and tried to push him back out the window. He struck her once, hard, on the temple, and then again, and at last she fell back into the room, unconscious. He hauled himself in through the window and sprawled on the floor, panting.

His breath came in short gasps and his mind was in upheaval; more violence, and they still weren't near safety! He tried to get up.

"Are you all right, Father?" asked Jonny. By the beam of the flashlight on the floor next to the hulk of the woman, Bartolomeo could see, standing over him, the handsome features of the tousle-headed boy in pajamas. He held his hand out to the priest to help him up.

"I'm fine," whispered Bartolomeo. But he could hear the clumping footsteps of the two guards already coming up the stairs. He struggled to his feet.

Where to go? He went to the window and looked down. It was too long a drop. But then he saw a remarkable sight: a table moving along the side of the house—the refectory table from the dining room. Under it, turtlelike, was Patrick Furst. He stopped under the window, positioned the table, and then scrambled up on its top.

Andrea di Grazia sat in his car and watched the two cardinals run down the driveway in the moonlight like a pair of thieves. Although it wasn't an official police car, Andrea had indulged in the luxury of two-way radio equipment, and he called back to the police station.

"Lori . . . slightly interesting situation here. I'd like you to check out who owns a big villa here in Calese." He went on to give the location.

"Might take a little while," Lori said.

"Like about five minutes, I trust."

It was five minutes when Lori called back.

"Belongs to a cardinal. Cardinal Tobin. It's his summer residence."

"Try calling the good cardinal in Rome . . . just to see if he's there. I'll hang on."

In a few minutes, Lori came on the radio. "Yes, he was there. I felt like a fool. I said, 'This is the telephone company,' and he said, 'This is Cardinal Tobin,' and I said, 'Just checking, sir,' and he said, 'Fine,' and that was about it."

"Okay, Lori, thanks. I'm going in the villa for a little look."

"Keep in touch."

"Sure. I'll write you regularly."

"Seriously, sir, I could dispatch a squad car."

"What's to fear? A couple of cardinals?"

"You were a cardinal, sir, when you nailed that hijacker on the plane."

"Right, Lori, but that was a disguise. Leave this baby to me—it could be nothing more than a routine matter."

"Right you are, sir. You're the big fish."

Andrea chuckled under his breath. A piece of cake compared to the hijacking job."

"Quick, Jonny!" cried Bartolomeo. "Sit on the ledge!"

The guards were pounding on the locked door.

"Nina! Nina! What's happening? Open the door!" They began throwing their weight against it.

The cardinal took Jonny's hand in his and lowered the child down to Patrick's arms. Then he swung his legs over the sill, hung by his fingers until he felt Patrick's strong hands. Then he let go and dropped to the table.

"You take the boy," said Patrick. "I'll lead them off the trail!"

Andrea suddenly heard a commotion from the house as he approached the front door. He saw three figures—the two cardinals and a boy—running quietly across the flowerbeds and down the driveway, and he heard shouts from inside. The front door burst open and two men ran out.

"Stop! I'm police!" shouted Andrea. But the barrel-chested man in the lead ran straight at Andrea with his fist clenched. The policeman crouched, and when the man started to swing, Andrea ducked to the side and lashed out with his foot and caught the man in the groin with a powerful kick. The guard howled and dropped to the ground, clutching himself. The second man drew his pistol, but before he could aim, Andrea was on him with a slashing chop with the side of his hand to the other man's arm. The gun flew to the ground, and with an oath, the man clutched his wrist.

"Hold it there!" Andrea commanded drawing his own

159

weapon. He was crouching down to pick up the other pistol, and didn't see the husky Sicilian woman come up behind him fast with an ax. She swung and hit him on the temple with the blunt end of it and he went down hard and without a sound.

"Hang on, Jonny!" whispered Bartolomeo, holding the boy by the hand. They raced away from the house, down the moonlit driveway between the cypresses. When they came to the end of it, they could already hear the guards' car being started.

"Barto," panted Patrick, "I'll be the fox. Give me five minutes' start. I'll give them a chase they'll never forget!"

"You always were the best driver in Brooklyn, Georgie!"

"Wait here with the boy for just a few minutes. They won't see your car. Then you can take him on into Rome."

Impulsively, Bartolomeo threw his arms around his friend.

"Patrick—Georgie—forgive me!"

"For what, Archbishop Bartolomeo?"

"For doubting your faith and your love, Cardinal Patricio."

Patrick's smile could be seen in the moonlight, and he said, "We'd better get going, Barto," for they could hear the car coming. Patrick sprinted to the right; Bartolomeo and Jonny ran to the left.

A car skidded out of the driveway and Bartolomeo hit the ground on the side of the road, pulling Jonny down with him. They lay motionless in the soft grass, watching as Patrick switched on his headlights and shot off with a squeal of tires. The guards' car swerved after it, careening around the corner.

It worked! God bless Georgie! God keep Georgie!

He looked over at the boy. The child was calm. What a fine boy this son of Taylor Phillips was.

"It's okay now, Jonny," said Father Bartolomeo as he stood up and they walked to the car and got in. While they sat for a few minutes to give Patrick the start he'd requested, Bartolomeo said, "We'll be heading for Rome now, Jonny. You'll be at your aunt's in no time. I've talked to your mother. She'll be very happy to see you again."

As Father Bartolomeo turned on the lights and started the car, he saw the woman running straight toward them.

"Father!" yelled Jonny. "It's her!"

And then it was as though a grenade had gone off.

But it was not a grenade. The explosion was an ax blade crashing through the windshield between Bartolomeo and Jonny, showering them with hundreds of diamonds of glass.

The jagged hole framed the enraged face of the Sicilian woman, her features twisted with fury, blood at the corners of her mouth from the cardinal's punches.

"Diavolo!" she screamed as she pulled the ax back to aim another blow. Instinctively the priest pushed the accelerator pedal down to the floor. The car shot forward and the woman sprawled over the hood of the car. Then, as it kept moving forward, she slid off with a great scream. Bartolomeo jerked the steering wheel to the right to avoid her, but when he felt the sickening bump of the left tire, he knew he was too late.

Braking to a sudden stop, he started to get out, but no, he could not. The boy's life was in danger. He should administer last rites, but the boy was more important. He looked in the mirror at the woman's lifeless body, a crumpled mound in the moonlight, then gunned the car down the road.

Oh, God! Oh, good God! A life! Another life! his mind wailed.

He was a mile down the road when he found his hands shaking so much, he had to pull over. He turned off the motor and opened the door and vomited onto the asphalt. Then he wiped his mouth on his sleeve and dropped his face into his fingers.

There was a moment of silence, then the boy's voice, quavering, said, "Father Bartolomeo, you couldn't help it! She was trying to kill us!"

The cardinal looked at the child and put his arm around him and hugged him. He shook his head and stared out into the night as he said, "A man of the cloth, killing someone! What would Christ have done in the same situation?"

"I don't know," whispered Jonny. "Can't you ask Him?"

Bartolomeo managed a weak smile. "Not a bad idea, Jonny."

He turned the key in the ignition. "We'd better get you back before those maniacs realize they've been fooled."

• • •

Cardinal Patricio, a dreamer and idealist, perhaps overly zealous in his dedication to the Church, was a superb driver. And he knew every turn, curve, and bend of these roads in this beautiful, moonlit countryside.

He started fast and could easily have lost the guards in their older, sluggish Fiat. It was tempting to gun it, get to Rome, get away from this ugliness, take a hot bath, and figure out how he was to go about divorcing himself from Tobin, Tertius, and the Guardians. The Pope! Bartolomeo had the Pope's ear. Tomorrow they would go straight to the Pope and tell him all!

He saw the pursuing car now in his rear mirror. He slowed up a bit. He stayed tantalizingly close for a while, then sped up, leading them farther and farther off the course that Bartolomeo would be taking back to Rome.

Suddenly there came the muted pop of a pistol shot. Patrick felt it thump into the rear of the car. He jammed his foot on the accelerator. Another shot, and he knew by the way the car slumped a bit to the left that the bullet had hit a rear tire. He kept going, but the other car was gaining on him.

Then he heard a siren and saw, screaming toward him, a police car, its light on top twirling. He skidded to a stop and jammed his hand down on the horn. But the car kept going, obviously on some other mission.

The police car was soon out of sight, and Patrick started off again with a jerk, but the guards' car was on him. One of the men leaned out the window and fired three shots at a front tire. The car slued from side to side. Patrick fought to keep it straight, expertly turning the wheel as the vehicle wobbled along at high speed. Then came another shot and the car skidded off the road, spun once, and slammed into a tree.

Patrick yanked the door open, jumped out, and lurched off toward the woods, holding his left arm with his right hand. Both guards got out of the car and followed him with drawn pistols.

"Lord," breathed Patrick as he ran, "let me make it to that clump of trees."

As he reached the trees, he quickly crouched down behind a fallen log. The men approached warily.

"Keep coming, you devils, keep coming!" he breathed. Once

they got far enough past him, he would race for their car—he prayed that they'd left the keys in the ignition.

He picked up a rock, waited until the dark shadows of the men were deep in the trees, then hurled it fifty feet from them. When the men heard the crash of the rock in the bushes, they fired, the spits of flame showing bright in the darkness.

And Patrick was up and running back toward the road and the car. He heard one of the men cry out, "There he is!" He heard a shot, but he didn't look around; he just kept running flat out. There was another shot near his feet, but the car was only two yards away now. He lunged and his hand was on the door handle when he felt the bullet strike his back. His hand slid down the car door. He sagged forward and hugged the ground dizzily as more shots came and the world went black.

The guards ran to the fallen figure, turned him over, and pointed a flashlight at his face.

"Oh, my God!" breathed one when he saw who the dying man was.

Cardinal Tobin, dressed in his expensive silk pajamas, was awakened by the phone. He listened silently, but his eyes narrowed. When the caller had finished, the cardinal merely spat out, "Fools! How did you manage to let this happen?"

He could guess who the other man in the rescue mission had been, and he was worried.

"Give me time to finish, Your Eminence!"

"I have no time for fools."

"We have another problem, Your Eminence. We have here a policeman."

"*What?*"

"We have a policeman here. He's down in the cellar, tied up. What shall we—"

A policeman! At the villa! Obviously that could be connected to that phony call he'd received from the "telephone company"...

"What did he see?"

"I guess . . . well . . ."

"He saw something?"

"Well, Your Eminence—"

163

"Our guest? Did he see him?"

"Perhaps."

"Perhaps? You know he did!"

"Perhaps, Your Eminence."

"Who is he?"

"Di Grazia, Your Eminence."

Andrea di Grazia! That was the one who'd achieved a measure of fame through impersonating a cardinal in the hijacking case. Bad enough, any policeman—but di Grazia!

"Is he injured?"

"Yes, Your Eminence."

"Is he conscious?"

"Barely, Your Eminence."

"Has he said anything?"

"Only moans, Sir."

"That's all?"

"That's all so far, Your Eminence. What are we . . . you know . . . what do we do with him?"

Everything would collapse if this policeman were to walk out of the villa.

Cardinal Tobin's voice was cool and steely. "I shall pray for this man."

Then he hung up the phone.

The guard understood. He went to the kitchen, opened a drawer, and took out a sharp knife.

Cardinal Tobin went to his small office in his apartment, and flipped through his black notebook. Only a small tapestry marred the room's plainness, plus a large brass crucifix on his desk. He found the number and placed a call to Thessaloniki.

An American voice answered.

"Melnick? Cardinal Tobin here. I think we may have a bit more responsibility for you to assume, but we know that you're most capable. Tell me, how are things there? Have you seen Mrs. Phillips?"

Melnick hesitated, then said, "Well, no, not really. She's been staying in her room, having her meals sent in."

Tobin said, "That's understandable. She wants to be near the phone to get word about— Well, actually, that's why you'll have more to do. You see, we've lost our bargaining position at this end."

"Lost the—"

"Lost our bargaining position!" Tobin pronounced the words carefully to remind Melnick to watch what he said.

"I get it."

"Melnick," Tobin went on, "you're sure she's still there? She hasn't left?"

"Positive. She hasn't come down from her room once. And we've checked the car every hour. Still there. It was still there five minutes ago."

"That's good. You're doing a fine job. Yes, by all means, keep an eye on the car. Citröen, isn't it?"

"Licensed in Turkey. Can't miss it."

"Good. And you understand, I will let you know exactly *when*. We have the usual arrangements with American Express for your payments. God bless you."

Tobin hung up and, looking up another number, dialed again.

"Signor Agnelli?" His tone was fawning and humble.

"Cardinal Tobin here. We know how generous you've been in the past, and it pains us to have to come again to you with our red hats in hand. But we have urgent need of thirty thousand dollars. Yes, sir, it is for a special disaster fund. Yes. In Brazil. Yes, I know... I know... it's a bit sudden, but so is the emergency. Excuse me? Ah, sir, you are too kind, too generous. You are a great Christian, sir, and the Pope shall hear about this and bless you, and so shall the poor souls in Brazil. Remember, Signor Agnelli, remember, and think upon Saint Paul's letter to the Corinthians, the one where he said, 'And now abideth faith, hope, and charity, these three; but the greatest of these is charity!' So bless you, Signor Agnelli, bless you!"

Although he sounded serene and confident on the phone, Tobin was beginning to feel the knot of panic high in his stomach. Patrick, dead on a road not far from his home! There would be an investigation. He had lost the Phillips boy, but that was all right for the moment, since no one—or almost no one—knew where the boy's mother was. Unless...

Of course, she could have disobeyed orders and telephoned

Bartolomeo. Of course! That was what had happened! How else would Bartolomeo have known about the boy? It was Bartolomeo and he alone who had managed to mess up everything! And unfortunately, he was the Pope's darling and in a new position of power.

He sighed. Then he opened a lower drawer in his desk and extracted a pistol. From another drawer he took out a silencer and fitted it on the barrel. Then he turned off the light and went out.

11

INSTEAD OF taking Jonny to his own apartment, Bartolomeo went straight to the Hudsons' house on the outskirts of Rome.

It was long after midnight, but there was a porch light on. Otherwise, the modest house was dark. Bartolomeo shook the boy awake.

"We're here, Jonny," he said gently.

The boy opened his eyes and looked around. "Wow!" he said.

"We're home."

"Home's with Mom . . . but this sure is second best."

The lights came on before they even rang the bell. The door opened and Jean Hudson, plump and pretty at forty, rushed out in her pajamas.

"I knew! I knew!" she gasped through her tears as she clutched Jonny to her. "I told Tom today . . . he'll be back soon . . . I could feel it!"

And she covered the child's face with kisses. Then she said, "Father, God bless you . . . oh, God bless you! Come in, come in."

The living room was decorated in California style, with ducks and decoys adorning the mantelpiece, reminding Bartolomeo of her husband's hobby.

"Has Tom been having any luck, lately?"

"The poor dear's been so busy, he hasn't had time to go out. And then, of course, this terrible thing with Jonny. He's in Milan tonight, trying to enlist the help of a friend on the police force there. Oh, God, I can't believe it!" She covered her eyes and sank to the sofa. Jonny sat down next to her and hugged his aunt, and she held him very close for a long moment. Then he went to Father Bartolomeo and buried his face in the now tattered and soiled sweater of the priest.

Jean Hudson jumped up, saying, "You both must be starved!" She insisted on making cinnamon toast and hot chocolate for them. As she went to the kitchen, Bartolomeo followed.

"My dear, please do not reveal anything to the police at this time—not as yet. I've talked to Jonny. He knows how important this is. We must buy time. I'll explain later, but it does have to with your sister's safety. I also suggest that to avoid questioning by the police, you take Jonny as soon as possible to the Fiumiccino airport and catch the first plane out. Perhaps you could join your husband in Milan. Be careful what you say on the phone."

"Let me ask you one thing," said Jean Hudson. "Why? Why did they do it?"

Bartolomeo shook his head. "Not now," he said. "It's too long and complicated. And dangerous to know."

She frowned, but nodded understandingly. "All right, then, tell me—and I think I have a right to know—who?"

Bartolomeo hesitated. "Yes, I agree. You do have a right to know that. A madman who will be summarily dealt with. His name is Cardinal Tobin."

Then he left and drove to his apartment, thinking along the way, *Now that the conspiracy has been exposed, I will have to see the Pope first thing in the morning. The police should in no way be involved. The Vatican has its own privacy to protect. Tobin and Tertius will have to be put away by the Vatican's own judicial system. Patrick and I will see the Pope together.*

He let himself in with his latchkey and snapped on the light switch. No light came on. He went to a table light and pulled the chain. No light. He felt his way to the telephone and picked it up. Dead. He headed for the front door, alarmed now, and then stopped when he made out the silhouette standing in the hallway lit only by the moonlight from the window.

"Tobin?" said Bartolomeo. Then, "Of course, Tobin."

"Too bad, Your Eminence," said Tobin. From the outline of his body in the dark, it was apparent that he held a gun in his hand. "Too bad you had to become involved."

He said it calmly, almost pleasantly. "Too bad you went against the Guardians . . . too bad you went against me. I say this with regret."

"And I say with regret, Cardinal Tobin, that you have totally forgotten that God called upon you to serve Him, and not Satan. Every fiber of your being is infected with evil. Don't you see you are blind to God's love?"

"It is you who are blind, Bartolomeo! All of you! It is I who love God the most—I, who want to return to the old values of the Church! I, who love the Lord enough to kill for His ideals! Under me, the Church shall return to the strict and just ways of the glory that once was hers!"

"And you think God wants you to kill for Him?"

"All is justified when it helps preserve the true Church."

He raised the pistol. Bartolomeo started to rush him, but there was no time, for he heard the muted spits from the silencer and felt the shots tear into his chest. He put his hands to the wounds and almost smiled.

"God forgive you," he whispered as he fell.

Cardinal Tobin made the sign of the cross as he stepped over the twitching body. He went to the fuse box and threw the switch, flooding the place with light. Then he went to the phone, picked up the plastic cord, and plugged it into the wall terminal. He took a piece of paper from his pocket and dialed the operator.

A few moments later he said, "Melnick? Sorry to wake you at this hour. But you may now proceed with *the* mission. Taylor Phillips is also to be considered as part of the operation. Understand? Good luck . . . and God bless you."

"Monks, they don't like strangers," Andoni was saying as they came down to where the boat was waiting. "Used to be, they let people come, stay at monastery all the time. No trouble.

Now, too many times things get stolen, valuable things, important books. Monks got to be more careful who come. You professor...they like professors. Professors don' do strange things."

"Do we really need him?" asked Jason, pointing to the donkey. "Is he going to get in the boat too?"

"He carry food and ouzo!" Andoni seemed a little offended. "Besides, boss, he my bes' friend. He go ever'where with me. And if you get tired walking, you can ride him."

The motorboat was thirty feet long, cerulean blue, with fading layers of peeling paint and a striped awning over the deck. Besides the boatman, there was only one other person aboard: a monk who sat in the stern, telling his beads. When he saw Jason looking at him, he turned away.

"I thought we were to have the boat all to ourselves," whispered Jason.

"Yes, boss, we were, but then the boatman say this here poor monk, he miss the boat last night and could we take him, so what could I say?"

Paranoid, Van Cleve, Jason said to himself. *You're even worried about monks now.*

Mangas, the burro, stepped into the boat obediently and stood quietly eating oats from the nosebag Andoni had brought.

"Very fine animal, boss...smart and loyal," Andoni said as they pulled away from the dock and the motor began its explosive *chug, chug, thunk, chug.*

"Exactly where are we, and where are we headed? The guidebook said Vatopedi is on the other side of the Athos peninsula."

"Long peninsula, thirty miles," said Andoni, "but skinny, only five miles across, so we go now to little port called Daphne, maybe halfway down the peninsula. Then we got to go to Karyes to get permission for to take you to Vatopedi." Andoni pointed and gestured as he spoke, although Jason could not see the shore through the morning fog.

"Supposing they don't give us permission?"

"They give it, boss. They give it to Andoni."

• • •

As Jason, Andoni, and the burro boarded the boat, a hundred yards down the quay, the small man who kept dabbing at his nose was hiring a similar boat.

"Hurry!" said McCue to the boatman. He was already losing Jason's craft in the fog. "Follow . . . follow!"

But the boatman pointed to an old man who had arrived on the dock with a cart full of sacks.

"We take potatoes to monastery of Xenofontos."

McCue shook his head and shoved a handful of drachmas at the boatman.

"We go now! Now!"

The boatman looked at the money, shrugged in apology to the potato man, and started up the boat's engine.

"How does he know where he's going in this pea soup?" Jason asked.

"Like wonderful machine they got on big boats, boss. He *hear* where he is."

"You mean he has sonar equipment on this little boat?" Jason said with disbelief.

"Nah, he just use his ears, boss. You get close to shore, the noise bounce back at you from the cliffs. Boat sound different. You do this all the time and pretty soon you know the way it should sound."

"I had hoped to see those cliffs and those monasteries. The photographs in the guidebook were spectacular," Jason said.

"You get to see them, boss. Later, fog burn off and you get to see them. Beautiful. And very old, boss. Twenty big ones on this peninsula."

"Where'd you learn such good English?" asked Jason.

"War, boss, war. I was war hero . . . had many English friends and we fight the Germans. They call me outrageous. 'Andoni the Lion' they call me. They give me money, cigareets, chocolate. You got cigareets, boss?"

Jason gave him one, and lit one himself.

"They all love me, the English. That because they say nothing can scare the Lion. Once I strangle two Nazis with my bare hands."

"Just your hands?"

Andoni shrugged. "Two hands and piece of rope. After the war I was very proud because I am only one in my village who speaks English. Other villagers, they think I am wise only because I speak English. When tourists start to come to Holy Mountain, they all want good guide who speaks English. I know all about Holy Mountain."

"Tell me about it, Andoni."

Andoni cleared his throat and, over the hollow chugging of the boat, began a recital, like a small boy in class. Jason felt sure that if he interrupted, Andoni would have to go back and start the memorized spiel from the beginning.

"Mount Athos, on peninsula sticking out into Aegean Sea, is earth occupied by monks for more than a thousand years. Mount Athos rise straight up from sea two thousand meters. Gets very cold on top, sometimes big snow. They got twenty monasteries"—he laughed his big laugh—"that why they call it Holy Mountain! Old days, three hundred monasteries, now only twenty. Used to be lots and lots of monks live here, but now not so many. Some monastery got twenty monks, some got hundred twenty." He laughed again. "Maybe mountain not so holy now!"

Jason smiled to show his appreciation of Andoni's little joke, and Andoni went on.

"Some monks, they don' live in regular monastery—maybe they live in *skete* or even smaller place. Some monks, they go off by themselves altogether. They live in huts or caves—like eagles' nests. That what they call them—eagles' nests—way high up on mountain. They got different way of living in monastery. Some, they all go to meals same time, do everything same time. Other monastery, they don' have to all pray or eat at same time. But mostly they got eight hours to pray, eight hours to work, and eight hours to sleep. And some places, the day start not at midnight but at sundown, and other places at sunrise. Some monastery, they got bells to let you know it's time to pray, other places they got big wooden thing they call *semantron*—they bong on it instead of ring bells."

"And why is it that no women are allowed?" asked Jason.

"Emperor Constantine Monomachos, almost thousand years ago, he say women bad for monks. He say no women on Athos.

Monks believe that in a storm long time ago, the Virgin Mary's ship was forced to land on Mount Athos coast. She so like the beauty of the peninsula, she say, 'This is my garden.' So it is holy ground now. The monks say a statue of the Virgin on Mount Athos spoke. It spoke to the visiting Byzantine Empress Pulcheria, sending her away like this: 'You go away. Here in this place there is another queen besides you!' Since then the monks don' let any other woman share the Virgin's garden."

"And you mean on this thirty-mile peninsula, there hasn't been a woman since?"

"Twenty-five year ago, French woman, journalist woman, she dress like monk, sneak in, stay four days. They catch her, put her in jail two years."

"How'd they catch her?"

"Young monk, he notice"—Andoni laughed as his hands described arcs in front of his chest—"he notice bumps. Woman go to jail!" He roared with laughter. "Funny thing, boss. In old days—real old days, before Constantine even—Mount Athos forbidden to men! Only virgin girls live here, girls preparing themselves to be priests—how you call . . . priestess. If man set foot on Athos in those days, they cut off his balls first, then kill him!"

"How many monks do you think there are at Vatopedi?"

"Vatopedi big—one of the oldest monasteries—rich too. They got maybe fifty, sixty monks there now."

"What do they eat? The guidebooks says they're mostly vegetarians."

"Special days, maybe three times a year, meat. Some places they got better food than others. They grow vegetables and have bread with olive oil, mostly. Some have a little meat, but mostly they do not eat meat. Some monks, like the ones live in those eagles' nests—who knows what they eat? But they all have wine, ouzo, coffee, maybe a little cheese."

"You are indeed a good guide."

Andoni beamed with pride and pleasure.

Jason turned his head and said under his breath, "That monk keeps looking at us."

"The monks, some of them don' see that many foreigners, like I tell you. They afraid of strangers these days." Andoni shrugged. "But you okay, boss. Monks like professors—people who 'preciate their treasures but don' steal them."

"I just hope he really is a monk," Jason said.

Andoni looked puzzled, but Jason didn't elaborate.

As they approached the harbor at Daphne, Jason said, "Where's Vatopedi from here?"

"Over the hill, but we don't go there right away. First we got to walk a couple hours to Karyes to get permission, like I tol' you."

"Walk?"

"Sure, boss. We jus' walk and Mangas carry everything for us. We not got taxicab like in New York!" Andoni laughed boisterously as he clapped Jason on the back.

As Andoni led Jason and Mangas up the dirt road toward Karyes, Jason said, "I read that there is some kind of complicated protocol for obtaining the permits."

"There's some funny things they do at Hazel Nuts—that what 'Karyes' mean. There's five men—they call it the Council of Five—and each man got a part of a seal, and they puts together all the four parts of the seal and that go into the handle and then they stamp the papers. If they like you."

"In other words, four men have a quarter of the seal, the fifth man has the handle—okay, I see. Now what about the tray? I read something about a tray."

"You important man, they bring out the tray. It got jam and water and liquor and you s'pose to eat it a certain way, but if you don't got lots of important papers, they don' bring no tray."

Jason was pretty sure he wouldn't have to cope with the tray, for he had no 'important papers.' He only hoped the papers he did have, an American passport and a press pass, would convince the council that he was sufficiently reputable to be allowed access to the monastery of Vatopedi.

The road—a mere path, really—became narrower and merged with scrub and thickets of arbutus and boxwood and judas tree, and then a dense forest of ilex and Spanish chestnut and pine. The harbor now was far below, and still they climbed.

Occasionally they would pass a lonely *kellia,* a little hermitage tucked back in the woods, with its little chapel.

The trail became rather steep as they neared the crest of the hill on the pathway to Karyes. Andoni stopped for a moment to adjust the cinch on Mangas, and Jason took the opportunity to remove his jacket, for now they were well above the fog. He looked around and saw that, some fifty yards behind them, the figure in the black cassock was trudging up the path through the trees. Then a spot of blue caught his eye, and he could make out another man coming up the hill much farther down.

"Seems to be a well-traveled road here, Andoni," Jason observed. Was it the same monk?

"Oh, sure, boss," Andoni replied. "Mos' ever'body come up this way if they go to Karyes."

Maybe.

Shortly after they had resumed their pace, Andoni stopped again and said, "Look, boss, look down there. That Hazel Nuts."

They were over the crest of the hill and could look out over the trees and down onto the red-tiled rooftops of the buildings of Karyes.

"Imposing buildings for such a small place," Jason said. He looked back and could spot neither the monk nor the other man.

"Monasteries all got at least one building in Karyes. *Konakia*—embassies—where monks stay when they come into town. They got representatives from their monastery, they got shops where they work, make things, maybe trade a little."

A train of mules loaded with logs and hay trotted past them. Not long after, they came into the cobblestone streets of the little town. Jason looked around at the stone-and-tile buildings, some with frescoes, many with deep, overhanging eaves. Black-robed men with brimless stovepipe hats, their hair tucked up into the tall cylinders, would emerge from one building and disappear into another. There were two vine-covered cafes, half a dozen little shops, and a big church. Another century.

There were no women, no children, no motorcars, no bicycles or wheels of any sort. There were a few dogs and a few cats. "All male, boss. They allow mules 'cause they got no sex. No cows, though."

There seemed to be no pattern to the layout of the streets

or buildings, many of which seemed to be at odd angles to one another, some close together, others far apart.

"We better get place to stay, Boss. Get some food, too."

"What about the food you brought?"

"We maybe need that on the trail. Better we go to *kellion* of Vatopedi. They give us something to eat and place to sleep tonight."

"Can't we just get the permit and keep going on to Vatopedi?" Jason asked.

Andoni shook his head. "Boss, you don' know how long those men they take! Hours, sometimes, to decide are they gonna let you go to Vatopedi. 'Specially since you don' got no papers except passport."

Was this man stalling?

As they passed the *kathlikon*—the church of Karyes—Andoni pointed to a building beyond, which could be seen in the space between the church itself and the separate tower. "That the headquarters, there, that place with all the steps and arches. We come back here later. You gonna see more church than you ever see in your life. Some monasteries, they got *kathlikon*, like main church, then they got chapel here, chapel there, and they got *sketes* that got chapels and *kellion* that got chapels and even *kalyves* got a chapel."

"*Kalyves?*"

"They place for monks, but only smaller than the *kellion* and bigger than a *kathisma*—they all places where monks live and they belong to the monasteries. Now we go over to that building and get permit."

They mounted the steps to the Holy Epistasia. Ecclesiastical gendarmes appeared, bearded and wearing battle dress of celestial blue with forage caps showing the seal of the double-headed eagle.

Andoni spoke to them and they were ushered into a dark room, lit by a single candle on a long table. Andoni gave a tattered paper of his own, along with Jason's passport, to one of the guards, who then disappeared. In a few moments five old monks filed silently into the room from a side door and sat at the table.

They paid no attention to Andoni, asking him to wait in the

anteroom. But Jason was scrutinized carefully. He was asked questions that seemed totally irrelevant at times, but was always handled with deference and courtesy.

One of the old monks pulled at his long, square beard and studied Jason hard, his narrowed eyes expressing some vague distrust.

"True—you are archeologist?" he asked.

Jason disliked lying and wasn't good at it, but he managed to say, rather convincingly, "Yes, sir, though I confess to knowing little of Athos and its vast history."

"You sure not art dealer?"

"Excuse me?"

"Art pirates come to buy or steal our art objects, our rare books. Unscrupulous people here help them acquire great treasures to sell to moving-picture stars and bankers in capitalistic countries, knowing full well they will be damned for all eternity for their perfidy."

"I assure you I am not one of them."

The monk was silent for a moment, then he nodded to the others. Jason was asked to wait in the anteroom.

Andoni looked up when Jason came out, but only smiled. He made no move to get up, so Jason sat down beside him.

"What happens now, Andoni?" he asked.

"We wait, boss. They gonna talk it over—like what you call jury—they talk it over and decide are they gonna trust you." Andoni nodded and said, "Like I tell you, boss, it could take a long time."

Jason did not have to wait long, for in less than twenty minutes a monk came out and asked him to return to the conference room, where he was told that permission would be granted.

He thanked the council, then watched as they performed the complicated ritual of putting together the assorted parts of the official seal. The ancient monk with the handle made an elaborate gesture as he stamped the paper that was finally handed to Jason.

"Here is your *diamoniterion*—your passport to any monastery on Athos. Go with God."

As they left the building, Jason saw a monk watching them.

He turned away, but not before Jason had seen it was the same one as on the boat.

Early the next morning, fog had once again settled over the Mount Athos peninsula as Andoni loaded his burro and Jason pulled on his jacket.

Karyes now looked eerie in the fog, and the donkey's clopping hooves echoed under the broad eaves and colonnades of the stone buildings.

"Not far, boss," Andoni assured Jason. "Maybe two, three hour, you gonna be in Vatopedi."

"How do you know where you're going this time, Andoni?"

"Jus' follow Mangas, boss. He jus' follow trail and I jus' follow him."

"But does he know where you want to go?"

"If I put him on right trail, he know."

In less than an hour the air had cleared and the warm sun felt good as they trod along through dwarf oak, holly, and myrtle. The path wove gently through the shrublike vegetation, parallel to the sea, which they could smell as the morning breezes wafted its ancient odors onshore.

Unlike yesterday, when they had been climbing over the ridge of the peninsula, the trail now gradually undulated along to the shore, where Vatopedi lay sprawled on the coast of the Aegean.

"There, boss. See, I tol' you. There the belltower, that Vatopedi!"

"What are those buildings with the little fluted and scalloped domes? They look Russian."

"That all one building, boss. That the *kathlikon* of Vatopedi. Back in old days, the tsars of Russia gave lots of help to the monks of Vatopedi. But lots of others did too. Maybe Serbians, maybe Constantinople, maybe Alexandria."

"Constantinople . . . reminds me . . ." How far could he trust this man Andoni? On the other hand, how far could he get without Andoni's help? Who would translate for him, now that Taylor was not at his side? And this man was Taylor's friend— she had said so.

"Reminds you what, boss?"

"Reminds me that the person I most want to see at Vatopedi is the abbot—Constantine."

"Oh, sure, that easy. He head man here. Sooner or later you *got* to see Constantine."

And how would he approach Constantine? Just come right out and ask about the scrolls? Suppose Constantine said it was none of his damn business and ordered him out of the monastery? There had to be a more intelligent approach.

"What's that strange sound?"

"That the *semantron* I tell you about. Big wooden thing. It tell you that it time to go to pray."

They entered the narrow archway after showing their passes to the young bearded monk at the sentinel's niche.

The courtyard of Vatopedi was bathed in morning sunlight. The church and its two dozen chapels, as well as towers, storehouses, refectory, library, treasury, guest houses, fountains, shrines, trees, tailored flowerbeds, and endless rows of cells, all were grouped within the fortified enclosure. One of the largest and richest of all the monasteries, it bristled with domes and turrets, strange and wonderful, the quintessence of a fairytale illustration.

As Jason stood marveling in the courtyard, the noise became louder and then he saw a monk banging with a mallet on a thick wooden plank hung from two posts. The resulting unique sound reverberated throughout the many buildings, and the courtyard was suddenly a beehive, with dozens of black-robed monks converging on the main church—the *kathlikon,* with the many scalloped domes. The monks paid little attention to Jason and Andoni, except for discreet glances at the newcomers.

"Pray time." Andoni looked at Jason and said, "You want to see Constantine, he maybe gonna be here." Andoni jerked his head toward the *kathlikon.*

They walked past orange and lime and peach trees laden with fruit as they mingled with the monks heading into the chapel.

Inside, the church was almost overwhelmingly ornate. Great

brass chandeliers hung from the high ceiling on chains, as did many intricately carved incense burners. Around the room, against the walls, were gilt chairs, and seeing the monks sit in them, Jason and Andoni did likewise. There was a huge, carved, locked cupboard near them. Could the scrolls be in there? Yes, they could . . . but they could also be in one of the dozen other cupboards, or even in the tower or in the cellar or in one of the other chapels.

Everywhere on the walls were icons and relics and frescoes and medallions. The church's musty, cluttered opulence contrasted sharply with the austerity of the monks' dress and mode of living. In spite of the gloom, Jason was immediately taken with a fresco of the Last Supper, close to where they sat.

With a gentle nudge of his elbow, he whispered, "How old, Andoni?" and nodded toward the painting.

"Almost a thousand years, boss," Andoni replied.

The interior was covered with frescoes—hundreds of stiff, gaunt saints looking like primitive El Greco figures.

At the end of the long chamber to the right of the altar was the imposing figure of a man who looked like one of the saints in the mural behind him. He was lit by a huge candle, which made him stand out in the darkness like a statue, as though illuminated by a spotlight. Jason didn't need Andoni's whispered "Constantine" to guess who he was, although the man was "cast against type," as theater people would say. After hearing about him from Yanni, Jason had visualized a ruthless, conniving dictator, but now he was surprised to see a small, reed-thin man with a short gray beard and round shoulders. But the eyes were large and black and looked as though they could pierce the lead shielding of an X-ray room.

The abbot started to speak, chanting the Mass, and his deep, resonant voice was powerful and hypnotic. Even though they were off to the side, Jason felt that Constantine was staring through the semidarkness only at them, like a portrait whose eyes were contrived to follow one around the room.

As Constantine spoke to the monks, although Jason could not understand, he noted the monks' rapt attention, as if they were riveted by the abbot's every syllable.

On the way out, Constantine seemed to stare directly at Jason and Andoni. But he went on by them and out of the chapel. As Jason and Andoni made their way out, two monks came up to them casually and said, "You are new here."

Andoni nodded.

One monk asked, "What monasteries do you plan to visit?"

"Vatopedi only, for we have come to see Constantine."

"Ah, then you must hurry, my friend. Constantine leaves now for Simonpetra."

"But he is abbot here, and it is known he never leaves!" Andoni exclaimed.

The monk shrugged. "A friend, a man in my *kellion*—Constantine goes now, he told me, to Simonpetra, after matins."

"What's this Simonpetra stuff?" Jason asked when they had left the throng of black robes.

"That is where Constantine goes now."

"Where is it?"

"Over hill . . . maybe four, five hours' walk."

"We just get here and he leaves?" *Another funny coincidence,* Jason thought.

"We will show you to your place of rest," said the monk. "Food awaits you there."

Jason was taken aback a bit. "You knew we were coming?"

The monk merely smiled.

They followed the monk to the far end of the east wing and up to a balcony. The second cell along the balcony was theirs, and one of the monks turned the key in the heavy wooden door to open it.

Lit by a kerosene lamp, the whitewashed walls were bare, and the room had only a crude table and two pallets for sleeping. A tray of fruit, cheese, bread, and honey was on the table.

"Eat well, my brothers," said one of the monks as he placed a carafe of wine in front of them, then withdrew, closing the door behind him.

Andoni fell upon the fruit and cheese. "Boss, one thing monks do is make good cheese—and good bread!"

Jason stretched out on the mattress. The utter quiet of the

monastery life seemed almost ominous. He thought of Taylor, back at the Macedonia Palace. How safe was she at this moment?

"Where are we in relation to the library and treasury?" he asked Andoni.

"Not far, boss. Jus' back there, near the *kathlikon*. Let's go."

As they walked through the courtyard, Jason saw a small shrine.

"That very holy, boss. That called Shrine of the Holy Girdle. Part of the belt of Virgin Mary they keep there."

Jason then saw the wall painting of All Saints in the chapel of Saint Demetrios, and the exquisitely decorated refectory with the sea-blue benches and dado, contrasting with the ivory-colored stone floors, the panels of religious paintings on the walls, and the remarkable patterns of the ceiling.

But Jason was not on a sight-seeing tour, and he reminded Andoni that he wanted to get to the library.

"Sure, boss, only I don't want you someday curse Andoni— say why Andoni not show you . . . say Andoni no-good guide."

At the library Jason restlessly looked at the many illuminated manuscripts on parchment, bombazine, and paper. Some of them dated back to the ninth and tenth centuries. The old librarian said proudly that it was one of the finest collections in the world.

Jason thought about the Ephesus scrolls as the monk showed him an ancient chrysobull. As an addition to this remarkable collection, those scrolls could be very significant, regardless of their content. *But where were they!*

Where would they be kept? It was too good to be true that they would be just sitting here in the library, but he described to Andoni the scrolls without telling him their content and asked him to ask if they might be kept here. The monk in charge, as ancient and dried out as the parchments he presided over, shook his head, but Jason noted that the sharp old eyes now peered at him suspiciously over his glasses.

If the monk understood, and Jason felt that he had, the man was probably lying. But perhaps not. Constantine was not here, either. Could he have taken the scrolls with him? Why? Why not? Since he had apparently known Jason was coming, would he now also know *why* he had come to this outpost? Of course, that was it! Constantine was taking the scrolls to another monastery for safekeeping. Simonpetra—wasn't that the most inaccessible fortress of all the monasteries, according to the guidebooks?

Jason gestured to Andoni and they left the library.

"There is other library, boss, but way down below our cell and locked."

As they returned to the *kellion* to go to their guest cells, Jason saw a monk. It was the one who had been in the boat with them yesterday. He went over to speak to him, but the man pulled his cowl up and walked into a chapel as they approached.

The evening meal in the heavily frescoed refectory was much the same as the midday one, with the addition of a large bowl of lentil soup, with fresh bread and olive oil.

The presiding monk rang a bell to tell them to sit down, then a bell for grace, and a bell to tell them to eat. During the meal, from a small pulpit at the end of the room, a monk intoned the life of the saint of that day. Jason and Andoni ate well, then went back to their cell, and prepared for the night.

When Andoni's snoring became low and regular, Jason opened the door cautiously and looked out. No one was about. He took the lantern and stepped out onto the balcony. He went down the first stone steps he saw. They led to another floor of cells, presumably filled with monks either asleep or at meditation, for it was very quiet. Still another flight of steps took him farther down into the monastery.

Then he tripped and tumbled down the steps. But he hung on to the lamp and got up, dazed but unhurt. On this floor there were no cells, just a long corridor, permeated with the cloyingly sweet smell of wine and lined with barrels.

He went slowly down the corridor, which intercepted another corridor coming in at right angles. At the conjunction was a great carved wooden door, secured with a huge, ancient lock. Embedded in the wall near the big ring that served as a door handle was a small cage, a recessed place with a little grilled door fitted with a modern lock. Jason could see that inside was a big, rusty key on a hook. How to get the key?

A wire. But where to get a wire? He thought of the tin cups on the wine barrels and retraced his steps. He knelt by a barrel and unwound the rusty wire from the cup.

He returned to the door, and, fashioning a hook on one end of the wire, he slipped it between the grillework of the recess. On the third try he managed to snag the big key, and he eased it cautiously out between the close bars of the grille. It clattered to the stone floor. Jason snatched it up and looked around. Then he shoved it into the keyhole and turned it, and the great door swung open soundlessly.

He stepped into the huge, dark room. As he did so, he noticed that his lantern was beginning to sputter and fade. He saw some large, ivory-yellow candles on a long table in front of him and managed to light three of them before the lantern flickered and went out.

The big candles lit the room as though by electric lights, and Jason looked around in amazement. This was clearly not a regular library, but a repository for rare books and scrolls; there was a wooden chair at the long table on which the candles stood. It was probably a workroom for translating and cataloguing the books. And what books! What scrolls! They seemed at first to be casually treated; a beautiful illuminated page from a Book of Hours lay under a magnifying glass, left there by whoever had been studying it. There were dozens and dozens of filing cabinets and cupboards. Around the wall were stacked rolls of labeled parchment, and papyri protruded from amphorae, probably going back to the first centuries of the Greek Orthodox Church.

On the table was a workspace, and several brittle scrolls were taped there in different stages of being delicately unrolled and photographed and translated. Jason glanced at them. They were not the Ephesus scrolls; they were not in Aramaic. He could not read the ancient language, of course, but he could recognize the look of the writing by now. He had to remind himself that there were thousands upon thousands of scrolls in the world; not all were from Ephesus.

Where to start—where to look? The scrolls he was looking for would not be treated so casually, not stacked in a corner.

So he started on the cupboards. In the second cupboard he found a carved wooden box. Gingerly, almost tenderly, he opened it. Inside were scrolls, a translation in Greek, and a stack of enlarged photos. Of course, he would not try to unroll the brittle papyri, but a glance at the corresponding photographs told him the writing was Greek, not Aramaic. He closed the lid. After five cupboards, he was getting discouraged. And then, in the sixth, right in front of him, he saw it: a silver box, rather large and ornate. It looked important, very old, and appeared to be a treasure in itself. It had a modern lock on it that was—miraculously—open!

This was all too easy, somehow.

Jason lifted the box off the shelf and put it on the table. He opened the lid with trembling fingers, and there were . . . scrolls. Scrolls, photos, and translations of the scrolls in Greek. But were they the Ephesus scrolls? He gently picked up a photograph. As he was about to examine it, there was a sound in the corridor behind him. He turned just as two monks came through the huge door.

"Yassou," said one. "Greetings."

He had been caught red-handed and could think of no excuse. But that would not be necessary, for the monks did not seem either surprised or angry. They simply pointed to the door, blew out the candles, and politely gestured him back to the guest cell he shared with Andoni.

Andoni was snoring peacefully as one of the monks gently shook him. When he sat up, fully awake, the monks spoke to him in Greek. Quietly but firmly, they told the guide that Jason had violated their trust and that Andoni would be expected to take Jason and leave at daybreak. They demanded the *diamoniterion,* the permit that had been authorized at Karyes, and tore it up, reminding Jason and Andoni that they would not now be permitted to travel to any of the other monasteries on the Holy Mountain.

"Go," they said. "Go with God, but go."

12

THE NEXT morning Jason and Andoni did not head back for Karyes, Daphne, and Ouranopolis as they had been commanded to do. Once out of sight of Vatopedi, Andoni set Mangas on a trail toward Simonpetra, at Jason's insistence.

It was warm in the sun, but still cool in the shade of the cliffs. The mountain in front of them grew more majestic, and the scenery became more and more rugged. As Jason, Andoni, and Mangas walked up the trail that looked from a distance like a coil of rope dropped at random from the mountainside, a game bird suddenly exploded at Jason's feet and whirred away to another patch of cover. Conifers, myrtles, dwarf oaks, rock holly, and various nameless shrubs gave way to groves of ilex, gnarled and shady.

They could see, to the west, a series of giant white glissades, slabs of stone waiting to fling themselves into the sea, whose blue edge ringed each inlet and cape like the gradations of a peacock's tail.

On the eastern horizon they could faintly see Lemnos and the Asia Minor coast, the plains of Troy from where, as Jason had read in researching his travel articles, Tozer had seen the platform where he and Andoni now stood as "towering up from the horizon like a vast spirit of the waters when the rest of the peninsula is concealed below." To the north, the wastelands of Cavalla, Thrace, and Dedeagach led to the junction of the Dardanelles.

At one point they looked up a canyon at a natural bridge, a great stone arch.

"Beautiful country, Andoni," Jason said.

They didn't see the man there, lying flat on his stomach with a pair of binoculars trained on them.

McCue was somewhat confused; Van Cleve and the big Greek arrived at the monastery yesterday before noon. Then, shortly afterwards, what looked like the big boss monk of the place left with some other monks. They didn't head for Karyes; they went down a trail to the south. McCue figured he had a good setup because he could see everyone who came or went from his spot on the wooded hill about a hundred yards above. By nightfall, Van Cleve had not come out, so McCue ate one of the candy bars he'd bought back at the Athens Hilton, had a cigarette, and went to sleep curled up on the soft mulch of dry leaves.

Then, early in the morning, before dawn, he heard some noise: the clatter of hooves. He rolled over and peered down at the monastery. It was Van Cleve and the big Greek, with the donkey. And they were heading out the same way the bigshot monk had gone.

He got up and watched his quarry through the field glasses as they made their way up the path. Well, he thought, it was probably time for him to make his move. No way to tell whether Van Cleve had the scrolls or not, and while it'd be nice to get the bonus for the scrolls, McCue was getting damned sick of the whole assignment and wanted to get back to civilization as soon as possible.

But this really looked like the time to finish the job, especially if they kept going up toward those cliffs. He could shoot them and throw them into one of those deep crevasses and they'd never be found; no bodies washing up on the shore to raise embarrassing questions. Then, if Van Cleve had the scrolls, fine, and if he didn't the Fat One in San Francisco would probably buy the story that Van Cleve's body had fallen into the sea with the scrolls. Either way, McCue would collect.

He put the binoculars in his jacket pocket, and picking up the woven market basket with his two-piece rifle in it, he set off at a dog trot on a trail parallel to the one Van Cleve was on with the guide.

"Sorry about last night," Jason was saying as they climbed and climbed. "They *wanted* me to find that box—it was a setup."

The big man was morose. "Constantine not gonna be happy when he hear."

"My guess is he knows already."

How could Jason explain the compulsion to find those scrolls to someone like Andoni, when he didn't understand it very clearly himself? And now, because the permit had been revoked, Andoni was having to take him to Simonpetra by this sneaky, difficult way, staying off the main path, stealing through the woods like hunters or outlaws. Now he understood why the Council of Five examined travelers so closely. He felt slightly chagrined when he thought of those five old men having placed their trust in him.

"We better go up this way, boss. We run right into Philtheou, we go down that way. And you don' got no pass no more."

"Another monastery, Andoni?"

"Right. We go this way now, toward the sea, and we come to Simonpetra. But it's gonna be rough. No trail down this way, and this side of mountain got lots of rocks."

"How far are we from Simonpetra?"

Andoni shook his head. "Don' you got enough, boss? Better we forget about Simonpetra. Constantine not gonna be happy to see you. He maybe not see you at all. He maybe put us both off the peninsula. Don't forget, boss, I still got my job to think about. I get banned from Vatopedi, Simonpetra, you think any other monastery gonna be glad to see me? That council of old men back there in Karyes—they gonna ban me off forever!"

"I've been thinking of not approaching Constantine openly. I was thinking . . ." And, knowing that it would be impossible to accomplish anything without Andoni, he told the old Greek the whole story about Lascaris and the scrolls. Later he wondered if he had done the right thing as he watched Andoni fuss over Mangas. Certainly, if there was deceit or dishonesty in that craggy face, Jason could not see it.

Andoni filled their canteens from a nearby spring and they continued up the hillside in the brisk morning air. There was snow in the ravines and snow hanging on the ledges above them, and, while the sun was warm on their backs, they wore jackets and their hands were cold. Snow in summer? But there it was, deep in the canyons on both sides of the narrow ridge that Andoni was leading him along.

Andoni told Jason about the passage: "The monks, they call this the Valley of Silence. They believe the Lord created it to test a man's faith in the Church."

A narrow ravine, slashed out of the mountain, was bottomless with perpetual snow. It was an approach to Simonpetra that monks were reluctant to take since the day that Father Emmanuel from the Grand Lavra met his death here.

"Avalanche here lots of times, in summer like now. I fix Mangas's feet," Andoni said. "Noise make snowslide."

Jason watched as Andoni tied rags around the donkey's hooves, then looked around to take in the beauty of the place. Back toward the great mountain, the canyon was an endless ribbon of white, undulating gently down toward them and becoming wider as one looked higher and higher toward Mount Athos, forming a huge V and finally disappearing into the clouds that hung about the top of the Holy Mountain. One could look down the other way and see the huge gray edifice that sprawled in the valley below. "That St. Paul's," Andoni said.

Slowly, carefully, they entered the valley, and it looked innocent and totally unthreatening. Then, suddenly, Mangas stopped, looked down, and stood motionless. Jason glanced over at Andoni, but he too seemed confused. Then Mangas opened his mouth wide and brayed. A tiny sleeping hedgehog unwound itself and scurried off into the bushes, but Mangas kept braying. Andoni fell on him and with both hands tried to close his mouth, but the damage was done.

The earth shook. Then boulders, rocks, and snow began to cascade down the mountainside. The donkey continued to emit shrieking sounds and reared in fright with Andoni clinging to him, trying to shut him up. The bulk of the falling material landed well in front of them so that no one was hurt, but the trail to Simonpetra was cut off.

"Oh, damn!" Jason stood looking helplessly at the impasse. "*Damn!*" he said again.

"Mangas sure fucked it up for us, boss," said Andoni.

"He sure did," Jason agreed.

Andoni shook his finger at Mangas, yelling, "You sure fucked it up, you crazy old..." Then he turned away, saying, "But what the hell, he jus' a jackass!" He noticed the serious look on Jason's face.

"So?" he said. "Maybe we go find shack some-place...rest...I fix something for you to eat."

Again Jason scrutinized the Greek's face. Why was he so eager to abandon this trip? Was there really a difference in his attitude since Jason had told him about the scrolls, or did he imagine it? But Andoni's good-natured expression revealed nothing, and his old brown eyes were guileless.

"Cards on the table," Jason announced.

Andoni frowned and said, "No, boss, I bring no cards. But we can play *tavli* when we get back—"

"I want the truth, Andoni!" Jason said. "Why are you so reluctant to take me to Simonpetra?"

"Boss, why you have to go there? You no can see Constantine. You tell me you gonna steal scrolls. How I gonna make a living if—"

"I have no intention of stealing anything! I simply want to verify that the scrolls do exist."

"Then why you got to see Constantine?"

"Because he's the only person I know of who can vouch for their authenticity, tell me whether or not they're the real thing."

"Why you got to do all that?"

Jason shook his head. "You've acted strangely ever since I said I wanted to go to Simonpetra. There's something you're not telling me."

Andoni hung his head like a small boy and said softly, "I jus' don' wanna go back there."

Jason looked at him quickly. "Back?"

"I was acolyte—like novice? Where you think I learn English? Not in war. I learn here at Simonpetra, and that why the English, they like me. Because I can talk with them. Oh, ever'one say, Andoni smart. When Andoni older, we send him away to school. But it never happen, boss."

"Why did you leave?"

"It was good life when I was young boy. But when I was young man, it not so good. I needed woman. I not made to be monk. My family very poor. Got six sisters, two brothers— who gonna feed them? I come along nex' to last. They give me to God, they say. And when I was young boy, it was good life. It good thing to do that time in my life. I no go back now, but good then. Like say you screw Queen of England eh? Good thing to have done, but maybe not so good when you do it, eh?"

"Then you know the layout of Simonpetra, Andoni. You know where the library is? Where they would keep the scrolls?"

"Library in big tower. Lots of books, maybe more valuable than books at Vatopedi. But they got guards, keys. Not easy to get in library."

"Tell me, Andoni—" Jason's mind was beginning to put together a few salient facts. "The work you did for Mrs. Phillips—did that have anything to do with the library?"

"Nah, boss," Andoni shook his head conclusively. "I never meet Mrs. Phillips. Someone call me and say a friend of Mrs. Phillips gonna visit me, ask for my services. I s'pose to do ever'thing I can to help him."

"Someone?" Jason asked. "Who?"

"A man I know long ago. He pay me lot of money to go to little *hesychasterion*—monk's eagles' nest—hut up on mountain. This man looking for papers too."

Lascaris's nest, Jason thought.

"What kind of papers?"

"Jus' some old papers, some papers s'pose to be wrapped in old linen sheet, he say."

"And did you find them?"

"Nah, boss. But he say that's okay. He pay me anyway. That same man call me about you and Mrs. Phillips."

"How long ago did he ask you to do this, Andoni?"

"The day before you come, boss."

Jason felt the hair on the back of his neck doing something strange. He felt a constriction in his chest. He felt very close to blacking out.

That was it! Someone had already looked for the scrolls in the aerie that Lascaris had once lived in. So now they were tracking Jason's every move, hoping he'd be able to lead them to the scrolls. And Taylor must be a part of this! Those mysterious phone calls she kept getting—he remembered how she'd close the door so he couldn't hear, how she gave such feeble excuses for them! No wonder she was so accommodating, so helpful, so eager to drive him around, so interested!

Jason's knees felt wobbly and he sat down on the ground, looking at the pile of rocks and snow blocking the path to Simonpetra.

This was the woman I trusted, he thought. *This was the one person in the whole world who knew what I was doing and why I was doing it. The only person who could have told the world what might have happened to me if I should be killed.* Jason had never felt so completely alone in his life. Even the death of his wife had not left him so totally abandoned, for his friends had all rallied around him in sympathy. This was different. This time there would be no one. Only Taylor knew what was going on, and she was apparently working for the opposition, whoever it might be. The Vatican? Constantine? Could the leader of this whole conspiracy be Constantine? Was it the almighty abbot who was drawing him closer, to control him, to find out how much he knew, to decide his fate?

But Taylor! How could she have deceived him so completely? Could she have fingered poor old Lascaris and Phillips Taylor? And who was this friend of hers who was here, trying to beat him to the scrolls? Was Andoni hired as hit man?

He looked over at the old Greek, who was now stroking the donkey and muttering to it benignly, and Jason's gut feeling was that the last supposition could not be true. But then, he'd been wrong about Taylor, hadn't he? Still, he knew his life was in danger and he could not afford to take risks.

Rage welled up in him and he stood up. *No one is going to do this to me,* he thought. *I am not going to go down to an unmarked grave, nor am I going to be swayed from my original purpose. I am going to find those scrolls and I am going to find out what in the name of Christ is going on here!*

"Andoni!" The force of Jason's voice made the old man jump. He left his donkey and came forward with his eyes widened. "What's matter, boss? You all right?"

"I want the truth and all of it!" Jason said. "Let's start with what Mrs. Phillips's friend said when he first contacted you."

Andoni started to talk hesitantly, then more freely. The story came out piecemeal, but how much was true? It was much the same as he'd already told Jason. He'd been hired to ransack the hermitage that Lascaris had once occupied; he found nothing, although he'd searched for a whole day, even removing part of a wall that looked like it might be a hiding place.

"But he pay me all the same. He nice man. She must be nice lady too."

"Oh, sure," Jason said. "Very nice." He looked hard at the old man, who had apparently not caught the sarcasm in Jason's voice. What could he believe? *Who* could he believe? Taylor had sold him out, and Andoni was working for Taylor or whoever her "friend" was. They could have told this old fool anything.

"I won't need you anymore, Andoni. I'll find my own way to Simonpetra."

"Boss, wait! I come with you!"

"No. I'll send the rest of your money to the *taverna*. I don't need you anymore."

"But, boss, what I do wrong? Why you don' want Andoni to take you to Simonpetra? You gonna need me, boss. How you gonna find your way out of Valley of Silence? You see how dangerous—"

Jason shook his head and said adamantly, "You've done nothing wrong. I simply will not need your services any further, and that is that."

Jason stepped off the path onto the crusty snow, and started crunching and sliding down the steep ravine. It had been many years since he tried climbing down a snowy mountain, and he realized that it was much easier to do on skis. Certainly it was less awkward. He had gone down about a hundred yards when he stopped and turned. Andoni was still there, with his head against Mangas's neck. Jason turned and continued his graceless plunge down the hillside as he fumed over the thought that while he'd been talking to Sister Eugenia in Tinos, Taylor had been working with the opposition to beat him to the scrolls.

Jason had walked what he guessed to be about ten minutes in the increasingly mushy snow when he saw the welcome stretch of pine woods in front of him and the path that led through them. He was relieved to see that he would soon be out of the snow. The path appeared to be a well-traveled trail, and it would surely lead to Simonpetra.

He stepped up the pace, lifting his knees high, and he was almost running through the hindering slush and ice.

Perhaps it was this clumsy gait that caused McCue to miss. Because of the crunching of his shoes in the snow, Jason heard nothing, did not detect the breathy thump of the bullet out of the silencer muzzle. All he saw was a patch of snow kicking up in front of him, and he knew that whoever was shooting at him had to be above and behind him.

He jerked the Luger that Taylor had given him from his pocket and whirled, crouching to make himself a smaller target for his assailant. Two hundred feet away, a cluster of boulders rose from the snow in a crude pyramid. It was the only place his would-be assassin could be hiding. He saw an opening in the rocks, fired once at it, a token shot to show that at least he had a weapon, and then turned and ran as fast as he could to get out of the open, unprotected ground. His only hope was the woods, the growth of pine trees some fifty yards away.

He found it impossible to run very fast in the sloppy snow, especially as he was also trying to zigzag to present a difficult target for the unknown sniper. When he was one hundred feet from the trees, a chunk of snow exploded ahead of him frighteningly nearby, and he knew the marksman was finding the range. He had no choice but to continue running as best he could. Now, for the last spurt, he abandoned the zigzagging and simply ran flat-out toward the nearest clump of trees.

He had almost reached the pine grove when he felt the bullet hit his right shoulder. There was little pain; it was simply as though a heavyweight boxer had struck him a savage blow to the deltoid muscle. The force spun him around and slammed him to the ground, sending the Luger flying from his grasp. He shook his head, then scrambled to his feet and literally dove the rest of the way into the trees, like a football player plunging over his center for those few precious yards to a touchdown. He ran on all fours until he was safely deep enough among the tree trunks to stop. Panting hard, he put his left hand to his shoulder and drew it away, the fingers warm and red with blood. He knew it was not very serious, but he also knew it would be painful soon.

He looked out through the trees. He could see a figure emerging slowly from behind the rocks, holding his rifle cautiously at the ready. So—this little insignificant man was the assassin. He didn't look like a killer, yet he loomed purposeful and lethal as he clumped down the mountainside toward the grove of trees.

Jason saw the Luger half-buried there in the snow, so near and yet so far; the hit man must have seen it also. Jason could step out and make a run for the weapon, but the odds were that this man would nail him before he could even reach the gun, much less pick it up, aim, and fire it. It was clearly a case of an amateur pitted against a professional.

He saw a thick stick lying off to one side of him. It had a sharp bend at the end, like a hoe. He picked it up and hefted it. It was a good club. As the assassin came closer, Jason retreated more into the trees. He saw the man bend over, pick the Luger up out of the snow, wipe it off, and put it in his belt.

Jason found the largest tree trunk close to the path and stationed himself behind it, club raised. He looked through the foliage and saw the hit man enter the path cautiously, his rifle half-raised, his feral eyes darting from side to side. He was no fool; he knew he had hit Jason, and the splotch of blood in the snow confirmed it. Probably hit him bad—too bad for him to be able to make a run for it. He was probably holed up here, maybe dying. Maybe he had another weapon . . .

The assassin took a few more steps along the path. He was some twenty feet from Jason when he suddenly turned abruptly and walked briskly back the way he had come.

Why did he do that? Jason puzzled. Maybe he suspected

that Jason was waiting to ambush him. What he was probably planning to do was to go around the woods, around Jason, and wait for him at the other end of the path with a bullet.

Jason would not fall into his trap. He would do the opposite. He would go the other way, go back and try to find the continuation of the first path that had been covered by the avalanche.

He waited a few moments. He felt his shoulder. The wound was starting to go cold, starting to throb and ache. But at least the bleeding had stopped. With the club over his left shoulder, he walked out into the path and retraced his steps toward the meadow.

As he stepped out from the path, he heard a flat voice with Irish overtones say chillingly, "You'll be droppin' the shillelagh now, Mr. Van Cleve."

Not three yards away from him, leaning casually against a tree trunk, an unlit cigarette dangling from his lips, the rifle resting in the crook of this arm, stood McCue.

Jason froze. "Shillelagh?" he asked ingenuously, while slowly moving his left hand up to get a better grip on the big stick still resting on his shoulder.

"I think you folks call it a club. Drop it."

"Listen," said Jason, playing for time. "I know you're going to shoot me, that you've been hired to kill me. But before you do, can't you just tell me who sent you? Taylor Phillips? The Vatican? Who? It's no skin off your nose to tell me now."

"No time for stupid questions," McCue growled. "You've seen too many movies, Van Cleve. The bad guy telling the good guy everything before he kills him. I'm not telling you anything, just doing my job."

"And your job is . . . ?"

"*Was* to kill you when you got the scrolls."

Jason said casually. "You don't see any scrolls on me, do you?"

"The Greek got 'em?"

"Do you see them on me?"

Jason edged a little closer.

"No I don't, and I don't care, either. Maybe the Greek's got 'em on the donkey. I'll find out soon."

"You didn't really buy that business about some crazy scrolls, did you?" Jason took a step closer.

McCue didn't say anything. He studied Jason with narrowed eyes and began to fish with two fingers into his breast pocket for a match.

"You think all this fuss was over some old papers?" asked Jason.

"What then, man?"

Jason leaned forward conspiratorially and said, "Gold, my friend. Solid Greek gold! Chests of it, just lying there in the monastery, waiting for us. And I could cut you in on it. Worth twenty times whatever your employers are offering you."

McCue shook his head. "They're paying me well, and—"

Jason gave a laugh. "They're going to pay you well, all right—with bullets. Cooperate with me and—"

"You don't really expect me to buy that bit of cock-and-bull, do you?"

He glanced down as he extracted the matches, and Jason took advantage of McCue's momentary distraction. He leaped forward, at the same time smashing the stick down in an arc as hard as he could. The club didn't quite reach McCue's body, but it smashed against his rifle and his forearm, and the gun was knocked out of the killer's hands. He stumbled backward with a cry and fell in a sitting position. But before Jason could raise his club to attack again, McCue yanked the Luger out of his belt and aimed it at Jason's chest.

"Drop it, Mr. Van Cleve!" panted the steely voice. "You interrupted me, and I don't like being interrupted. Now I shall finish—"

It proved to be an ironic ending to a sentence he was never to complete. A large, black-hooded form stepped out of the trees behind the seated man. One wide-sleeved arm shot out and its hand closed around the wrist of McCue's shooting hand. The monk's other arm went around McCue's throat. Having thus secured the assassin, the monk banged the hand that held the pistol against a rock until the fingers loosened their grip and dropped the weapon.

Then Jason saw the flash of a knife in the monk's hand and the fingers of his other hand entwined in McCue's hair, jerking his head back and exposing his round white neck.

With horror, Jason watched as the man's throat became, in two seconds, three different kinds of melon. At first the flesh was pristine, like the skin of a honeydew; then, as the knife was drawn across it in a slow but expert sweep, the slice made by the blade looked like a thin wedge cut into the orange meat of a cantaloupe. But then, as the knife bit deeper, the cantaloupe changed into a great scarlet gushing watermelon.

The blood gurgled in the man's throat. His eyes rolled back until they were totally white, with no sign of irises, and then his torso pitched forward against his own legs.

The monk looked at Jason for a moment from under his hood, the black, intelligent but fierce eyes gleaming on either side of the falciform nose, and Jason saw that it was the same monk who had been on the boat with them. He started to say something, but he could not tell whether or not the monk intended to kill him too, and he could make no sound.

Then, as Jason tried to clear his throat, his benefactor, after wiping his knife blade on the back of McCue's jacket, extended his hand.

"My name is Paul Krenski."

Jason took a breath. "Thank you," he said.

He stared down at the motionless body of McCue. Chalk up one more death to the scrolls, those accursed pieces of papyrus. Who was this man who had been hired to kill him? Was there anyone who would mourn his demise, out here in the middle of nowhere?

"I'm not by nature a killer," said Krenski. "But perhaps I did the world, as well as you, a favor just now."

Jason heard a noise behind him. He grabbed the Luger from the ground and whirled around.

"Boss! It's me!"

"Andoni!"

The big man was standing there, tears in his eyes, his donkey behind him. He nodded at Krenski.

"Boss . . . I hear a shot . . ." Then Andoni saw the blood on Jason's jacket. "You wounded!"

He stripped Jason's jacket off and whistled.

"You damn lucky, boss." He took out his knife and cut

some strips from Jason's shirttail, soaked them in liquid from his canteen, then expertly applied the cloth to the wound. Jason winced.

Then Andoni offered Jason the canteen. "Ouzo . . . gasoline for the motor."

Jason took a swallow of the harsh liquor and coughed.

He offered the canteen to Krenski, who shook his head.

"Good stuff, eh, boss?" Andoni grinned. "Best damn medicine in the world."

"Especially for surgery," Jason agreed. "Anesthetize the patient and sterilize the wound all with ouzo—great!"

He found himself inordinately glad to see the big man again.

"Look, boss, you got to let Andoni take you now. No more fool around, okay? Andoni take you to Simonpetra."

Krenski spoke up, saying, "If I may, I will go with you."

"Why?" asked Jason.

"I will explain as we go."

They set off together, and Krenski talked. Some of the story was familiar to Jason, but most of it was not.

"For me, the scrolls—from the beginning, from the first time I saw them—became an obsession, the very core of my life. As Gogol wrote, 'And from that day forth, everything was, as it were, changed and appeared in a different light to him . . .'" He smiled ruefully.

"I met Sister Eugenia when I was young. We've been friends ever since, even after she went to the nunnery at Tinos. You know my name because her father gave the scrolls to me to translate—until he took them away and declared them blasphemous. Even I haven't read them all. That's why I've followed you and Andoni, knowing that he was once a monk here at Simonpetra and would know where such things might be kept."

As they walked along, they were aware that their presence was a disturbance to the idyllic peace of the forest; birds hushed their songs, lizards scurried into the underbrush, and occasionally a wild dog's mournful howl could be heard.

Jason said, "I'm not sure that the scrolls are here at all. At Vatopedi, I happened upon scrolls in their translating room that

I'm almost sure were what we're looking for, But dammit, they caught me and there's no chance of my ever getting near them again."

"Ah, yes, the scrolls of Vatopedi. Don't feel badly; they're fake."

"Fake?"

"A doctored version that alters the story to coincide with accepted doctrine. I've seen the originals. Remember, I was the second man to see them. Lascaris was the first. Except for the author, of course."

"And the author was?"

He hesitated, almost apologetically, and said, "The Apostle John."

"How much of the story of Lael do you know?"

"About three-quarters, I would guess. How much did Eugenia tell you?"

Jason told him where the Sister's tale had left off.

"Then, while I know more than you, neither of us knows the end, and we shall not know it until we find the real scrolls." He pounded one hand into the palm of the other. "I know they're in Simonpetra! Constantine must have them with him right now. He'd never let them go, nor would he destroy them. You see, you were getting too hot on the trail."

"But how do you know those scrolls at Vatopedi are fake?" Jason asked. "Have you seen them?"

"I'll explain it all," said Krenski. And he started telling how, after Lascaris made off with the last part of the scrolls before the translation had been completed, Krenski became obsessed with the need to find out the rest of the story, so he left for Rome and visited the Vatican. Young and naïve, he thought the Catholic Church would assist him in obtaining more information.

"How wrong I was! The cardinal I talked to promised to help me—a man named Tobin—and let me do research with the precious books of the Vatican Library. When I went back to my hotel to wait for the phone call Cardinal Tobin would make after authorization had cleared, someone tried to kill me."

"Who?" asked Jason.

"God only knows. But I managed to club him senseless. As far as I know, the only person who knew I was staying at that hotel was Cardinal Tobin."

Krenski then fled from Rome and went to Yugoslavia with the help of friends. He assumed that if the Vatican was after him, then they surely knew about the existence of the scrolls from other sources. He felt that he had to go back to Izmir at any cost and try to find the scrolls so that he could translate the ending.

"I was afraid for my life, so I took another name and avoided appearing anyplace where I might be recognized. Then I found out that Lascaris had disappeared, and I wasn't able to get any information about where he'd gone."

When a sailor was murdered in the hotel room next to his, Krenski felt sure that it had been a mistake on the part of the killer, for when he had checked into the seedy hotel, that room had been assigned to him. Seeing that it was a room with three bunks, Krenski had offered to pay extra for more private accommodations. It was possible that the killer did not know about the change and had murdered the unlucky drunken sailor who'd been given the bed Krenski had rejected.

Having figured out this probability, he placed his passport surreptitiously on the dead man's body and slipped away. To the authorities, it appeared as if Paul Krenski had been the murder victim, and he had no doubt that the killer's employers would be satisfied by this news and he'd be off the hook.

"Phillips Taylor—yes, the psuedo-vice-consul who involved you in all this—he managed to get me a stolen passport and I hitched my way to Greece. I met people and made some friends, and finally I learned that Lascaris was living on the Mount Athos peninsula as a monk. I went to Thessaloniki and, by working at various jobs—waiter, bus driver, and guide for a tourist office—I kept track of Lascaris and learned a lot about the religious community of Mount Athos as a whole. The gossip was that the abbot of Vatopedi, Constantine, was at odds with the Vatican, that a cold war existed between Constantine, who was head of the richest and most important monastery on Mount Athos, and Rome."

As time went on, Krenski gleaned much information about

the political climate of the clerical enclave, but very little about the scrolls. Lascaris himself, Krenski never saw again. First the old man was lost in the vast confines of Vatopedi, in the multitude of other monks. Then Krenski heard that Lascaris had been condemned by Constantine and was hiding out in a *skete* somewhere in the wilds of the mountain itself. By the time Krenski learned the exact location of the hideout, it was reported that Lascaris had left Mount Athos and returned to Izmir.

"I contacted my old love, Eugenia. She told me she thought the scrolls had been destroyed—that her father had burned the photographs of the translations as well as the originals."

Knowing that Lascaris had spent a lifetime cosseting those scrolls, when Krenski recalled how avidly interested Lascaris had been during the laborious translation, he simply could not accept Eugenia's story. Then, when he learned that she had embraced the Church as a nun and was at Tinos, forever lost to him as a possible wife, he became even more compulsive about the story of Lael. He suddenly saw a way to win the confidence of both the woman he loved and the people who would know the most about the scrolls; he would become a monk on Mount Athos. Eugenia would then reveal the truth and he might be able to infiltrate the powerful Vatopedi security that Abbot Constantine was building up.

"Things went along very well, surprisingly well, and I couldn't believe my luck. When I finally 'discovered' the scrolls in the same silver chest that you mentioned, I soon realized why I'd made such phenomenal progress. They were fake."

Jason said, "Then they actually *wanted* you to find them. Wanted both of us to find them?"

"Exactly."

"But why?"

"Because we want to know the ending, right? And at the end of the bogus scrolls, John the Apostle abruptly breaks into the story saying that he had just recovered from a serious illness that has kept him in a hallucinatory state for six months. During that time, he confesses, he made up the scrolls out of whole cloth based on nothing more than his disturbed imagination. He acknowledges that the 'forces of evil' gained power over him and manipulated him into writing the blasphemies, and that he had decided to burn the scrolls and to terminate his life, and he begs forgiveness of God, Jesus, and Mary. Period. And so ends the Ephesus story and the threat to the Church."

Jason thought for a moment, then said, "Supposing it's true, this business about John being deranged when he wrote them?"

Krenski shook his head.

"The codicil is an obvious forgery. Whoever wrote it was clever and erudite, but he showed inconsistencies in style and actual errors in the Aramaic that aren't in the first part. Even the papyri themselves have a subtle difference in texture, although an excellent job was done in making them *appear* ancient. No, it was ordered by Constantine or someone else, higher up. A perfect way to squash the story of Lael that was beginning to leak out and threaten the Church."

Krenski went on to tell Jason that he had been in touch with Eugenia and had learned of Jason's visit to her. She'd told him that she was sure Jason would go to Mount Athos, so Krenski kept the Ouranopolis departures under surveillance. It wasn't difficult to spot Jason from Eugenia's good description, and follow him, and being dressed as a monk made it easier to get around. It was reasonable to suppose that the other man he saw tailing Jason might be a hired assassin, so he stayed behind and managed to save his life.

"But why?" Jason asked. "Why risk your life to save mine?"

Krenski smiled. "I was in no danger. That killer had no idea that anyone would be following *him*. Anyway, we're obviously both after the same thing. And I need help. I figured you and Andoni might have some information that I didn't." He looked over at Andoni and said, "You grew up in Simonpetra, didn't you, Andoni? You must know that place pretty well."

Andoni nodded. "That right."

"But," Jason protested, "Andoni, you were so young. They wouldn't have told you where the true treasures were hidden."

Andoni laughed. "They no tell me, but I know! One day I s'pose to be sweeping chapel floor. I get tired, boss, so I curl up on bench, go to sleep. Then I hear noise, I wake up, I see . . . oh, what I see!"

"What exactly did you see?" asked Krenski, his eyes glittering eagerly.

"I see two monks. They go right past me, they don' see me. They go to take something to put it away, put in hiding place. When they open, I see gold, all kind of gold!"

"But did you see scrolls?" demanded Krenski.

"I see gold cups and gold chains and gold crucifix and gold—"

"But did you see a silver box?" Krenski stopped walking and indicated the size with his hands. "About so big?"

Andoni shrugged. "I see so much gold I blind to silver. But if it valuable, it there."

"And where in the chapel is it hidden?"

"I show you, boss, I show you!"

And they set off once again for Simonpetra . . . only faster.

13

TAYLOR LOOKED at her watch for the hundredth time. It was still only eleven-twenty in the morning. She had talked to Father Bartolomeo less than twelve hours ago. He could not have accomplished much during the night—or could he? She remembered with a smile his tenacity and enormous capacity to concentrate his efforts upon the problem at hand, whatever it might be. There had been the time when she realized that her son would have to be enrolled in a school, as he was soon to be six years old. Alone in Istanbul, she had no idea where she might be able to send him. Father Bartolomeo had immediately arranged for the child to enter a fine school where he would be taught in English as well as Turkic, and also took care of the transportation problem as well.

Still, it was difficult just to stay in this hotel room and wait. She wanted so desperately to be doing something, anything, to help Jason. As she paced up and down the room, she wondered how close he had come to guessing that she was the Judas goat, leading him into the trap. But hadn't she begged him to give up his stubborn search for those scrolls? Hadn't she almost confessed her involvement? But then, when he had begged for her support, how could she undermine his confidence and courage by letting him know that she had been informing on him? How could she know that her calls had come from someone who was using Father Bartolomeo, using her faith in him and their long-standing friendship, using her faith in the Church itself, using her love for her child. And kidnapping! Despicable! And now the first man she really cared for was in jeopardy because of her. Her guilt and apprehension made it impossible for her to concentrate on any plan to assist Jason. She simply had to put her trust in Father Bartolomeo.

Now she sat looking at the luncheon tray of ratatouille with bits of lamb that she'd had sent up by room service. It looked good, it smelled good, but she simply couldn't eat it.

With shaky hands she poured a cup of tea and took it to a chair by the window. She was looking absently out the window at the hundreds of boats on the quay of the perfect horseshoe harbor, when the telephone rang.

The room clerk said, "There is a gentleman here."

He will ask for you by your maiden name, Father Bartolomeo had said.

"And he asked to see me?" Taylor said cautiously.

The clerk sounded perplexed. "He is asking for Miss Wright. What shall I say, Mrs. Phillips?"

"Send him up, please," she replied.

She opened the door to a middle-aged man in a business suit. His ruddy face crinkled into an ingratiating smile and his blue eyes gave her an appreciative once-over as he said, "Al Rozmyslowski. I'm told you'd be expecting me, Mrs. Phillips."

"Mrs. Phillips?" she asked, suddenly defensive.

"Or Miss Wright. Naturally, Father Bart had to tell me that you were really Mrs. Phillips. He had to tell me a lot of things . . ."

"How'd you get here so soon?" she asked. Not only had he arrived sooner than she'd anticipated, but he was not the sort of person she'd expected.

"I fly fast," he said laconically.

"You're a friend of his?"

"I pilot a plane for a big company. I was on my way to Athens. Had a stopover in Rome, so I gave the Padre a jingle. For old time's sake, you know. Korea."

"Korea? Was Father Bartolomeo in Korea?"

"Oh, sure, we go way back. Oh, I see. He never mentioned it. Well, that's okay. People always think of priests as leading sheltered lives. I guess some of them do. But lots of them have seen more and heard more than you or I ever will. The Padre's a tough little guy."

Little? She'd always tought of him as— But then, this man was well over six feet tall. But if he was a pilot, why was he dressed in a business suit? Lord, she *had* to trust someone!

"Mrs. Phillips, do you want to go check on Van Cleve's whereabouts? I got a helicopter, and I gather that's why I'm here."

She shook her head as she paced. "I'm worried to death about him, but..."

"But?"

"How much did Father Bartolomeo tell you about this?"

"Everything."

"Well, then, you can see that—"

The phone rang. Before she could think about waiting, she snatched it up. Thank God, it was her sister's voice. And the words were so beautiful:

"Tay, he's home! He's safe and perfectly all right! I can't say anything more, not a word, right now."

Taylor gasped, "Let me talk to him!"

"No, not allowed. He's asleep, anyway. No more for now— can't—" And she hung up abruptly.

Taylor sobbed uncontrollably for a minute, then she pulled herself together, laughing and gulping as she blew her nose.

"Now what were you saying about a rescue mission?" she said to Al.

"I gather the boy's safe."

She nodded. "I feel as though Christian Barnard had just given me back my heart."

"I'm mighty glad," he said. "Now about this little foray— you'd better change into some warm, comfortable clothes. Slacks, good walking shoes, just in case. Might help if you could cover your hair. We can pick up a fisherman's cap for you. Better if you didn't look quite so feminine. They don't like women on Mount Athos or anywhere near it. No females of any kind. Not that I don't like the way you look, understand." He grinned.

And she grinned back—her first smile in days.

As they came out of the hotel, she remembered Father Bartolomeo's warning about her being followed. Just because Jonny was safe didn't mean she and Jason were. She looked around as they got into her car.

"You drive, Al," she said. "I'm still shook up."

As they drove down Phillipou Street, the wide boulevard through the city, traffic seemed deliberately choreographed to hamper their progress, and Taylor felt her nervousness increase as Al patiently started, stopped, and crawled along.

"It's this damn fair they're having," he said.

Soon they saw crowds on the street and heard music and saw the Ferris wheel turning.

"I keep thinking everything in Greece has to be old," he went on. "Hell, I thought Thessaloniki was going to be a cute little cobbled one-street town and here it is, looking like Barcelona, all modern and a hundred thousand people and about as quaint as Omaha."

"Important city," said Taylor, mechanically. "Always has been. Named after Alexander the Great's sister."

"Thessaloniki," said Al. "That's some first name. Wonder what her last name was."

A tan car moved in behind them.

"Probably the same as his—the Great."

"I wouldn't mind that. It'd be easier than the one I got."

He glanced into the rearview mirror from time to time, then he asked suddenly serious "Tell me, can you handle a gun?"

Taylor looked at him quickly, saw that he was not joking, and replied, "My father taught me skeet-shooting, but I haven't done it for years."

"Okay," Al reassured her. "It probably won't be necessary. I just wanted to be sure you wouldn't panic if I gave you a gun and told you to use it."

"I won't panic," Taylor said.

They came to a vacant lot near the square that housed the fairgrounds, and Taylor could see the helicopter with a crowd around it.

"Here we are," Al said as he pulled over. "Now to find a parking space." He looked over at Taylor and said, "I'd better let you out here so you won't have to walk so far. They let me land the copter here because of the fair. It makes another attraction. You go over there and wait for me. I'll park the car and join you as soon as I can. Don't talk to anyone!"

Taylor nodded and jumped out. She watched as Al slowly drove away to park her car, but soon lost sight of him. She had the feeling she was being watched and looked around, remembering the car that had been behind them for a while. It was not in sight now.

Sauntering, she pretended to look at the displays of pottery and television sets and dreadful plaster statues of Achilles, as though caught up by the holiday spirit of the throng and the music. But she kept looking back in the direction Al had gone, still feeling uneasy and very alone as she worked her way toward where the helicopter was.

Someone bumped into her and she stumbled, lurching into the arms of a man with spiky red hair.

Then she felt the hard muzzle of the gun stuck in her ribs.

"Keep moving, lady," he said quietly. "Let's just keep moving."

"Who are you?" she said, desperately looking for Al.

"Move!" he commanded.

With one arm around her waist, he walked her briskly away from the display booths. An old lady selling honey cakes from a tray slung from a leather strap around her neck stood in front of them, chattering eagerly. The man pushed the woman aside and they kept going through the crowded square toward the empty lot and the helicopter, the old lady following closely, with a persistent sales pitch in Greek.

"What's the old bitch saying?" the man asked.

"The way you're holding me, she thinks we're newlyweds," Taylor said. "She wants you to buy me a cake."

The man said nothing and continued to guide Taylor toward the helicopter. The sleek brown craft was surrounded and being much admired by the crowd.

The old lady was still nattering, then she darted in front of them and, walking backwards, kept saying, "Goo' luck! Goo' luck!"

"Oh, for Christ's sake!" The man stopped and, holding Taylor by her wrist, fished out some change for the old woman, slammed it on the tray, took the proffered cake, and shoved it into Taylor's hand.

He steered her through the crowd, right up to the copter, and helped her up to the craft's step, muttering, "Smile, Mrs. Phillips, they're taking your picture."

She turned, standing on the step. Incredibly, there was a photographer aiming at her. "Smile!" the red-haired man ordered her, and she felt the gun in her spine as she looked around for Al. Should she yell?

"Don't even think of screaming," he said, as though reading her mind.

He opened the door of the tinted bubble. She stepped into it and her captor followed, then crouched down in the seat behind her.

About thirty years old, he had hair like a red hairbrush and the thinnest rodent face—two profiles put together—and very pale blue eyes. A large brown splotch on one side of his face looked like the burn made by a chainsaw on the end of a log.

"Who . . . who are you?" She'd seen him before.

"You can call me Melnick, lady," he said, "'cause that ain't my name."

"What do you want?"

"What I want is for you to be a nice girl and you won't get hurt. Just keep your mouth shut and wait for your friend." He looked over his shoulder. "And right on schedule, here he comes."

"Hey, pretty girl," Al said as he opened the bubble's door, "all set for—" He stopped talking when he realized he was looking into a gunbarrel. He froze.

"Get in," Melnick ordered. "Come on, let's get this thing off the ground."

Al slowly got in the pilot's seat and fastened his seat belt. "Well, this is a new wrinkle. What kind of flight plan you got in mind?"

"Just shut it up and get it up," Melnick said. Then he muttered, "Never did like finks."

"I've never even seen you before, mac."

"Nah, but the lady here knows what I'm talking about, don't you, lady?"

Taylor's mind was spinning. *How could they know I called Father Bartolomeo? Of course! I called him from the room they had reserved for me at the hotel. They had either the room or the phone bugged.*

Then, suddenly, Taylor wheeled around and confronted the man. "It's because you cowards no longer have my son, right? You don't need me anymore!"

The woman's vehemence caused the man to lean back, out of her reach. "Take it easy, lady!"

Al was clearly stalling for time when he asked, "How'd the kid get away?"

"Hell, I don't know. Not my department! Now get this thing flying!"

Al inserted the keys and switched on the ignition, and the great blades began to rotate. Then he pulled up a handle by his right side and the crowd fell back and watched in awe as the helicopter rose slowly from the ground. He shoved the stick forward and the craft tilted and sped across the square and then up over the roofs of the stores and over the Ferris wheel and the fairgrounds and the statue of Alexander the Great.

"Okay, mac, any particular destination you got in mind, or do you just want the scenic tour?"

"Yeah, smartass. There's a little paradise island off the tourist circuit where we can have a picnic." He pointed to the baklava cake still in Taylor's hand. "With that." Then, in a different tone, he added, "Bear south, buster, and stay low."

As they flew along the coast, Taylor was inwardly damning herself: *Stupid, stupid, stupid!* But what could she have done differently? Just sit in the hotel forever? She looked at Al and he gave her a reassuring nod. Surely he had some plan. When they landed, he would somehow take care of this maniac. He'd asked her if she could use a gun; that meant he must have one aboard somewhere. But where?

How ironic! Jonny was safe—God had answered her prayers. But now she might not live to see him!

In twenty minutes a cluster of five islands not far off the barren coast came into view. Actually, they were little more than flat rocks, and none was longer than a hundred yards, nor did any of them have vegetation.

"Ease her down on the little gem to the right," ordered Melnick. "Got a nice little beach."

The copter started going down slowly.

"How long have you been following me?" Taylor asked, stalling. "There's something familiar about you. I think I've seen you before."

"And you could never forget my handsome face, I know," said Melnick.

"You . . . dammit you were at the bar! You were at the Golden Sphincter the day Phillips Taylor got killed! You killed him, didn't you?"

He laughed easily. "Lady, what makes you think I go around killing people?"

"And you're probably the one who took Jason's film and tapes from his stateroom, and—oh, God!—you're probably the one who killed that poor old man and cut off . . . oh, no!"

"Lady, do I look like a killer?"

Al was pale as they hovered over the island, but he said coolly, "Okay, mac, if you kill me, how do you get off the rock?"

The man gave a wry grin. "You're not the only flyboy in the world, you know. Ever hear of 'Nam?"

The helicopter sagged down on the rocky beach, tilting slightly in the strong wind, and settled delicately there, its blades still turning.

Al said quietly, "Okay, now what?"

"Out."

"Out?"

"Out," repeated Melnick with finality, looking at both of them.

Taylor got out first, crouching under the blades, her knees shaking. Ridiculously, she was conscious of the baklava's stickiness in her hand. She looked down. A wave broke over the rock's edge and slithered around below her feet.

Melnick followed Al as he got up to get out of the craft, never taking his eyes off the pilot as they stood under the slowly spinning blades.

"Nothing personal," explained Melnick to Al. "It's the girl they want. You just got in the way."

He slowly raised his pistol and pointed it at Al's chest.

Suddenly Taylor uttered a great scream. The gunman's head spun and she smashed the handful of baklava into his eyes. She dove to the ground at his feet as the man fired blindly. Almost at the same moment, Al brought an open-handed chop down hard on Melnick's wrist, and the pistol spun and clattered to the rocks below, and bounced into the water.

Melnick's arms shot out, and Al felt the thin, steely fingers sink into his neck like the tines on a rake. He felt his face flush, felt the searing pain behind his eyes as they bulged from his head, felt the world spin as he started to pass out. Al tried striking and kicking blindly, but he was helpless. Then he managed to thrust his hands out and into Melnick's armpits. He felt his own fingers dig into the other's ribs. The two swayed and strained there for a moment bouncing against the fuselage of the helicopter, Al fighting to stay conscious.

The blades, he thought, the blades! With a great effort, Al tensed his arm muscles. Then, with every bit of strength left in him, he suddenly jerked the man up and off his feet. The shadow of one turning blade went past as he lifted Melnick higher into the air, and then he was able to boost the hit man up just high enough for the next blade to catch him on the side of the head.

The blow was of such force that Melnick's body was yanked from Al's grasp. It was flung across the rocks into the shallow water, the top of his head gone, like the top of a boiled egg severed by a table knife. A big wave surged in and took the body out with it in a swirl of crimson.

Al lurched to where Taylor lay on the ground, rigid with horror.

"You all right?" he gasped.

"Guess so," she whispered.

"Let's get out of here," Al said. "You were great. There's a shotgun in the back seat but no way I could get to it."

"Oh, Al!" Taylor said as she turned her face away from the sight of the body floating in the sea.

"Come on. Let's go. There's probably another one just like him trailing your friend right now."

• • •

Taylor's shivers subsided as Al sped the helicopter on its way to Vatopedi. He shouted to be heard over the noise.

"There it is, Mount Athos—the Holy Mountain. All six thousand gorgeous feet of her."

Taylor looked silently at the beautiful, thin finger of land stretching ahead of them, jabbing out into the sea with the cone of mountain at the tip rising into the sky. She could see the incredible architecture of the ancient monasteries dotting the rugged coastline, and she wondered which of them might be Vatopedi.

"Do you think we'll be in time?" she whispered.

They cruised offshore for an hour, looking at the monasteries and trying to find Vatopedi. Taylor remembered looking at Jason's guidebook, and Al had brought only the usual charts and maps, which did not identify the monasteries by name. Since he had not known to which monastery he might be going until he spoke with Taylor, his flight plan had simply specified Mount Athos.

"I can radio the tower at Thessaloniki," he said.

"I think I see it! Yes, those look just like the funny fluted domes! And the courtyard from the picture of Vatopedi I saw in Jason's book!"

He hovered around as she confirmed it, then said, "Okay, you'd better get that cap on. Tuck your hair up into it."

She started to search through her purse. "I could pencil on a little mustache with eyebrow—"

"That won't be necessary. You won't be getting out. I'll do all the talking."

"You speak Greek?"

He shrugged. "Enough to get by. There's more to this job than just flying the plane. Bosses often find themselves tongue-tied in foreign countries."

He banked around the spacious courtyard and they could see the gradual swarming of the black robes streaming from every direction as the chopper finally came to rest behind the belltower of the *kathlikon*.

Al lifted up the transparent canopy. An aged monk approached the craft cautiously, and Al asked if he could tell them where to find Jason Van Cleve.

The old man tugged at his umber beard and turned to the

others. Al repeated it several times, but the monks only buzzed back and forth among themselves.

Taylor suggested, "Ask for Andoni, the guide."

This brought an immediate response that Al didn't understand.

"What are they saying?" he asked Taylor.

Taylor replied, "It seems that Andoni and Jason had their *diamoniterion* revoked—their permit—and were asked to leave."

Al then asked where they had gone, and it appeared that nobody knew. Two of the monks pointed to the south, others argued with them.

Al asked Taylor, "What do you think?"

"They probably went back to the Pegasus Taverna in Ouranopolis. That's where Andoni lives, and that's where I dropped Jason off."

"Ouranopolis it is," said Al. "And I'm hungry."

The Pegasus Taverna was dark. Al pounded on the door, then tried it.

"They could be around here somewhere," he said. "The door's not locked."

Several of the people who had observed their landing in a field at Ouranopolis were still in awed attendance. One of them, a very old but very agile man, whisked past Al and went into the house.

Al looked at Taylor and they followed. The old man was greeted with obvious pleasure by both the black dog and the yellow-striped cat. He nodded curtly to Taylor and Al, and said in English, "Feed...I feed for Andoni...when not here...when he be guide...I feed..."

Al said to Taylor, "You stay here. I'm going to find a phone and call my office in Rome. Be right back."

The old man was pouring milk for the cat. He worked about the kitchen like one who knew where things were kept.

Taylor asked him in Greek, "Where is Andoni?"

The old man reverted to his native tongue with relief and told her at length of how Andoni had been approached by someone who wished to go to Vatopedi.

Taylor told him that Andoni had lost his permit to be at

Vatopedi. Could he have gone anywhere else, since he had obviously not come home?

The old man just looked at her for a moment, then he brought out the food for the dog—bones and cornmeal mush from the cellar, all cooked together—and Taylor waited as he ladled it into a long, troughlike container. The man was thinking. One could see the process working as first his lips would move silently, then his eyes would roll heavenward, then his brow would wrinkle.

Finally he came over to Taylor and said, "I am sorry. I not know."

She was about to turn away, then she asked, "How long have you known Andoni?"

"Since he little boy. I know his father! I know his mother! I know him when they send him to monastery!"

"Andoni was sent to a monastery?" she asked.

The old man nodded as he concentrated on putting the milk container back in the pantry.

She asked, "What monastery was Andoni sent to as a boy?"

The old man said, "Simonpetra." He indicated the direction with an impatient clutch at the air and shouted, "Simonpetra!"

"Simonpetra," echoed Taylor.

Just then, Al came in. "Taylor—" he began.

"Al, I think we've got it! The monastery at Simonpetra, that's probably where Jason is!" Then she gasped, "Al, what's the matter?"

He looked distraught and white, but he tried a weak smile.

"Called Rome . . . got good news and bad news. Confirmed the news about your son . . . he's unharmed and safe with your sister."

Apprehensively, Taylor sank down at the kitchen table.

"And the bad news?"

"Vatican news release announces, quote, much lamented deaths of two esteemed cardinals, of apparently natural causes, unquote. One of them was our friend."

Taylor whispered, "Father Barto?"

Al nodded.

With a sob, Taylor let her head sag down to her folded

arms, and her shoulders shook. Al put his hand on her shoulder. "Let it all out, girl. Then we'll find out about this Simonpetra."

"I can lose a friend like him by *my* death," she murmured, "but not by his."

14

IT WAS three-thirty in the afternoon when the three men first saw Simonpetra. Andoni had been leading them seaward, off the high ground, the better to approach Simonpetra, for the terrain was less rocky and precarious closer to the shore below them.

Jason had been looking out to sea, appreciative of its varying shades of blue as seen from above. He wondered how they would get away from Simonpetra, once the scroll business had been taken care of. Would there be a boat harbor, or would they have to make their way back the way they had come? He was about to ask when Andoni led them out of a grove of gnarled olive trees.

Jason suddenly murmured, "God!"

Compared to Simonpetra, the Empire State Building and all the skyscrapers of New York seemed somehow insignificant to Jason. He caught his breath.

Andoni was patriotically proud. "That 'Rock of Simon,' boss. You like?"

"Incredible!"

Krenski said, "Incredible it is. And everyone said it was impossible when Simon wanted to build it there on that precipice, but there it is and there it has been since about 1365."

Before them, shooting almost straight up from the sea, was

an enormous pillar of sheer rock, on top of which were the overhanging balconies of Simonpetra. On each of the seven stories there was a balcony that seemed to be supported by wooden poles that appeared no more substantial than a spider's web.

The three of them contemplated this architectural wonder for some moments in silence.

"That really is a fortress," said Krenski finally. "The monasteries of Mount Athos were once much plundered by pirates, but Simonpetra was not one of them."

Jason said, "Their library and treasures must be intact. I'll bet nothing's ever bothered them."

"No, boss, seem like every century they got big fire. Last time in 1891. Lots of relics burn. But they still got the left hand of Mary Magdalene."

Jason repeated, "Mary Magdalene?"

"That right, boss. They got her hand. That never burn."

Jason thought, *That's like telling me the left hand of Lael is up there! No wonder Constantine brought the scrolls here! Not only was this fortress impregnable, but the scrolls could be guarded by Lael's own hand! Maybe Constantine himself believed . . . ?*

Looking up at the amazing monolith, Jason recalled Byron's description of it that was quoted in the guidebook he'd read. "Athwart its great crag, the monastery's architecture resembled the barracks of Potala, the last palace of the God-king of Tibet." But until now, the description had been just words. Now he saw that the monastery seemed to be erupting out of the rock, and at the top of this seemingly inaccessible monolith were the unexpected balconies. Jason could only admire men with faith enough to walk on such balconies; he wondered if he could do it. Then he thought, *For a look at the genuine left hand of Lael, I could do it. And if she is called Saint Mary Magdalene, I could still do it.*

As they moved forward now, the massive golden rock was turning a brilliant coral hue in the afternoon sun. Jason saw the terraces of the vegetable gardens—rows of beans and tomatoes hanging nervously fifteen feet above one another, an unlikely garden suspended high above the sea.

At the base of the great rock were dozens of beehives. Straw skeps in rows dotted the shale that covered the uncultivated areas.

When they arrived at the base of the escarpment, Jason looked up at the great forbidding walls. No one was visible at the top.

"How do we get up there, Andoni?" Jason asked.

Andoni pointed to a large gondola-type basket in front of them, hanging from a thick rope.

Jason looked at the basket and then up again at the awesome structure. It looked like a giant dovecote; he half expected to see black-robed birds flying out. This was certainly no Vatopedi, where one could just climb a little hill, show a pass, and walk through the gate. Visitors here would be highly visible and thoroughly scrutinized as they tried to enter.

"They're not going to let us in here without a pass, Andoni," said Jason.

"Yes they do, boss." Andoni reached under the tarpaulin on the donkey's back and pulled out some cloth vestments.

"Ever'body know Andoni." He pointed to Krenski. "And he all right in his cassock. Now, you put on cassock and you be all right too."

He handed Jason the robes and sandals. "I borrow when we leave Vatopedi."

Jason laughed. "You are a wonder, Andoni!"

He slipped the cassock on over his clothes.

"But supposing they speak to me?"

Andoni shrugged. "They got monks from lots of countries. Besides, I do talking."

Jason looked again at the reed basket; shaking his head, he said, "That *can't* be the only way."

"Yes, boss, only way."

"What's the bell for, Andoni?"

"You ring, somebody bring you up. Better we don' tell ever'body we coming, huh, boss?"

Jason nodded.

Andoni tethered the donkey and said, "I go up first, boss, then I pull you up."

Andoni went to the basket and stood in it.

"You can't climb up there!"

Andoni laughed. "I do this all time when boy. Sneak out, come home late. Have to get to cell without the monks find out!"

Andoni grabbed the rope and started to shinny up it. It was an amazing display of strength as his powerful arms hauled his great body up and up in a humping series of movements. Up and up he went, his legs scissored around the rope, his arms straining as he grunted himself up foot by foot.

At the top, he swung his legs over the parapet and looked down and grinned. He motioned for Jason and Krenski to get into the basket. Jason climbed in first and then helped Krenski in. He waved to Andoni, and in a moment they felt a jerk and heard the ratcheting as the winch lifted them up into the air.

As they were winched up, Jason looked out over the Aegean, orange now in the hot sunlight. He ventured to look down at the blue grapes against the verdure of the receding earth, far below. He saw the peaches ripening, the fig and walnut trees, the ubiquitous olives, and the rows of hives in the apiary. The pole beans formed green tepees as he looked down on them from above.

Suspended in space, high above the sea, he felt also suspended in time; he could already see how this primitive way of life might have a profound attraction.

"I hope you have a plan once we get up there," he said to Krenski.

"The plan, as I see it, is no plan. We lie low and wait for a chance to get at the chapel, and hope that Andoni was not exaggerating about knowing where the treasury hiding place is."

"Supposing we just play it straight. Confront Constantine, tell him what we know, and demand to see the originals?"

"Insanity." Paul shook his head. "My friend, you are dealing with fanatics."

"But if we tell him that we have seen the photos, that I have the negatives of some of them—"

"Jesus, you don't have those with you?"

Jason shook his head. "I'm not that dumb. But, knowing that, won't he want to talk to us?"

"Knowing that, he'll want to expel us, denounce us, and probably burn the originals. No, believe me, theft is the only way."

"Then what do we do with them?"

"That, as Mr. Kipling said, is another story."

They were nearing the top.

"Paul," Jason started hesitantly, "may I ask you something?"

"I think I can guess," He said with a small smile. "Do I believe in the scrolls' authenticity?"

Jason nodded.

"Of course I do," Krenski said. "Otherwise I've wasted a good part of my life. When not actually working on them, I was thinking about them. Of course they're authentic. That is, they are old, they are of the era they purport to be, and the language is faultless."

"But—"

"Now, if you ask whether I believe the story they tell— who's to know? A hoax? I seriously doubt it. They didn't play religious games in those days. Writing materials were too hard to come by then for frivolity. That was back about 60 A.D. That kind of hoax—holy shrouds and pieces of the True Cross and all that—didn't come in until the fifteenth century."

"So, then . . ."

But they had reached the top. Andoni locked the winch and helped them step out of the basket onto a little landing platform. "Welcome to Simonpetra," the big man said in a hoarse whisper.

Bells began to ring, some deep and full-throated, some metallic, some pealing melodiously. Bells on every balcony rang out.

"Vespers? This early?"

"No, boss, matins!" Andoni said. "Monks here on different time schedule. Different calendar, too. Thirteen days later than us."

"Good," said Krenski. "We won't be noticed."

They walked through an arch and down a narrow, cobble-stone-paved tunnel to a big square. They hung back in the shadows and watched the monks, like columns of black ants streaming across the courtyard and around the huge fountain in silent rows toward one of the chapels.

"Outrageous," said Andoni with a smile. "This afternoon they use that chapel, not *kathlikon!*" He pointed to the opposite side of the square, where the huge red church stood. "Used to be, they keep those important things in *kathlikon*. That where I see when the monks open the...how you say, script?"

"Crypt."

"Altar table look like regular altar. Got beautiful linen on it, all embroider and lace and candles. But the top—big white marble slab. Under that slab, they keep treasure. They bring out treasure for special time, like saints' days. That why some things, they no get burned in big fires. They safe in that marble script."

"How do we get in?" Jason asked. "There are two big monks standing in front."

"They sort of guards," said Andoni. "We go around back. But we gotta cross square first. Gotta act natural."

He stepped out into the courtyard, and Krenski and Jason followed. In his attempt to "act natural," Jason held his hands behind his back and strolled out onto the big flagstones.

Andoni looked back; then, frowning, he hissed, "Boss, don' do that! Monk never put hands behind back!"

"It's a sign of the denial of Christ," explained Krenski.

They went across the square, not quite ambling, but not walking too purposefully either. Andoni led them past the fountain, past the marble wellhouse, to a corner of the square about one hundred feet from the *kathlikon*. There was a narrow alley, and, after glancing around to see that the monks weren't watching, he stepped into it, motioning Jason and Krenski to follow.

They ran down the alley, turned the corner, and dashed to the back of the big church. There was a small wooden door with blistered blue paint peeling off it; a rusted lock hung above the rusted knob.

Andoni cursed. "I forget about lock!"

He took a large folding knife from his pocket, snapped it open, and began prying at the hasp. He cursed in Greek as he worked at it, digging into the crumbling wood around the screws. In a few minutes he was able to yank the screws out of the wood and the door swung open. It was pitch black inside.

Andoni crossed himself and said, "You go in, boss. I stay guard here. Don't stay long. We get the hell out of here. I don't like this job."

There were three lanterns on the floor inside the door. Jason took out a match and lit the wick in one. By its light he could see a long, narrow corridor, almost a tunnel. He stepped in and motioned to Paul, and they went down the corridor cautiously. The stench was almost overwhelming, a mixture of hundreds of years of mustiness and urinations, both animal and human. There was no sound except the slapping of their sandals and the scurrying of two black rats in front of them.

After thirty feet, they came to some steps. Jason stopped, took off his sandals, and put them in the pocket of his cassock, and Krenski did likewise. They went up the steps slowly and came to a wooden door. Jason eased back the bolt and opened the door slowly and stepped through. Krenski followed. They were behind the altar, and Jason could see, by the light of one great candle, the Byzantine icon of Christ. In the incensed mustiness, Jason sneezed. As it echoed, they looked around quickly and waited for disaster to strike, but there was no one in the church, which, in the gloom, seemed as big as an airplane hangar.

Jason whispered, "The altar table!"

Krenski's eyes flashed and he led the way past the *iconostasis* screen to the area behind: the *bema*. There was the huge marble table. It was a sarcophagus.

Paul pointed to it and hissed, "Yes! The only place it could be. God bless Andoni!"

He quickly grabbed up the objects on the table, the silver chalice, the gold cross, the candelabra, and handed them to Jason, who put them quietly on the floor. Then Paul whipped off the ornately embroidered cloth, exposing the great white marble crypt.

"See!" Krenski exulted. "Andoni was right. It *is* a vault!"

A barely discernible crack outlined the lid cut in the marble.

"Help me!" Krenski bent, the palms of his hands pressed against the lip of the marble lid. Jason did the same.

"Now!"

They both strained, and the heavy lid gave a little. They

227

pushed and slid the marble slab inch by inch until they had a fair clearance to the contents inside. Jason held the lantern over the opening, and the sight that met their eyes was staggering. The light reflected off great piles of jewelry of incalculable beauty and value: tiaras, raw gold, worked gold, cut diamonds, uncut diamonds, swords with dazzling pearl and ruby hilts, crosses inlaid with emeralds, lapis lazuli, sapphires, jade, turquoise, and golden topaz. There were small jeweled boxes with glass windows revealing rare and sacred relics.

"Lord God above," whispered Krenski.

In one corner Jason saw what appeared to be a silver box almost buried under gold medallions. He leaned far down into the crypt and brushed the medallions off the box and pointed it out to Krenski.

It was an ornate, ancient box, a twin to the one Jason had seen in the locked cellar he'd broken into at Vatopedi.

"Yes!" breathed Krenski. "Oh, yes, yes!"

He helped Jason lift it out and put it on the side of the crypt.

Then Jason saw it: a small leaded-glass box, much like the others in the crypt that contained relics, but this one was not jeweled. Through the heavy glass, Jason could see the withered remains of a small brown hand! Could it be that he was actually looking at the hand of Lael? He stood gazing down at it for a long moment; an engraved plate had Greek writing on it, and Jason glanced at Krenski, but the man was in a frenzy of activity, releasing the catches on the silver box, his hands shaking, perspiration dripping from his face. Jason watched as he pulled out a scroll gingerly.

"It's Aramaic!" Krenski hissed with elation. He flipped through the rest of the contents in the box. There were scrolls, photos, and Greek and English translations.

"This is it! All of it!" He grabbed the translation and went toward the last pages, the unknown part.

"Listen . . . listen!" he whispered as he began to read, faster and faster in his excitement. Jason stood listening to the words as he looked down into the little glass box, transfixed. How long . . . how long had the left hand of Mary Lael been hidden away here on Mount Athos, here with the scrolls, the story of her life . . . Mary—Lael—Magdalene . . .

Krenski's voice was low and urgent.

Then Lael came near and said, "Come, John, for we have work to do."

And so we went to the tomb and she spoke to the guard, and such was her power that he fell fast asleep against the boulder. And she commanded me to roll back the great round stone that blocked the tomb. And I said, "I am but one man, and small. It would take four men to remove that rock."

And she said, "John, move the rock." And I tried, and the great rock moved as though it were a small stone. We went into the tomb, which was lit only by the light of one candle. And Jesus' body was on a shelf, wrapped in the linen cloth and facing toward Jerusalem. She quietly moaned over Jesus' body when she saw it, and she embraced him and held him in her arms. It was then that the spirit of the Divine departed from Lael, and left her body to return to Heaven. And this explosion, this blinding light, this separation of the Divine from the human identity, was like lightning, and I could see that it burned an imprint on the shroud in which Jesus' body was wrapped.

From that moment on, the rest was deception. Lael and I brought out the body of the Master and we placed it lovingly across the donkey's back. Then Lael started away with the animal, and I, too, walked along on the other side. Lael turned to me and said, "Thank you, John. I will now take Jesus to a secret place and bury him."

She wanted to do this alone, so then it was that I took my leave of her.

And I said to her, "When you are ready, come to us in Ephesus, for it is there that Mary and I are to go. None of us will ever be safe here again. I can already feel evil forces moving about us, threatening us."

And she answered, "When I am ready and finished with what I must do here, I shall come to you."

And I watched as she walked the path, and I wondered where she would take Jesus. And she looked so desolate and alone that I called after her asking, "Can I be of no help to you?"

And she only shook her head. Her eyes answered no ques-

tions. Yet in those all-knowing eyes I saw the knowledge of her own doom, and, I feared, mine.

Again she started up the path, leading the ass that bore the body of Jesus; and over the city of Jerusalem, night fell.

And it came to pass that the news spread over all the nation that Jesus was risen from the dead. People were looking for him in the street, and the disciples believed they recognized him under all manner of disguises. The legend was alive; the fires were burning; the Word was being spread.

But already evil people are gathering in the name of Christ, and if God chooses to leave me on earth to continue the fight for the souls of men, my next task will be to deal with those who do evil in the name of the Christ. And tomorrow I must . . ."

"That is the end," said Krenski, and he sighed.

"Just like that?" Jason said.

Krenski nodded.

Jason again looked down at the little hand in the box and said, "But then . . . then what happened to Lael? Did she go to Ephesus with John and Mary?"

"There is a short codicil here about what finally happened to hers. And all this is the true word of John; it is no hoax."

Suddenly another voice rang out in the *kathlikon.* "Mr. Van Cleve!" It echoed in the dome of the church.

The words came from behind them. Two monks with wooden staffs flanked Constantine. His small body was erect, his voice calm but strong.

Jason instinctively reached for his pistol and drew it.

"A murder weapon, Mr. Van Cleve?" Constantine said, not slackening his pace. "You, a man of peace, a man of culture, dealing with murder weapons?"

Jason put the pistol on the altar next to the lantern. There was something in Constantine's voice that made him obey instantly.

The monks marched toward them relentlessly, like executioners, but then the abbot put out a restraining hand and they stopped. Constantine's eyes moved from Jason to Krenski and back again.

"We have committed no crime," Jason said.

Constantine pointed to the scrolls and the treasures.

"Not even sacrilege?" he suggested.

"Nor sacrilege either," said Krenski. "We are not after anything here but the truth!"

"Whose truth?" asked Constantine contemptuously. "Yours or mine?"

"There can only be one truth," Jason said.

"Wrong, Mr. Van Cleve," Constantine replied. "Truth wears many faces. Some of them are deceiving."

Krenski said, "And you, sir—does it constitute truth to masquerade as a holy man, yet at the same time suppress historical biblical documents?"

"Who is to say whether they are either historical or biblical?"

"Why not get them out in the open, out where experts can examine them, test them, and either accept or denounce them?"

"Ah, you would like that, wouldn't you, Mr. Krenski?"

Paul was startled. "You remember me?"

"Of course," said Constantine. "I also recall how quickly you lost your vocation, your desire to serve God as a monk, when you thought you had found the Ephesus scrolls. How could I forget your determination to tell the world about them, to destroy the faith of millions? You would make a great name for yourself as translator and champion of the scrolls, while destroying the greatest religion the world has ever known."

Jason couldn't help interjecting, "But you have read them. Are they so blasphemous? Just because they tell the same story, the same philosophy in a different way? Do you regard Christians as so unknowing and unbending and unintelligent that they couldn't accept this new version without losing their faith?"

"Regrettably, Mr. Van Cleve, most of the world, Christian or otherwise, is uneducated. What they have believed, what their families have believed for centuries—the Gospel, in all sense of the word—should not, *must* not, be so casually stripped from them. Perhaps these new revelations, whether they believed them or not, would not shake their faith. But there is a great risk. No one has the right to test the faithful of the world, especially when the Church has so many enemies, both religious and political, who would like nothing better then to come across such a weapon with which to split Christianity."

"You mean to deepen the existing split between the Roman

231

and Orthodox churches?" said Paul. "In other words, you don't want *me* spilling the beans about the scrolls. *You* want to hang on to them for your own political use when the time comes to up yourself in the Church!"

Constantine's eyes narrowed into black slits.

"Your remarks are as untrue as they are impertinent. My reasons are strictly moral ones."

"And it is moral to do *anything* to suppress these scrolls?" Jason asked. "Even to kill?"

Constantine's ivory brow wrinkled above his black eyebrows. "Kill, Mr. Van Cleve? I have killed no one ever—either personally or through an agent."

"You didn't have Phillips Taylor and Nestor Lascaris killed?"

The old abbot shook his head vehemently. "I do not kill. We do not kill here on Mount Athos. Look to Rome for your killers, not to these blessed monasteries. Now you will leave Simonpetra. We harbor no ill will, but we wish you to leave this sacred peninsula at once and return to your own world."

"And if we tell that world about the scrolls?" asked Jason.

Constantine smiled. "Without proof, your allegations will be dismissed by all but a credulous few."

"Ah, but we have proof!" said Paul, as he grabbed the papers from the box and brandished them. "And the world will judge. The scientists and experts will judge!"

"Put them down, Paul," commanded Constantine in a calm, low voice.

"I have them now," panted Paul, and Jason heard the hysteria in the man's voice. "I have them and you will never get them back until the world knows about them! The entire world!"

"Put them down, Paul," repeated Constantine with a sigh, and he and his monks moved toward him.

Paul snatched up Jason's pistol from the altar and pointed it at the abbot.

"Stop where you are!"

The abbot held out his hand, pointing his finger at Paul's eyes.

"Come, Paul, we should not be enemies. Put away the gun. Put the papers back in their rightful place."

So hypnotic, so forceful were his words that Paul hesitated, then turned slightly, mechanically, and put the papers back in the silver chest. But then he whirled and leveled the pistol again at Constantine, his hand shaking.

"We will take the whole box! The scrolls, the photographs, the translations—"

He grabbed at the box, still holding the pistol, and lifted it off the altar. A monk leaped forward and brought his staff down on Krenski's arm. The pistol went off as it dropped from Krenski's hand and clattered to the floor. A second staff arced in a backhand swing, caught Krenski on the side of the head, and slammed him to the foot of the altar.

Jason dropped to one knee.

"Paul!"

His brow was split and blood seeped from it; he was unconscious, but he was not badly hurt.

Then Jason raised his head and saw Constantine. The old man was lying on the floor, and the monks were hovering around him in consternation. Jason went quickly to them. He saw that there was a bullet hole in the abbot's neck, and blood was spurting out. Jason knelt down and pressed his thumb against the carotid artery, stemming the flow of blood.

"Get a doctor! Do you have a doctor here?" Jason asked the monks, who were mumbling prayers. One of them got up and ran out of the church.

"Father Constantine," Jason said, a catch in his voice. "It was an accident! He did not mean to shoot you, I'm sure. We meant no harm, ever!"

Constantine moved his hand feebly, as though he understood and forgave. Jason took the wrist of the old man; his pulse was getting weaker.

"The story of Lael," Constantine gasped hoarsely. "All because of that story . . ."

Jason stroked his head and asked, "Sir, is it a true story?"

Constantine smiled slightly. "What do you think . . . my son?"

A monk folded a clean linen cloth from the altar and pressed against the wound. Jason held it in place. The bleeding was subsiding.

"The scrolls," Jason said. "I think Krenski was right; they belong to the people. They should know—"

The old abbot narrowed his eyes and gathered his strength.

"No!" he rasped. "Wars! Betrayals of faith! This story . . . if published . . . means bloodshed of epidemic proportions!"

He grabbed for Jason's hand and squeezed it.

"Promise!" he begged. "Promise to forget . . . forget . . . promise you will not . . ."

His eyes closed and he caught his breath with the pain, then let it out a little at a time, testing the pain as he exhaled. Finally he opened his eyes and went on, "Your own safety . . . people will always . . ."

"Who are these people, these anonymous people?"

"Guardians! Fanatics! Unoffical . . . Guardians of the Faith . . . in Rome."

"The Vatican, then?"

"No, no!" Constantine closed his eyes again for a moment. "A cardinal at the Vatican, yes . . . Tobin."

"Tobin?" The one Krenski had mentioned!

The old abbot opened his eyes and nodded, and the action started the bleeding again from the wound in his neck. He tried to sit up and started coughing. Blood came gurgling out of his mouth.

"Sir, do not try to talk anymore," Jason said as he tried to support the man in a more comfortable position.

Constantine went on. "Tobin . . . a maniac . . . head of a secret society. Uses it . . . for personal power. Goes back . . . to early history of the Church. First victim . . . was John."

"John?"

"In Ephesus. John."

"The Apostle John? He was murdered."

The old man nodded. "The Guardians."

"And Lael?"

Constantine whispered something.

"What? I don't understand."

He whispered it again. Jason wasn't quite sure of what he said. Three gasps and a shudder, and the old man was dead.

The monk who'd been giving Constantine last rites began to weep silently. Then the front doors of the chapel burst open and a dozen monks rushed in, most of them brandishing sticks and clubs. At the same time, Andoni appeared from behind the altar.

"Boss! What's goin' on in here?"

Then he saw the oncoming monks. "Let's get out of here, boss!"

Jason got up hurriedly as the monks ran to their fallen abbot. They glanced briefly at the corpse, then started menacingly toward Jason.

"Tell them, Andoni," Jason said out of the corner of his mouth as he backed up. "Tell them in Greek—I didn't kill him!"

"Who did, boss?"

Jason jerked his head toward Krenski, still unconscious at the foot of the altar. "An accident!"

Jason edged back to where Krenski lay, and picked up the pistol as the band of monks, clubs raised, advanced slowly, muttering and growling.

"Tell them!"

"No use, boss, they no believe me! Back way, boss, quick!"

Andoni kicked over the lantern and it crashed into the silver box. Then, with a backhand slap, he knocked down the big candle.

"Run, boss!" shouted Andoni. "Forget Krenski."

Jason froze. He didn't know what to do: leave Paul to the enraged mob of monks and save himself as well as Andoni, or try to rescue the unconscious translator who would do nothing but impede their progress out of the monastery and lead to no one's escaping.

But his mind was made up for him. The blazing kerosene from the lantern ran over the photographs and scrolls in the box and over the altar, creating a barrier of fire. Deciding he'd alert authorities anonymously when he reached town—if he did—and leave it to them to retrieve the translator, he jumped in behind Andoni as the guide cried "This way!" They passed behind the altar to the little door in the rear, bolted it, and raced down the steps. Krenski would be fine until the authorities arrived. The monks could do no more than imprison him, and with help from the American Embassy in Athens, Krenski's imprisonment wouldn't last long.

"Hang on to my belt, boss!"

They went through the black corridors fast, and then down some steps, through the last door, and finally they were outside in the fading light of the afternoon.

It was dusk, and the air smelled fresh and clean after the dank corridors and the incense of the musty chapel. Jason took the sandals out of his cassock and put them on quickly. They dashed across the yard and into a short tunnel. When they emerged from the tunnel, they could see the elevator basket and they sprinted for it. They got in and Andoni released the ratchet. He controlled the speed of their descent with a handle that pressed against the rope.

"Faster, Andoni!" said Jason as he looked up and saw the heads of the angry monks appearing over the wall above them.

"Fast as we can without we jus' fall, boss!"

About ten feet from the ground, the basket came to an abrupt halt. Then it started to go back up. Jason looked up and saw the monks winding them back up as though reeling in a big fish.

"Jump, Andoni!"

Andoni looked down as the basket continued to rise. Then he looked up at the monks.

Jason pushed him over the side with his foot, and Andoni fell to the ground, landing awkwardly in a sitting position near the rows of beehives. Then Jason spilled over the side and lit on his feet with a great jolt. He went over to Andoni, who sat moaning on the ground. He helped the big man to his feet, but Andoni cried out, "Boss, I think I got broken foot!"

"Lean on me, Andoni."

He put his arm around Jason's shoulder. "Get me to Mangas. I can ride him." He hobbled to where the donkey was tethered. Jason boosted the man onto the animal's back, then glanced up toward the monastery. The elevator basket was descending with four monks in it.

Andoni saw it too, and said, "Your pistol, boss!"

Jason shook his head. "I can't kill a monk!"

"Then they kill you, boss! Me and Mangas too!"

Jason swatted the donkey on the rump, saying, "Get going, Andoni! Mangas can outrun them! Get going!"

"Boss, wait . . ." Andoni called, but the little burro had started down the trail as fast as he could go with Andoni clinging to him, and they were soon out of sight in the trees and underbrush.

And then Jason heard a familiar sound, a strangely modern sound in these environs of antiquity. It was the *whack-whack-whack* of helicopter blades. Jason looked up, shielding his eyes against the setting sun, and saw the aircraft. He waved his arms frantically.

The monks were down now, climbing out of the basket, and heading for Jason at a dead run, clubs raised.

The helicopter swooped down and swung in toward a level patch of ground, its whirring blades kicking up dirt and pebbles.

The monks were closer than he'd expected when he looked back. They were taking a shortcut through the apiary toward him, zigzagging through the skeps, the conical beehives made of straw.

Jason raised his pistol and sent his last bullet into one of the hives. The shot tore into the side of the bees' straw home, and a small swarm came out. The insects flew around the monks, who batted at them as they kept running and running. Jason turned desperately toward the helicopter as it landed.

He froze when he saw who was getting out of the craft. It was Taylor, and she had an automatic shotgun, which she was raising to her shoulder.

God, Jason thought. *She's going to kill me herself!*

But no, she was pointing the gun toward the onrushing monks. There was a blast from the gun, and one of the beehives exploded from the force of the pellets. Then another and another and still another. Great brown clouds of angry bees swarmed out and attacked the closest things to them—the monks. Screaming, the men slapped at their assailants, rolled on the ground, and ran back in panic toward the monastery.

As Jason started to go to Taylor, he heard a voice calling "Bravo! Bravo!" It was Andoni's voice.

"What are you doing here?" Jason asked.

The old Greek smiled. "Come back to save you, boss. I always do, don' I?" He limped and placed his hands on Jason's shoulders.

"Besides," he said, "I want to make sure you get out of here okay."

"Why?"

"What you mean, why? You still owe me half my money!" He gave a thunderous laugh. "Outrageous!"

Jason pointed to the helicopter.

"You are coming with us," he said.

Andoni's eyes narrowed as he looked at the chopper.

"Oh, no, boss," he said. "I . . . I can't."

"What's the matter, Andoni? Are you afraid of the flying machine?"

"Me? Afraid? That's outrageous! The way you speak about me, boss, the lady will think I am some kind of coward."

He leaned forward and whispered, "Besides, how can I go on flying machine? I have to take care of Mangas!"

They embraced each other and smiled, then Andoni limped back to his donkey.

Jason turned and walked over to where Taylor stood by the helicopter.

"Hello," he said awkwardly.

"Hello," she whispered.

"Thank you, Miss Oakley," he said.

She smiled. "And to think, my mother disapproved of my taking up skeet shooting."

Jason took the shotgun from her and kissed her gently, then harder, and she kissed him back fervently and clung to him.

"Oh, Jason, I've got so much to tell you," she said. "Jonny is okay and I couldn't tell you about the kidnapping—"

Al leaned out of the copter and yelled, "We'd better get goin'! If those monks find out there's a woman on their sacred soil, they'll really be mad!"

Jason smiled down at Taylor and they walked the few yards to the helicopter and he helped her into the cabin.

Even over the whir of the turning blades of the aircraft, Jason could hear the plaintive chapel bells of Simonpetra, spreading their vibrant sounds of grief through the valley.

As the helicopter lifted, he took Taylor's hand in his and thought of the tumultuous days, of the people whose lives he had invaded, and who had changed him in ways he still could not quite appreciate. And all for some scrolls that might now be reduced to mere ashes, to remain only as a memory in his mind. What to do with the wealth of information he'd been exposed to in less than a week?

"Forget them! Forget them!" the dying abbot had begged.

Forget Paul Krenski's dream? Forget his own yearning for the truth about them, which by now bordered on obsession? Forget the several lives that had been lost over them? Was he a reporter or not? Quit a story in midstream?

Like Scarlett, he would think about it tomorrow. Right now he was safe, next to the woman he'd grown to love. He could see Andoni, waving happily, on the path down below them. The very last rays of the sun were turning the Aegean into a tranquil white-gold carpet. One by one the magnificent façades of Simonpetra, Gregoriou, Dionysiou, and the other monasteries gradually cloaked themselves shyly in the lavender of the twilight.

Jason said, "God, I'm glad you're safe!"

She squeezed his hand. They were silent for a moment, then she asked, "Did you find what you were looking for?"

"More, much more. The very hand of Lael—I saw it."

"And . . . and what happened to her? Did you find out?"

Jason swallowed and said, "Constantine said that John the Apostle was the first victim of the Guardians . . ."

"Yes?"

Lord, why was he moved almost to tears? Was it fatigue? Or had he too begun to swallow the story of the scrolls?

"And the second was . . . I think he said . . ."

"Yes?"

"The second was Lael."

Taylor sucked in her breath.

Al swiveled in the cockpit. "Hey, fun-seekers, where to? I mean, the Rozmyslowski Travel Service may be a little hard to pronounce, but we aim to please! So anywhere you want to aim, folks, we aim. Fiji, Katmandu, Moorea, or Fresno, just say the word!"

Jason's mouth widened slightly, but it really wasn't a smile. "Rome," he said flatly. "A little unfinished business in Rome."

15

THE AFTERNOON sun filtered into an elegant apartment not a quarter of a mile from the Vatican. Cardinal Tobin seldom drank anything but the wine of Communion and caffe espresso; back in Ulster, as a boy, he'd pulled his besotted father out of too many pubs, seen his father maim his mother too many times, dodged too many paternal roundhouse rights, ever to have anything but disgust for alcohol.

But in the last months he'd found that he was taking wine when there was no Communion, and from time to time he'd had a martini, maybe two, if one of the other cardinals was drinking. And this last week, well, he didn't need anyone to drink with; at least two martinis was the rule before dinner, and sometimes three, instead of dinner.

Things were not going at all right with the Guardians and his plans. The wiry little man in gray slacks and black sweater paced up and down in his apartment. He paused by his desk, picked the martini up, and gulped it. He sat down, then, just as quickly, got up and paced again.

When was he going to get that call from McCue, telling him that the meddling Mr. Van Cleve was no longer a problem? Or the call from Melnick, assuring him that Taylor Phillips was no longer a threat?

Things here in Rome had been difficult enough, but he'd

taken care of them rather brilliantly. Yes, in all modesty, since there could be no way to link him with those deaths . . . brilliantly. He'd dumped Bartolomeo's body in the woods near the spot where Patricio's corpse would be found. A mystery—two cardinals found murdered not far from a lonely country road—front-page stuff requiring an investigation, even while the Vatican was releasing the baloney about "natural causes." Ha!

Already the newspapers were speculating that while the two clerics were being held up in their car by bandits, an off-duty police officer, Andrea di Grazia, chanced by and tried to intervene, and all three were killed. There were holes in the story, but it didn't matter. He, Cardinal Tobin, was in no way involved; he was totally in the clear.

And it was good that Patrick had been eliminated. He'd gone as soft as an eclair lately, and didn't seem to understand what the Guardians were all about. He'd begun to worry about Patrick, about how far to trust him. A man like Patrick could be dangerous, very dangerous. Yes, that part had all worked out for the best.

As for Bartolomeo . . . poor, blind idiot, blundering around in matters that didn't concern him—

The phone rang and Tobin jumped. Good! At last, McCue or Melnick. He picked up the receiver eagerly.

"Yes?" he said.

A genial American voice said, "Cardinal Tobin? Hi, this is Ed Matthews, over at UPI."

"UPI?" repeated Tobin.

"Yes, the news service? As opposed to Associated Press?"

"Oh—oh, yes," said Tobin. "Newspapers."

"I happen to be in the neighborhood, and I wondered if I could come talk to you for a few minutes?"

"What, pray tell, about?"

"About a couple of things, Your Eminence. Like about the sad death of Cardinal Bartolomeo . . ."

Tobin felt a tightening in his stomach. "What about it?"

"There's a rumor that the Pope was going to appoint him Archbishop of New York. I'd like to check your ideas on that, and any thoughts you might have about who the replacement might be."

Tobin's stomach relaxed. He hated newsmen, but this was not the time to antagonize them. In fact, he could use them right now.

The voice went on. "I'd only take up a few minutes of your time."

Tobin sighed. "All right, then. I am very busy, but come ahead. I am in apartment 3A. But no photographer!"

"No, sir."

In ten minutes, Jason, carrying a briefcase, rang the bell to the cardinal's apartment. Tobin opened the door.

"Matthews," said Jason as he stepped in. "Ed Matthews." He showed his press card and silently prayed that Tobin would not wish to examine it closely.

"Yes, yes, yes," said Tobin, his black salamander eyes taking in his caller in sharp, darting looks. "Welcome. Come into my office."

He led the way through the foyer to the small room off the living room, and took a seat behind his desk. It was barren except for the empty martini glass, a few letters, and a large brass cross supported by a marble base.

"So, here we are." Tobin gave his best attempt at a jovial smile. "How can I help you make the newspapers of the world more lurid?"

He pointed at a chair, and Jason sat down.

"Well, Your Eminence," said Jason, "there's a rumor floating around over at UPI that you might be the next Archbishop of New York."

"How terribly interesting," said Tobin. "Any other rumors?"

"Yes," said Jason. "There was also some comment made on the coincidence of those three dead men being found fairly near your country place in Calese. And one of them, the policeman, was rumored to have said he was going to call on you that night."

"Interesting rumors," mused Tobin. "I heard a good one myself just a few minutes ago."

"Yes?"

"I called UPI and they never heard of Ed Matthews. The rumor is that you are Jason Van Cleve."

"Not totally inaccurate, Cardinal," said Jason, dropping the

243

geniality. "And I am sorry to disappoint you with my aliveness. I can't say the same for the spook you sent to kill me."

"I will tell you the truth—"

"Don't break any habits for me," said Jason.

Tobin gave a grunting laugh. "What wild imaginations you writers have. Me, send someone to kill you? What will you think up next?"

"No, what will *you* think up next? I'm going to the police now and tell them about everything—Lascaris, Phillips Taylor, Jonny's kidnapping, and—"

"And of course you'll tell them about the objects in here," he said as he opened a drawer and pulled out Lascaris's briefcase, the handcuffs still dangling from it.

"Of course. And I have the negatives of those photos in here." He patted his own briefcase.

Tobin asked, "And Constantine, does he not have the originals?"

"At this point he has nothing, except tenure in the next world."

"He is dead?"

"Yes, and the scrolls burned."

Tobin's face broke into a genuine smile. "You have done well, Van Cleve! You've done our work for us, like a proper Guardian!"

"I've done no work for you. I was only interested in finding out the truth."

"How noble," said Tobin, leaning forward. "And now you plan to tell the police everything."

"Yes," said Jason.

"No," said Tobin in a steely tone.

Jason was looking into the barrel of a pistol that Tobin had been holding in his lap.

"There is an unsightly bulge in your breast pocket," said Tobin. "Kindly remove it and drop it to the floor."

Jason extracted the pistol and dropped it.

"Now stand up, Mr. Van Cleve."

Jason got to his feet.

"Before you shoot me, I have a request."

"If it is a modest one."

"Let me see how Lascaris's photos compare with what I saw of Constantine's originals."

"The seeker after truth to the end, eh, Mr. Van Cleve?" He hesitated, then clicked open the briefcase, turned it around, and shoved it toward Jason with the barrel of his pistol. "I too would like to know if there are any major differences."

Jason took out a handful of the photos and began to riffle slowly through them. He stopped at one.

"Well . . ." he said thoughtfully as he held it closer to his face.

"Yes. You found something?"

"This sort of changes things," Jason said, pointing to the bottom of the photograph. "Look here!"

He leaned over the desk to show Tobin, who craned his neck forward.

"You see that sentence?" Jason said, and at the same time he flung the photos and papers into Tobin's face. The pistol went off, but not before Jason had grabbed the brass crucifix by its marble base and swung it. One of the sharp arms of the cross caught Tobin on the right temple, slamming him out of his chair. He crashed into the wall and then fell back and lay still on the floor. His eyes were open and glazed, as blood pumped from the deep wound in his head.

Jason dropped the cross. It clattered on the floor. Panting, he lurched over to the phone to call the police. He lifted up the receiver . . . then put it down again. He knew what he had to do first. And fast before he changed his mind.

He gathered up the scattered papers and photos and put them in a big metal wastepaper basket. There were some more left in Lascaris's briefcase, as well as the tape and film stolen from his stateroom. He threw them in too. He opened his own briefcase and took out the negatives he'd taken from the burning camera shop in Izmir, and tossed them in. Then he put a lighted match to the lot and went back to the phone and dialed the police.

To the detective who answered the phone, he merely gave the address and said tersely, "Cardinal Tobin has been killed."

He hung up. Then, as he watched the flames cast weird shadows around the room, he lit a cigarette and dialed the number of the Hudson residence, where Taylor was reunited with her sister and her son.

Bestselling Books for Today's Reader